Truth Game

Douglas Hurd

timewarner
paperbacks

A *Time Warner* Paperback

First published in Great Britain in 1972
By William Collins and Sons
This edition published in 2003 by Time Warner Paperbacks

Copyright © Douglas Hurd, 1972

A CIP catalogue record of this book
is available from the British Library.

ISBN 0 7515 3457 9

Printed and bound in Great Britain by
Mackays of Chatham plc, Chatham, Kent

Time Warner Paperbacks
An imprint of
Time Warner Books UK
Brettenham House
Lancaster Place
London WC2E 7EN

www.TimeWarnerBooks.co.uk

The Rt Hon Lord Hurd of Westwell, CH, CBE, PC was educated at Eton and Cambridge, where he obtained a first-class degree in history. Following terms as Minister of State, he became Secretary of State for Northern Ireland (1984–85) and Home Secretary (1985–89) before his appointment as Foreign Secretary in 1989. He was MP for Mid-Oxfordshire (later Witney) from 1974 to 1997. Upon his retirement as Foreign Secretary in 1995, Lord Hurd joined the Nat West Group, leaving in 2000 to become Deputy Chairman of Coutts Bank. He is also President of the Prison Reform Trust charity.

Lord Hurd is the author of thirteen books and lives in Oxfordshire with his wife Judy and their son and daughter. He has three grown-up sons from his first marriage.

For Thomas

Nineteen-Fifties

'You may sit on the floor if you wish.' The man slipped gratefully on to the polished parquet.

The Sultan of Rajnaya looked over the white walls of the palace to the jagged blue spine of his island. From those hills had always come the strength of his family. From them his ancestor had swept down to cut the throats of the Portuguese. He had been just such a ragged village chief as now sat before him.

'Six of our boats tonight, you say?'

'Two to each of the northern harbours, Highness.'

'Rifles or sub-machine-guns?'

'Rifles,' the man said, 'The last consignment until the next big boat comes to Aden.'

'And the British customs cutters?'

'The engines of both are sick this morning.' The man grinned. The Sultan did not trust men who grinned. He stroked his luxuriant white beard to show that the interview was at an end.

When the man had gone the Sultan spun the big bright circular table which was the main furniture of the room. It had just come from Harrods, and since its coming the Sultan could eat alone throughout a meal. Before retiring the servants put all the plates together on the table at the same time, the hot ones nearest him, and as he ate he rotated the table to bring fresh dishes within reach. If his great-grandfather had thought of this he would not have been stabbed in the back by a servant while at dinner.

The Sultan tasted a pink jelly, of which he kept a stock at the end of the table. Little cubes of fruit had risen to the top of the dish. The jellies came in tins from Australia. They were very economical, and as they were almost tasteless it would be difficult to put poison in them. Even so he opened the tins himself. If his grandfather had known of the jellies, he too might have lived until his beard was white.

The Sultan pressed an electric buzzer in the shape of a tortoise in green glass. The tortoise gave a piercing cry, but nothing else happened. The Sultan clapped his big soft hands, and a servant at once appeared, white shirt and trousers under the red turban which marked the royal household. He bowed to the Sultan with a sideways grimace at the tortoise. The whole household was sure it would bring the Sultan bad luck.

'I pressed the bell.'

'I heard nothing except the clapping of your Highness's hands.'

In the old days men had been executed for less. The Sultan instinctively felt at his side for the curved sword which was no longer there.

'At what hour does the British Commissioner come?'

'At eleven, Highness.'

'Bring me the paper which he gave me yesterday. Then go.'

The servant brought a slim blue booklet in paper covers from the embrasure overlooking the sea. His bare feet moved silently, and the heavy tasselled curtain in the arched doorway fell back into place behind him.

Report of the Constitutional Advisory Committee
July 1954

Our terms of reference were as follows: To devise and recommend a pattern of constitutional reform in Rajnaya which would lay the foundation for democratic institutions while having regard to the special status and characteristics of the island, and in particular

(a) the responsibility of Her Majesty's Government for defence and external relations,

(b) the traditional suzerainty of His Highness the Sultan.

(c) the multiracial character of the island.

Summary of recommendations

1. A Legislation Council should be established of thirty members, of whom ten would be directly elected within the municipality of Rajnaya (paras 1–7) . . .

Paper, it was all paper nowadays. His brother in Aden told him that even the men who brought the rifles from Vladivostok talked as if they were reading pieces of paper. His nephew at Cambridge wrote him many clever letters, but what was the use?

The Sultan hoisted his corpulent little body to its feet and moved slowly to the embrasure. Once it had looked on to a long fringe of palm trees and a beach of white sand, from which the lighters went to load and empty the occasional visiting steamer. The trees had been grubbed up, replaced by the big cranes building the new harbour. Squat glass and steel buildings, most still swathed in bamboo scaffolding, were poking up from the white houses and mud huts along the shore and for a mile or so inland. Money, new money pouring into his island from the oil rigs out to sea.

Everyone told the Sultan he should be glad. But money meant more Indian immigrants, carrying their suitcases down the gangplank of the ancient steamer from Bombay, buying up his city of Rajnaya. Money meant the Commissioner coming once a week to tell him how to spend it. Money meant emptying villages, more blue booklets, strange teachings in the schools, seditious newspapers, women flaunting their limbs in the streets, drink and drugs. Who could tell the end of all this money? It was not thus that the Sultans of Rajnaya had been used to rule.

Luckily there was another way, and he thanked God that his brother the merchant in Aden had found it for him. The rifles came to Aden every three months, at the bottom of a hold full of timber. His brother bought the timber and sold it to the British Army. The rifles, which were cheap and good, came on dark nights to the little fishing harbours on the poor side of Rajnaya beyond the blue hills, where there were no Indians and the coastguard cutters rarely came. There the rifles waited in the rafters for the day when the Sultan would rule in the old way.

He knew how to do it. A clear word passed through the villages by a fast horseman, then a chosen few with sure eyes waiting behind the rocks. After a little fighting there would be much shouting and feasting and firing in the air. There would be plump Indian bodies to comfort the sharks and encourage the others to leave. The British, being clever, would go in time, and the Russians, also being clever, would not come. There would be an end to the talk of schools and American hospitals and elected councils which so unsettled the people.

The Sultan smiled and looked at the gold watch which hung on his plump wrist. The Commissioner was late.

The same servant rushed in, forgetting to bow. 'The Commissioner is here.'

'Of course.'

'He has come with soldiers and a thousand tanks.'

There were two bren gun carriers, in fact, and the palace was surrounded by the local levies under their British officers. The Sultan saw at once what had happened. It had always been possible that he would be betrayed before he was ready.

There would be no fighting.

He knew the British, and the fate which lay in store for him. He thought on the whole the Dorchester Hotel would suit him best.

2

In a few minutes Anne and Francis Trennion would be there, and Richard looked at his familiar surroundings with their eyes. Roses everywhere, but especially on the yellow brick of his parents' house, twined now with the sparse second flowers of the wistaria. The swimming pool by which he sprawled was much smaller than the Trennions' pool at Chailton and quite different in character – blue and neat, whereas theirs was huge, green and scummy. His parents were in their usual summer posture, upside down at either end of the tangled but vivid border. Silence, except for the terrier yapping by the woodpile beyond the back door. Afternoon heat, scorching brown patches on the lawn, justifying his new blue and black striped swimming trunks and the bottle of Asti Spumante in a bucket beside him.

And himself, Richard Herbert, son of the Professor of Tropical Medicine at the University of Cambridge, at the end of his second year reading history as an exhibitioner at St Catherine's, secretary-elect of the University Labour Club, a good swimmer and tennis player, conscious of his good looks and ambitions, and the fact that the two went forward together. As he lay by the pool, feeling the pleasure of the sun burning his thighs and shoulders, Richard thought again of the coming year. 1954 had been pleasant, 1955 must be decisive. He wanted to make a splash in the world of undergraduate politics, big enough for the ripples to be noted in London. He wanted to grapple the Trennions, twin brother and sister, so closely to him that he could draw from them some of their magic.

Francis Trennion was always punctual except when betrayed by the age of his Morris Minor. As it clanked up the drive Anne forced the side door open and jumped out before the car had stopped.

It was four months since Richard had met her for the first time at Chailton, four months during which he had tried to keep in his mind each detail of her face and body and the way she moved. When he was with Francis in his room on the staircase which they shared at St Catherine's he looked every five minutes at the double photograph which stood on the desk, Anne in a fishing boat surrounded by mackerel, Anne on the shingly beach below Chailton, frowning and fully dressed with a book in her hand. Brotherly photographs he had thought, no help to a lover trying to recreate the glamour of his mistress.

The term was flimsily based. One tentative kiss on the last evening at Chailton before he returned to Cambridge, standing in the dark Victorian embrasure of the landing. They had looked out through leaded panes across the headland to Michael's Mount and the lights of Penzance.

Now she was finding her way through the little maze of rose bushes. He could see the blue dress with a white sash emphasising the slim waist. But it was the eyes which had caught him. They were big and blue, not in the least silly. After eighteen years they were set already in a frame of tiny wrinkles, proof of Cornish wind and weather. Now in July her face was sunburnt, her black hair short and tied back, and it was hard to imagine her spending the next few weeks, as was planned, in serious study at the house of a nearby aunt.

She came towards Richard, holding out her hand a little obviously to avoid a kiss. Before they met there was a final explosive clank from the drive, as Francis stalled the Morris. He caricatured deliberately his hopelessness with any piece of machinery. It was his only parlour trick, the others laughed and constraint vanished.

'Swim? Come in and change.'

Richard took her hand and kept it as he led her into his father's study. He cleared an untidy mountain of papers from an upright chair, and left her to it, photographing busily with his mind for future reference. By the side of the pool Francis was already deep in a book.

'Not going to bathe?'

'D'you mind if I don't?'

'What's the book?'

'De Tocqueville. There's such a mass of stuff on my special subject I must get a grip on it before next term.'

Small and dark, face ordinary and dull till he smiled, slightly pointed ears, a thin body of which he took no account; and he would actually be enjoying de Tocqueville. In all these things the opposite of Richard, who vaguely wondered from time to time how they had become friends. Francis had taken the initiative, shyly asking him to tea, to walk the Backs, to drink and talk through the night, and finally last Easter to stay at Chailton. For Richard it was pleasant to be sought after by the cleverest undergraduate of his year.

'Put it away, for God's sake, Francis. I've got too much to ask you. Gaitskell's turned us down, and I must have one star speaker for the Labour Club next term, or our dear comrades will lynch me.'

Francis knew much more about politics than Richard, but lacked a taste for the undergraduate variety.

'You should try a European, they have all the ideas nowadays. Nenni or Mendes-France, someone like that.'

'We couldn't afford any fares.'

'What, not even with Revani on your Committee?' They laughed. If Francis was the cleverest member of their year at St Catherine's, Johnnie Revani was the richest. His uncle was the Sultan of Rajnaya and his father a merchant in Aden, from whom Johnnie had inherited a comfortable combination of considerable wealth and revolutionary opinions.

Anne appeared in the doorway, ran across the lawn and dived straight into the pool. Richard was after her; in his hurry he miscalculated his dive and the water from the splash cascaded over Francis and de Tocqueville. It was only seven strokes to the shallow end, he caught her round the waist and they stood laughing. It was different from what he had expected, as if he had known her for years and they had swum in that pool since childhood. He had carefully timed the phases of his campaign that afternoon, meaning to keep his main news till after the wine. But now he flung in all his forces, like a general who sees the enemy melting after an hour of battle.

'You remember I said I'd be looking for a cottage. Well, I've got one for a month beginning next week. A bit tumble-down, in a wood beyond Melbourn, the farmer let me have it for ten pounds. You'll like it. I thought we might picnic and work there every day until you have to go back to Chailton. All three of us, I mean.'

He heard himself talking too quickly and like a love-sick upper-class youth, which was less than half the story of Richard Herbert. But he had already learnt to trust his own knack of speaking to people in the way they liked.

Anne stood close to him, both thigh-deep in the blue water. She looked back across the pool to where Francis sat, uncomfortable on a stone bench beside the deck chairs, bent over his book. Clumsily she touched Richard's skin at the hip and slid her hand round to his spine, just under the top of the costume. Her touch, cold and light, lasted for a second, then she was thrashing back towards her brother. Richard was there before her.

'You'll come then?' He had to get an answer now, or the afternoon would spoil.

'Of course, we'll come,' and towelling her shoulders she began to explain vigorously to Francis.

Richard felt there was now endless time available to talk about the whens and hows. He twisted the cork and opened the wine with the right sort of controlled explosion. The sun was still hot, though the shadow of the high Victorian house had begun to dominate the lawn. The two neat piles of weeds on the verge near each of his parents had grown perceptibly, though neither of them appeared to have moved. The terrier, for Richard the chief of many small irritants in his own home, had stopped its yapping. He filled the three green glasses, each in a woven straw holder, wondering if his mother or father had ever felt exhilarated as he did now. But Richard's excursions into the feelings of other people never lasted long.

This one was interrupted by an Alfa Romeo. Long, low and scarlet, and an arm in a blue blazer waving strenuously behind the windscreen.

'They've arrested my uncle.'

It was an absurd thing to shout across Cambridge rose bushes on a summer afternoon in the mid-fifties, and Johnnie Revani was usually careful to avoid appearing absurd. But for once his excitement won over the rules.

'My father rang from Aden. They surrounded the palace with tanks. At least fifty people were killed, the bodyguard fought to the last man. My uncle is being flown to England tonight, in chains my father said.'

The three of them could see from the flash in Revani's eyes that all this was good news. But they had often heard him attack his uncle as a medieval despot and tool of the British.

'I know he was an ogre, but I can't help feeling sorry for the old gentleman,' said Anne.

She lay on her front on a faded pink Li-lo. The wet black hair straggled down her back.

'Sorry, sorry, what is sorry? He was the worst tyrant in Asia, and that's saying something. But now we can call him a martyr. Now we can get to work and throw the British out with all those fat Indians who help them.'

'And put your uncle back?' asked Francis.

'You must be making a joke.'

Johnnie Revani wore a spotless white shirt and tie, very light grey trousers fiercely pressed, and a dark blue blazer with Leander buttons. His skin was not too dark to be English. It was the sleekness of his thick hair, the hook of his nose, the polish on his shoes and the perfection of his upper-class speech which showed the Arab.

'I thought the Indians were a majority in Rajnaya,' said Francis quietly, looking up again from de Tocqueville.

'The census was a lie and even so, it is not their country. We will send the Indians home, that is easy once we have the power.' He checked himself. 'This is your chance, Richard, if you really want to make your name next term.'

'What do you mean?' Richard was angry at the intrusion into an important afternoon. He had not stirred from his deck chair, long legs crossed, the water drying on his chest. He refused to become interested. Revani came and stood over him, and Anne enjoyed the contrast between them. Dark fair, dressed undressed, tense relaxed, stocky tall, 25 21, attractive attractive.

'It's perfectly simple. You said at the last Labour committee you wanted to make a splash next term, and everyone said people were bored with politics, nothing sensational was happening. And you all went on with a bourgeois little conversation about which members of the Shadow Cabinet you would invite down to talk to us. Well now, don't you see, you've got a cause now, something real you can act on so that the newspapers will notice. I began to work it out as soon as my father had phoned.' Revani pulled a neat notebook out of his pocket. Anne got up and looked over his shoulder.

1. Opening day of term: Demonstration for withdrawal of British troops from Rajnaya.
2. Deputation to Colonial Office.
3. Emergency resolution in Union.
4. Exclusive interview with Sultan . . .

'I'm sorry to interrupt.' No one had noticed Professor Herbert join them. He seemed dressed for midwinter in old clothes which hung shapelessly; he carried a trowel. 'I'm sorry to interrupt, but have any of you young people seen Kilty?' He assumed they all knew that Kilty was the terrier.

'For God's sake, he was yapping his head off a few minutes ago, over there by the woodpile.' Richard was impatient with his father for butting in.

'He's not there now, and your mother and I have searched thoroughly both the house and the garden.'

The last terrier had been killed on the road on just such a gardening afternoon.

'Oh, he's all right, he'll have nipped through into the Fletchers' garden.'

'The connecting door is shut, and I mended the hole in the fence last week.' The Professor's tone had something expectant in it which nettled Richard.

'Dad, I'm sorry, but we're busy, we've got a plan to work out for next term. This is Johnnie Revani, by the way. I don't think you've met him before. I'm sure Kilty's all right, he can't have got out on to the road, we'd have seen him go down the drive. He's just hiding somewhere, he'll turn up when he's hungry.'

'Oh, I'm sorry. I didn't realise you were working.' The Professor put a slight accent on the last word as he looked down at his son, still sprawled in the deck chair. He ambled off to consult again with his wife. Richard got up and joined Anne in her inspection of Johnnie Revani's bit of paper.

5. Boycott of lectures, rally of all progressive groups in Market Square.
6. Lobbying of M.P.s.

The three of them talked quickly, with growing enthusiasm.

Anne jumped ahead from one item to another, and her keen-ness nudged Richard on. They sat together on the stone seat, and his arm crept round her back as they listened to Johnnie. His skin was still warmer than hers.

A cloud passed over the sun and Anne asked: 'Don't you think it'll be fun, Francis?'

For the first time they noticed that Francis was no longer there. Indeed they were sitting where he had sat without realising.

As they all looked up, there was a fresh burst of yapping, feverish and excited. Francis and Richard's parents were coming towards them across the grass, the terrier spinning happy circles round them. The Professor reached the pool first.

'He was hung up by his collar on a branch under the woodpile. Must have gone in after a rat. Couldn't bark or do anything except slowly suffocate. Lucky that Francis found him in time.'

3

Mr A. Pancratz (Camden East):

. . . we felt it essential that at the earliest opportunity after the recess the House should debate a situation where British troops intervened in August to depose a ruler linked to us by treaty, just at a time when he was about to introduce wide-ranging constitutional reforms. From the statements which the Sultan has made since his arrival in London it is clear that he was also proposing to demand the revision and updating of his treaty arrangements with Britain. The

Parliamentary Under-Secretary will have to work hard to convince us tonight that this was not the motive for the British action. As things stand, on the basis of what has so far appeared in the press and on television, the Government stands condemned of violent and arbitrary action to prop up a policy of imperialism which in this day and age is a glaring anachronism.

In the box to one side of the Speaker's chair the two Foreign Office officials whispered together. It was 9.30 p.m. A trickle of members were returning to the Chamber after dinner, but for the most part the long lines of green benches on either side of the House of Commons were empty. The officials had listened to the whole of the three-hour debate, and were hungry. They were also vaguely conscious that they had let their parliamentary Under-Secretary in for a difficult time. No feeling of guilt of course, for they had done their duty; but as he rose to the despatch box, smoothing his hair then ruffling his papers, they felt a faint relief that they were not in his shoes.

There had been two good reasons for deposing the Sultan of Rajnaya. The first was that he had secretly stuffed his villages full of Soviet rifles which could only be for use against the British presence, or the Indian immigrants whom he so detested. But this information came through intelligence sources, and could not be used without compromising them.

The other reason was that he was a bigoted bloodthirsty old man with a household of slaves and dungeons packed with political prisoners. He refused to spend money on his subjects, Arab or Indian, or let them take the first fumbling steps towards political responsibility. For five years he had not stirred from his palace. But to depose the Sultan because of his internal misrule went beyond the letter of the Treaty. So of this too the Parliamentary Under-Secretary could say little or nothing.

In preparing for the debate the Foreign Office officials had followed the honoured principle that the less your spokesman knew of the subject he was handling the less likely he was to make compromising mistakes. Mr Alistair Simbury-Smith had a brief of sorts, and a pleasant speaking voice, but that evening he knew very little about Rajnaya.

Mr A. Simbury-Smith. (Putney North-West), Parliamentary Under-Secretary of State for Foreign Affairs:

We have had an interesting and lively debate this evening, and I would like to pay tribute to the many excellent speeches which we have heard on both sides of the Chamber. It would be a poor day for this House when it could no longer find time to debate with sympathy and understanding the affairs of a distant country like Rajnaya, an island like our own, and an island with which we have strong ties of interest and history.

Hon. Members. Get on with it.

Mr A. Simbury-Smith: I propose to make my own speech in my own way.

('I can't think,' whispered the Head of the Indian Ocean Department, 'how he's going to last the full twenty minutes.' 'That's what he's paid for,' said the desk officer for Rajnaya.)

At the same time I cannot disguise from the House that I do not share, nor do my colleagues in the Government share, the analysis put forward from the front benches opposite and in particular in the able but not wholly temperate speech of the right honourable gentleman the member for Camden East (Mr Pancratz).

Mr Pancratz: On a point of order, Mr Speaker. Is it in order for the honourable gentleman to imply that I was not in control of my faculties when addressing the House?

Hon. Members: Disgraceful.

Mr Simbury-Smith: I was far from implying, Mr Speaker, that the right honourable gentleman's intemperance was caused by anything other than his own flamboyant character.

An Hon. Member: Cheap.

Mr Simbury-Smith: If I have caused him any offence by my remarks I am deeply sorry . . . Perhaps it would be for the convenience of honourable members if I briefly rehearsed the sequence of events which led to the deposition of the Sultan of Rajnaya. Before I do so I would like to associate myself with the tributes which have been paid in many parts of the House to the character and achievements of his Highness during the many years of his reign. It is a matter of deep regret to His Majesty's Government that this distinguished reign should have come to an end in circumstances of controversy and personal distress . . . Many references have been made here tonight to the Treaty of 1899. I would merely wish to point out that in 1912 . . . Again in 1933 . . . It is thus clear that the responsibility for determining the existence of an emergency rests fairly and squarely on the British Commissioner in Rajnaya, acting of course in close consultation with the Foreign Office.

On 9th May this year the British Commissioner received information that the Sultan was in contact with a certain foreign power . . .

An Hon. Member: What's wrong with that?

16

Mr Simbury-Smith: I must get on. During the weeks which followed it became clear to the Commissioner that these contacts were of a nature to imperil both the external security of Rajnaya and the maintenance of civil order on the island. On 30th July therefore . . .

Mr Pancratz: Is the Parliamentary Secretary aware that his story will carry no conviction unless he is able to tell us the exact accusation which he is making against the Sultan together with the source from which the Commissioner obtained his information?

Mr Simbury-Smith: For reasons of national security . . .

Hon. Members: Oh.

Mr Simbury-Smith: Hon. members must allow me to make my speech in my own way. For reasons of national security of a kind which were entirely familiar to hon. gentlemen opposite when they were in office, I am not at liberty to be more precise. On 30th July the Commissioner felt bound to issue an immediate declaration of emergency and to assume responsibility for internal security in accordance with the Treaty. Accordingly on 5th August . . .

Mr Pancratz: Did the Commissioner give the Sultan any advance indication of this decision?

Mr Simbury-Smith: I am afraid I do not have that information immediately available. (Interruption.) I will write to the right hon. gentleman, or he may like to put down a question.

An Hon. Member: Where is the Foreign Secretary? This little chap is no good.

Mr Simbury-Smith: Accordingly on 5th August the British Commissioner proceeded to the Sultan's Palace and informed His Highness . . .

The Chairman of the Cambridge University Conservative Association swore at the telegram which he had just picked up at the Porter's Lodge.

'Regret must cancel meeting tonight detained London important duties deep apologies Simbury-Smith.'

'Couldn't face it, I suppose,' he said to the Secretary. They were drinking washy coffee at the Union.

'He certainly had a lousy press after that speech in the House last night. Blast the man. Too late to put cancellation stickers on all the notices. What'll we do instead?'

'Another discussion group, I suppose. With luck we'll escape lynching. No one will come expecting much from Simbury-Smith.'

In their concern the Conservatives did not notice that the telegram originated in Cambridge. It was a risk that Richard Herbert and Johnnie Revani had decided they could run.

Alistair Simbury-Smith looked at the pile of neatly folded newspapers on the empty corner seat opposite him. If he picked them up his detective would assume that he was going to read once again the cruel notices of last night's debate. He was not used to having a detective and found it irksome. Too many Rajnayan waiters in London for the risk to be acceptable, Scotland Yard had said. Perhaps it would all die down now, and this shadow could be dispensed with. At any rate he must tell the Secretary of State quite firmly that he, Simbury-Smith would not, repeat not, be responsible for negotiating the revised treaty with the new Rajnayan Government. The name clung to him like a bad smell.

At least tonight he could talk to the undergraduates about his old love, the social services. He had thought of cancelling the meeting altogether, but the Crossbencher column might have got to hear of that. He got out of his briefcase the pamphlet which he and two other gay sparks had written seven years before on a Negative Income Tax. Distant carefree days of the Bow Group, argumentative dinners on winter evenings at the House, sausages and cabbage at Swinton College in Yorkshire, walks in October sunshine along the front at Brighton during the Party Conference. How he wished he could crawl out of foreign affairs back into that little English world where everything was sane, progressive and certain.

The evening light had almost gone, and a thin rain fell on the heads of commuters heading homeward down the platform. Bishops Stortford already, only another thirty minutes; he must hurry if he was to write any coherent notes for the meeting.

Both rain and darkness had thickened by the time the train reached Cambridge, and the thought of dinner at the University Arms seemed increasingly attractive. Fortunately there were no delays or uncertainties on the platform such as in his experience sometimes occurred when arrangements were in the hands of undergraduates.

'Mr Simbury-Smith? I'm Hugh Colybeare of the Conservative Association. This is our secretary, Nicholas Ralli. Let me take your case, sir, it is really very good of you to come at a time when you must be so busy.'

'Well, yes, we are rather hard pressed just at present.'

An exceptionally civil and good-looking young man,

19

thought Simbury-Smith. Hardly looked more than eighteen; just the sort of chap that was wanted in the Foreign Service. A little surprising that the other one, the Secretary of the Association, was evidently an Arab of some kind, but a thoroughly good thing of course. They escorted him past the barrier (courteous of them to have bought platform tickets), and out of the main station entrance. For some reason their car was parked on the farther and darker side of the street, opposite the buses, but the Secretary had an umbrella and Simbury-Smith hardly felt the rain. He got into the front seat. The fair young man drove rather fast to the War Memorial and then turned left, which Simbury-Smith found odd.

'Traffic diversion, is there?'

'That's right. Quite a major diversion it's going to be.'

As the car headed for Trumpington Johnnie Revani leant forward from the back seat with the gag in his hand. The strap lay beside him, ready for his second movement. They had practised the technique many times, and he made no mistake. Within twenty seconds Simbury-Smith was silenced and immobile.

Johnnie Revani sat in the only armchair in the cottage; its springs almost touched the floor. He was flushed with excitement and his eyes shone.

'The plan was perfectly clear,' he said. 'We turn him out on to the road in the morning and at the same time spill the story to *The Sunday People*. That way we get maximum publicity for our cause and maximum ridicule for the Government.'

Richard lay on his elbow on the hearthrug with his back to the fire. The logs which he and Francis had cut together in the summer were still damp, and every now and then smoke eddied into the room. Richard disliked Revani now. He disliked him for taking so seriously the present operation, which in Richard's mind had never been more than a good joke at the expense of a Tory. He disliked him for intruding on the cottage and displacing the splendid images which had accumulated there so fast during the vacation.

Walking with Francis on paths beaten through the ripe corn. Talking and reading with Francis under the beech trees. Swimming at dusk with Francis among the reeds in the deserted cut a mile away across the fields. But of course above all Anne. Anne lying in the soft thick grass which had long ago submerged the garden; Anne at the sink when the three of them washed up together. Anne burning sausages and hanging his clothes on the line; Anne upstairs under the white bulging ceiling with the thatch low over the windows, on the truckle bed with the mattress so elderly that two bodies side by side were bound to tilt towards each other. For him there had never been a time like it. It went far beyond what he had hoped for when the idea first came to him.

Into this idyll Johnnie had intruded. An urbane figure, always handsome, always intense, always political. In September he had taken to coming to the cottage almost every day, forcing the big red car up the bumpy chalk track soon after they had finished breakfast and settled down to the morning stint of reading. Francis would then disappear with his books into the wood, Johnnie would take off his blazer but not his tie, and they would sit in the kitchen or the sitting room sharpening their thoughts and their plans. Anne was clearly fascinated. She brewed extra strong coffee and it was usually Anne who made him stay and eat with

21

them. Johnnie would talk for an hour at a stretch about Rajnaya – a tumbling flow of anecdote, analysis, rhetoric, scheming, always ending with revolution and the British expelled and humiliated. Then he would talk about Britain, sharp malicious talk which fitted the intolerance of his listeners and made them laugh. He knew exactly how far he could go without offence. Richard himself enjoyed each session while it lasted. It was afterwards that he regretted the wasted sunshine and the hours which might have been spent alone with Anne.

Now it was late October, and the cottage had been deserted for six weeks. The farmer had used the two upstairs rooms to store sacks of newly harvested grain, and it was on a pile of empty sacks that Simbury-Smith, tied hand and foot, was now gnawing at his gag, midway between fear and anger.

'I'm not sure,' said Richard slowly. 'I'm beginning to think it would be more sensible to put him on the last train tonight, and not to tell the Press at all.'

'But that would destroy the whole purpose of the operation.' Johnnie Revani plucked at the sharp creases of his trousers. 'Simbury-Smith must be humiliated publicly, and because of Rajnaya. Otherwise, if it is all to be hushed up, why have we taken these risks, you and I?'

'He will have had a lesson.'

'A lesson? That kind are past learning. A good dinner and a bottle of burgundy at the Carlton, and he will be as pleased with himself as ever. In a fortnight he'll have forgotten all about it, and in his memoirs there'll be a piece about the stirring speech he made at Cambridge tonight.'

'He's not important. He just does what he's told. Not worth worrying about.' Richard hardly meant it. But of

22

course it was partly true. Simbury-Smith was a human being. If you pricked him he was hurt, and if you locked him up in a Cambridgeshire cottage all night you made him a laughing stock for years to come.

Johnnie Revani got up in one smooth quick movement, not using his limbs separately like a European, and began to pace up and down the little room. Although he was not tall he had to stoop to miss the beam, and this made his anger slightly ridiculous.

'So in the end after all the talk you treat it as a game.'

The sound of his raised voice brought Anne in from the kitchen. She had been heating a pan of soup to go with the sandwiches they had brought for supper. Now she stood in a corner of the room by the grandfather clock, almost invisible. To reduce the risk of being seen by a stray passer-by, they had drawn the curtains tight and lit only the small lamp with the brown parchment shade.

'It is always the way, the same story I was told and only half believed. No one in this bloody country will give a damn for anything. To make a joke, to make money, to make a woman – these are the only things you respect.' The glow from the logs caught his brown face and supple figure moving among the bric-à-brac of the cottage sitting-room. Richard wished that Francis had been there, but Francis had always refused to be drawn into their plans. It was Anne who spoke, from the dark corner, in a voice with an edge which he had never heard before. She was carrying the tray of sandwiches.

'You are wrong, Johnnie. It's not the British, it's just Richard. He's not serious.'

Richard got to his feet. The logs spat out of the grate. He did not know what to do. It was not going to end well.

23

'If you worked your plan, by tomorrow afternoon the man upstairs will be very angry,' Anne went on. 'Richard is afraid of what he will do.'

'Of course, of course, we've discussed this dozens of times.' Johnnie caught her wrist and pulled her out of the darkness as if it was Anne he had to persuade. 'He will get us sent down probably, perhaps even if we are lucky, sent for trial. There will be journalists and publicity everywhere. They will send me back to Aden or Rajnaya, and Richard will be famous for the rest of his life, a hero.'

Anne laughed. 'Ah you discussed, you discussed. But when it came to the point did you really think Richard thought it was more than a joke?'

Richard Herbert stood in front of them, face flushed from the fire, hair untidy, purple sweater rucked up round his waist. He knew he did not look his best and this was always important. His one need was to bring the whole silly episode to a close.

'There's no point in being melodramatic. I'd no idea you were taking it all so seriously, Johnnie. I'm going upstairs now to tell Simbury-Smith I'll put him on the train back to London tonight if he says nothing about it to anyone. It'll be in his own interest to keep quiet. And we'll all have had a good laugh.'

'You can't, you can't. The car is mine, and Anne won't let you take hers, she's on my side.' Revani's voice shot up and he was suddenly less impressive, like a child which sees its toy disappearing.

'It's no good, Johnnie,' said Anne. She stepped between the two men and stood looking at Revani intently for a second. Then to Richard: 'Come on.'

The two of them untied Simbury-Smith and hustled him

down the narrow stairs. His mouth was so sore that he simply nodded as Richard explained. Outside the rain had started again and they slopped through puddles to Anne's elderly Morris, parked on the track behind the big Italian car. Revani watched them passively from the cottage doorway, his figure just outlined against the dim light from the sitting-room.

Anne opened the front left-hand door of the Morris and began to push Simbury-Smith in.

'Put him in the back,' said Richard. 'He'll give no trouble, you can ride in front with me.'

Anne continued to push, and shut the door as soon as most of the bulky figure was inside.

'Off you go,' she said, and the edge was back in her voice. 'I'm staying here. And I don't ever want to see you again.'

She ran off across the squelching track to the doorway. Richard hesitated. The wet was coming through his shoes and he had left his raincoat in Johnnie's car. The door of the cottage shut without a noise, and the darkness was complete.

He got into the Morris and drove Simbury-Smith fast to Cambridge station.

Nineteen-Seventies

Barney Tyrrell, head of the Current Affairs Division of Enterprise Television, ripped open the white envelope marked 'Personal and Secret'. It had become a Thursday ritual during the election campaign.

'Bloody awful,' he said. He was just over forty, grey hair brushed back from a sharp dark face, the only waistcoat in the room and a yellow rose.

They shifted in their seats. It sounded worse even than last week. And last week two men had been summarily sent to other less exposed departments.

'Only fifteen per cent can remember hearing anything about the election on "Our Life". Even the nine o'clock news did better.'

The nine o'clock news was on the other channel. The editor of the 'Our Life' programme twisted his wispy beard, consumed with a sense of unfairness. He had been plucked into television from a weekly magazine on the understanding that he was simply window-dressing. His job was to produce one heavy sententious programme a week to keep the critics happy and make sure Enterprise Television got its franchise renewed when the time came. Now, just because there was an election he was told that everything depended on his ratings. That white envelope from the Research Department had become a nightmare.

'The cannabis petition,' he said. 'What about a group of

teenage students from some College of Art firing questions at two front benchers? Have you ever smoked pot? Have your children signed the petition? We could get some of the students to storm out in the middle.'

Tyrrell thought through a puff of Panatella. From the fifteenth floor of the Enterprise building, London spread before them. The boardroom, which he had the right to use for this occasion, was oak-panelled, and expensively lighted. Reproductions of Canaletto alternated round the walls with framed awards and carvings in fourteen languages of the Enterprise slogan 'Great is Truth'.

'The Tory whips wouldn't agree,' he said. 'And even if they did the police would arrest most of the kids at the studio door on the way out. Good for ratings but bad for the image.'

And bad for Labour too, he thought: no votes in cannabis, even in the mid-70s. A Labour government would mean C.B.E.'s for the communicators, above a certain salary level of course, and drinks again at Downing Street for their wives. These Tory years had been a lean time for the dignity of the industry. Last night he had even canvassed a street in Hampstead himself. But these were not thoughts for the meeting.

'Any ideas, Richard?'

Richard Herbert, at thirty-eight, was the senior and most successful of the corps of interviewers cherished by 'Our Life'. He looked younger than his years; it was only in daylight that the flesh below the chin hung a little heavy, and the cut of the suit seemed three or four years too young for his waist. But the sleek fair hair was unimpaired, and anyway it was not just good looks which had kept Richard Herbert afloat. He did have ideas and an instinct for diplomacy which turned them to good effect. All the anxious faces round the table suspected that the wispy beard would go after the election and that Richard would slip smiling into his place. He might even be aiming higher than that.

Richard sipped his coffee. The words were ready in his mind, but a little suspense was always useful, particularly in a gamble like this.

'Rajnaya,' he said. They gaped.

Richard had got into the train at Barnes that morning flummoxed and undecided. He guessed the ratings would still be bad, but he had been able to think of no answer to the question which would be put to him. Breakfast had been taken up with an argument whether his wife had time to drive him to the station or whether he should walk. He had walked, not noticing the roses in the magnificent little gardens, not thinking of the election or the ratings, just fighting the silly argument with Roberta over again inside himself.

Once seated in the train he had broken out of this frustration by reading the bulky letter from Francis which he had jammed into his inside pocket when the postman had knocked at the height of the breakfast quarrel. He expected little from it except a sense of guilt, for he knew that Francis, unmarried and thousands of miles away, had kept an investment in their friendship more substantial than his own.

'Dear Dickie . . .' no one called him that now. But suddenly his attention was caught, the idea leapt into his mind, and by the time he reached Waterloo it had so flourished that he caught a taxi to Enterprise House instead of queuing for the usual bus. If he replaced the wispy beard, it would be goodbye to buses for ever.

'Rajnaya,' he said. 'You read about the riots last week.' They hadn't. 'Middle page stuff because of the election, but

28

a dozen admitted killed, probably a hundred. And I have just heard that next week is going to be worse, much worse. Monday is the anniversary of independence, and they'll be lucky to get by without civil war.'

'You must be out of your smart little mind.' Joe Steel had a big pale face, and a scruffy mass of grey-brown hair. New York was his home, but he had quarrelled with the *New York Times* while working for them in London, and on the rebound had snapped up an offer from Enterprise. He disliked Richard for being better-looking, more successful and less able than himself. There were normally five hours in the day when Joe Steel was sober, and during any of them he was a dangerous opponent. 'No one in Britain cares a snowball in hell about foreign affairs at any time, and during an election they're total poison.'

'Usually I'd agree with Joe, of course,' said Richard, putting on his diplomatic mid-Atlantic manner. 'But Rajnaya is special. The Government there has reached the end of its tether. One more whiff of grapeshot and they'll invoke the treaty with Britain – bang in the last week of the election campaign. There's the issue we've been waiting for. The question is simply this – does Enterprise want to be in on the act before it starts?'

They didn't like it; he could feel caution rising like a mist round the table. Nothing like high-paid creative talent for running away from an idea.

Joe Steel had his knife out first. 'Before we spend thousands of pounds and send a team to die on a street corner the other end of Asia, perhaps we should be a little surer of our facts. You are always brilliantly informed, Richard, but I didn't realise you actually read the Foreign Office telegrams.'

'Better than that.' Richard pulled out the blue airmail

envelope with the crest on the back. 'Letter from the Acting High Commissioner in Rajnaya, dated three days ago, via F.O. bag.'

At the head of the table Tyrrell crunched a chocolate biscuit from the plate reserved for him alone. It was a sign of interest. 'Does the letter bear out all that you said just now?' Richard had not meant to go so far, but there was no retreat. He found the right passage and read aloud.

'Things are rotting so quickly that it seems President Lall could ask for British troops if there's trouble at the anniversary parade. He's got plenty of proof of external interference, so it would be a good case under the treaty. And the answer can't wait, certainly not as long as polling day. At least it'll give the politicians your end something to talk about as well as cannabis.'

'It certainly will,' said Tyrrell. 'I like it.' He liked it, they all liked it, there were smiles and second cups of coffee. Only the wispy beard, watching the ebb of his authority, felt bound to make a stand.

'But what if after all the trouble and expense nothing happens at the anniversary on Monday?'

Tyrrell laughed, and this time the crunch on the chocolate biscuit was final.

'Of course if we stay away, it may turn out sweetness and light. But if we're there you can bet your last luncheon voucher something will happen, that's for sure. A scuffle in a bar, a bit of swearing, a gun or two – that's quite enough of a happening if you've got a camera in the right place and someone who can ask the right questions. Richard'll do it fine.'

This was the difficult point. Richard had foreseen it as the taxi rounded Trafalgar Square.

'I don't think I can go myself.'

A dark cloud built up again at the end of the table. 'Why ever not? It's your idea and you're the right man.'

'You forget you've fixed for me to do a programme on the Foreign Secretary's speech on Saturday.'

'Forget it, I'll unfix that. I'm not going to lose the chance of a civil war and a big election issue because of a piddling little fête in Downshire.'

Richard was in confusion, so obvious and so uncharacteristic that Joe Steel laughed.

'Look hard, gentlemen, you'll never see the like again – young Richard's got an attack of shyness. He's dropped his letter-writing friend in the shit, and doesn't want to be on the spot to watch it swallow him up.'

Richard felt them all look at him, some curious, some malicious.

'I honestly would rather not go. I don't think I'm the right man.' He did not really believe in his own idea, certainly not enough to traipse off to a godforsaken little island at the height of an election campaign in which he was doing good work.

Tyrrell accepted this, to the general surprise.

'Stay at home then, and polish your soul at the Ridingley fête. Joe, you're for Rajnaya – subject of course to your editor's approval' – with an elaborate bow to the wispy beard, who was already plunged in thought of a future incarnation with the British Council.

Joe Steel grinned elaborately, and emptied the chintzy coffee cup as if it held brandy.

'Richard, I suppose your F.O. type usually changes for dinner? Just time to clean my white tuxedo, the one with the bullet holes.'

2

When Richard woke up next morning it was raining hard. The sky through the gap in the curtains was still half dark. The danger signal was the splash of water from the roof where the gutter had broken. It cascaded into the little walled courtyard to one side of the house and if the drain was blocked with leaves, the level of the water rose quickly over the sill of the door and into the kitchen. This had happened two months ago, and since then he had persistently forgotten to telephone the builder or clear the leaves out of the drain.

Richard looked at Roberta, humped asleep beside him. They had quarrelled again last night, about Rajnaya of all things. He had come home waving like a trophy the fact that he had refused to go there.

'I was tempted, but I didn't want to leave you just now.'

But it was a mistake in his marriage to expect applause. He should have learnt that by now.

'You mean to say they seriously meant to send you abroad while I'm like this?' Roberta was two months gone after a boy and a miscarriage. The doctor said rest. 'I hope you made it absolutely clear it was out of the question.'

'I told you, I'm not going.' He had also brought home two avocado pears bought at Waterloo, but she had not even looked in the paper bag.

'But they might send you to some other bloody country, next week, perhaps? D'you mean to say you haven't even told them . . .' And so on; she had found her opening.

She always looked attractive when really angry. Her short dark hair fell forward, and the white skin flushed just below the cheekbone. Five years earlier he would have stopped the words by sweeping her off to bed. That didn't work now, nothing worked; the evening was wasted, not in misery (they were past that too) but in wary patrolling between bursts of her anger. She was pregnant, she was bored, she was married to a man whom everyone found attractive except herself. He knew all the reasons now and none of the answers. Three years earlier he would have gone out for a drink and perhaps a girl. This time he had been in bed by eleven.

He threw aside the bed clothes, not minding if he woke her. He fumbled with the keys, opened the kitchen door to the leaden morning, and leaning from the doorway poked at the drain with a broom handle. The wind veered for a moment and blew the rain in at the door. He returned to bed half-wet, half-dry, shedding his pyjama jacket. Roberta had not stirred.

He had twenty minutes before the baby woke – no time for more sleep. Lying there in the grey light, listening to the ugly music of loud rain and his wife's breathing, thinking of Tyrrell and Joe Steel and back to Francis and again to Roberta, Richard Herbert was seized with anger.

Between them they had trapped him. Here he lay, half-naked in a bed in S.W.13, still young, intelligent and handsome, with all his thrust and dash unimpaired. But he was their prisoner, satisfying none of them completely, because of them incapable of satisfying himself. Francis wanted him to answer his letters and be an honest friend. Roberta wanted him to ring up the man about the gutter and be back in the house by 6.30 to pour her gin and tonic. Tyrrell wanted him as editor of 'Our Life', a second spider so that the web could be more elaborate and the flies more juicy. And what did he want for himself? Money, power, a loving woman – of course. But what they really denied him was excitement, the real excitement towards which Cambridge had seemed to point.

Rajnaya, was that where the excitement lay? Perhaps his idea for the programme had been a good one after all. He thought for a moment of Joe Steel flying eastwards at that moment. First-class of course, and gaining hours fast; Joe would be fuddled with whisky by now, eating a plastic lunch and scribbling unreadable malice on the acre-sized menu. Perhaps after all he should have gone to Rajnaya himself. The wrong kind of excitement of course, because he would be there as an observer of other excited people, but even so nearer the mark than a Tory fête, God keep us. And if Roberta was going to have another miscarriage she would have it, into whatever continent her husband had by then strayed. An ambulance could drive her faster to Queen Charlotte's Hospital, and he had used up all the words of comfort last time.

The baby woke and began to cry – half past six, a child punctual in each disagreeable turn of its daily round. It was now a question which parent got up to give it the bottle of pink liquid which would keep it quiet for another hour. Probably the nappy would need changing. Roberta lay motionless, but he knew she was awake. He had refused to find the six pounds a week for an au pair girl. But it was he who had cleared the drain, and to show that his conscience was easy he turned on the light. He began to read the papers which he had brought back from Enterprise the night before.

ENTERPRISE FORWARD PLANNING SCHEDULE NO. 2873
Commentator's copy
Transmission times: Bulletins throughout evening.
Feature: Foreign Secretary's Speech.
Unit: Outside Broadcasting.

Length of transmission: 3–5 minutes depending on interest.
Location: Ridingley Hall, Downshire (Conservative fête).
Commentator/Interviewer: Richard Herbert.
Commencement time for feature: 2.30 p.m.
Editor's Note: Sir John Pastmaster's first speech during the current campaign. Unlikely to say anything new (Broadcast required to balance Leader of Opposition's Jarrow speech same day). Suggest short extract from speech itself (Central Office will suggest passage, but you have free hand) followed by *either* Tory fête scenes *or* short exclusive interview with Pastmaster after speech. B.B.C. do not at present intend to cover.
Local contact: Conservative Wessex Area agent
                   (Salisbury 44903)
or   Chairman of Fête Committee (wife of owner
                   of Ridingley House) The Hon. Mrs . . .

There had been moments earlier in Richard's life when he had suddenly seen luck coming to him. The sight of a sword not his own hacking at the thicket in front of him had given him more pleasure than any achievement of his own. The history tripos paper with two questions leading straight back to the books he had just finished; the rustication after the Pitt Club Ball of the young Tory who would have beaten him as President of the Union. Then the luck had veered away and stayed away. Not since those Cambridge days had he felt the same tingle at the back of his neck as came to him now at the thought of Anne Trennion.

'The Hon. Mrs Anne Charteris.' Of course that had been the name on the wedding invitation seven years before. Captain the Honourable James Charteris, then just out of the Army and soon after chosen by a West country constituency on account of his profile, pleasant smile and pretty wife. Richard had not gone to the wedding of course. His memories of Anne had nothing to do with the girl whom he saw next day in the *Daily Telegraph,* long dark hair outshining the veil and a thin fair man with a long nose beside her.

Now he would see her again. And of course more than see her. Tomorrow his would be a position of power at Ridingley. He would be treated at least as deferentially as old Pastmaster. If they knew their stuff all those local Tories would offer him drinks and small talk, coax him into a good humour, try and find out which extract from the speech he would take, steer him away from shots of Pastmaster with a glass in his hand. A private talk with 'Chairman of the Fête Committee (wife of owner of Ridingley House) – nothing could be more natural. And after that, God helping, there could be a means of escape and a new chapter. The coincidence was too great to be meaningless. The rain would stop and the drains would clear and this time nothing would smother him again.

It was a brave early morning thought and he knew its limitations. He tried to give it substance by composing his end of the telephone conversation which he would have as soon as he was safe in the office. 'Could I speak to Mrs Charteris, please?' very silky, no 'Honourable' of course. 'This is Richard Herbert of Enterprise Television.' The pause, the quick steps across the parquet floor, the cascade of excited words, the invitation to lunch, to dinner, to spend the night.

And so, almost dozing, back to the earlier Anne. Not nights but afternoons, hot with the high meadow grass around them, and the sound of boats on the river not far away, cheerful half-heard voices to give a spice of danger.

Short hair then and a brown eager face, and he himself slim and quick-moving, with not enough knowledge of anything to spoil his confidence. It had been easy in those days to be sure. Until that evening in the cottage when things had gone abruptly wrong.

Half-awake, he turned to Roberta beside him. Under the soft night-dress her breasts were heavy, and still thinking of Anne, he moved his hand up to touch them. She turned sharply to her own side of the bed and then was out groping for her slippers. 'The baby,' she said, and shuffled from the room. Richard turned out the light, for a clearer view of his new vision.

Goodbye baby, goodbye drains, goodbye Barnes, I declare this fête well and truly open.

3

'I forgot if I told you, Johnnie Revani has stopped coming to the house. Till lately he came to parties, even sometimes just for chess like the old days when you used to brew the coffee. Never talked politics, or about Rajnaya at all, and I never pumped him though *he* pushed me to. But now he doesn't answer the cards, and I can't get through to him on the telephone. It's as bad a sign as any.'

Anne Charteris sighed over the blue airmail paper and put it down beside the grapefruit. This was the third letter from Francis in a fortnight, all three long, and from experience she knew this meant he was worried. But he never said so or gave her a peg on which she could hang something helpful when she wrote back. Just page after page about

Rajnayan politics, assuming a knowledge and an interest which were beyond her.

At the other end of the table her husband was reading the *Downshire Gazette*. They were breakfasting half an hour earlier than usual because of all the work still to be done for tomorrow's great event.

'What about Rajnaya, then?' she asked. 'Is it going to be dangerous?'

'Rajnaya?' James Charteris was always running mental races with his wife in which he felt he deserved some sort of a handicap. Then he remembered. 'Ah, of course, Francis. What's up with him now, then?'

'But you must remember that riot last week, and how worried I was.'

'Yes, yes of course.' He had even got the atlas from the gun-room and looked the place up.

'Francis goes on and on about it all, but doesn't tell me what I really want to know. If there's more trouble there, will he be in danger?'

Charteris put aside the *Gazette* and took off the horn-rimmed glasses which looked so absurd on his outdoor face. 'Of course not, darling. In that sort of place there's trouble all the time, it doesn't mean anything particular. One good thing about our getting out of all these countries is that they don't shoot at us any longer, too busy hacking at each other.'

'Francis says he's moving into the Residence.'

Charteris saw how he might give reassurance. He had never resented the fact that his wife was more ambitious for her brother than for him.

'If there *is* more trouble while the High Commissioner's away and Francis is in charge, it'll be the making of him. Best thing that could happen to his career, I should guess. I don't know the exact form in the F.O. but he might well put himself right in line for a Knighthood next time.'

'But if it's nothing to do with us, how can Francis get so much credit out of it?'

'Oh, of course, we've got a treaty with the Government out there, we had some P.Q.'s about it the other day. Bound to be a mass of telegrams, consultations, that kind of stuff.' He was about to take up the paper again, but saw in time that he had not hit the target.

'Look, Anne. I never have time to go to the Foreign Affairs Committee nowadays. I don't know the ups and downs of these things any longer. But you've got old Pastmaster coming to lunch tomorrow. He never has anything to say to me, so you can spend the whole time quizzing him. But don't talk up Francis too much, they never like that sort of thing.'

Yes, that was right, she would make the Foreign Secretary sing for his Vichyssoise and cold salmon. But Anne was irritated that she could not assess the situation herself. James had never been able to distinguish foreign countries except by their sporting achievements. But in the old days, with Francis and Richard Herbert, yes and Johnnie Revani, she had known it all. Of course they had not really known it all, just under half she reckoned, just enough to be voluble and passionate about a riot, assassination or coup anywhere in the world as it flickered across the headlines.

Francis had gone forward fast; Richard and Johnnie Revani she never saw now, but imagined them leading exciting lives. Only Anne Charteris, nee Trennion, had gone back, out of the game altogether. She looked out of the window across the newly mown lawn to the marquee and the shimmer of the lake. One couldn't have everything, as

James was always pointing out. But for a moment, gathering together the rest of her letters to read upstairs, she missed the excitement of all that righteous and committed anger.

'What have you decided about the detective?' asked Charteris as she passed him on the way to the door.

Quite right, these were the things which concerned her now. 'Oh, don't worry about him. He and the secretary from the Foreign Office will eat in the gallery next door to us. There'll be red boxes and a special telephone, they're going to fit it all up there. That'll leave the Parliamentary Private secretary and the Conservative Area agent to have lunch with us.'

'You'll be the only woman.'

'You'll be there to protect me.' She kissed him and he was happy.

There was a great deal to settle in her own mind before the fête committee came for its final meeting at eleven. They took their lead from her, as they had learnt to do over the last three years. She had tried to work out an exact routine, but each year there were special problems and this one had brought the usual crop of small difficulties. The band were insisting on payment in cash and special billing on the programme. The big elm at the end of the rose garden had shed three branches lately and would have to be roped off. There was a feud still to be resolved between the home produce stall and the tea tent about the price to be charged for cakes.

But above all of course the fête this year fell during the election campaign. This meant a crowding in of the outside world, more charabancs from farther afield, journalists, candidates from neighbouring seats, television. She almost wished that Pastmaster had cancelled the engagement when the election was announced, as everyone had expected he would. But secretly she thrived on extra action and a touch of fever. Unlike James, who would spend the whole morning in his study making himself miserable over his three-minute vote of thanks.

The telephone beside the desk rang, and she had a presentiment of bad news about Francis as sharp as a physical pain. The relief when the voice said, 'This is Richard Herbert' was so great that without thinking she answered the man as if he had not been out of her life for more than fifteen years.

'Richard, darling, where are you?'

After that false start it was difficult to get back on to a normal footing, nor did she really feel that she wanted to. For Richard was part of Francis, part of the past, as real at that moment as the election or the fête or her husband. Not really understanding the flow of words, she gathered that Richard was actually coming to the fête because of something to do with television and that he would like to be invited to lunch. At that a small alarm sounded in her mind. James would not like it, and Sir John Pastmaster might well dislike it. But in her mood of the morning this was not enough, and she said yes. Richard's voice went on. He was talking in a somewhat forced way, almost as if reading from a script. She multiplied her words of welcome.

'Yes, of course, Richard, come as early as you can . . . don't worry, we'll find time somehow for a proper talk . . . you mustn't hurry back, stay and have a quiet supper.'

She could talk to Richard about Rajnaya. Richard would know about it, he moved on the fringe of that world, he would understand about Francis.

Later Anne Charteris came to regret that she had not listened more carefully to what Richard said and the way he said it. But for the moment there were eight telephone calls on her list, and the cook and the gardener to see, all before the committee arrived for coffee at eleven thirty. Somehow she must prevent them from spending the whole meeting in speculation about the weather.

4

'Labour lead of two and a half per cent, I see. The Secretary of State will not be best pleased.'

'And just over a week to go. It'll be touch and go or worse.'

The two men talked in a detached way, for they were contemplating the misfortunes of others. One was a member of the Diplomatic Service and the other had the second safest seat in the country. On this Saturday morning they were waiting for the arrival in the Foreign Office of Sir John Pastmaster, Secretary of State for Foreign and Commonwealth Affairs, whom they served.

'Anything much in the telegrams?'

'No, very dull. That's one thing about this campaign, it's dead quiet in the world and no one's had an excuse to drag in foreign affairs.'

'Touch wood. How about the speech for this afternoon? Did you manage to clear it with all the departments in time?'

Donald Pringle, the official Private Secretary, made a face. The Foreign Secretary's political speeches were drafted by a bright-eyed young man in the Conservative Research Department, whose ideas and adjectives were then winnowed by officials until the result was sufficiently drab to be safe.

'Had trouble till almost midnight with the "vision of

Europe" bit. Western Organisations Co-ordination Department dream no dreams and see no visions. In the end we got by with "concept of intracontinental co-operation". – Tell me, why is the Secretary of State doing this fête at all?'

Jack Mellon, Parliamentary Private Secretary, was not quite sure how much Pringle knew about Sir John Pastmaster's political standing. It was a subject difficult to discuss across the subtle frontier which separated their two worlds, those of the member of Parliament and of the Civil Servant.

In the political world it was well known that when, six months earlier, the last Foreign Secretary had fallen into the Atlantic with his airliner on the way to Washington the Prime Minister had appointed Pastmaster as a stopgap. He had wished to postpone until after the election, which he expected to win, his substantive choice for a post of such importance.

It had been a risk. Pastmaster, though of sound mind and respected in the Party after five blameless years as Chairman of the 1922 Committee, had a reputation as a poor speaker. One of the Prime Minister's first acts after the dissolution of Parliament had been to tell Central Office that because of the pressure of international events the Foreign Secretary could not be expected to take any part in the election campaign. Sir John, conscious of no such pressure, was irked to learn indirectly of this guidance. When soon afterwards it was suggested that the Ridingley fête should be cancelled, he insisted crossly that it must proceed.

But these were not matters which could comfortably be discussed with an official.

'James Charteris down at Ridingley is the son of an old friend, and Central Downshire has never been a really safe seat.'

'Good morning, gentlemen.'

The Foreign Secretary was wearing a light brown tweed suit, shining brown shoes, and a pink rose. His thick grey-white hair was brushed smoothly back from the high-coloured face. He looked exactly what he was: a conventional Conservative about to make a weekend speech in the garden of a country house.

'Nasty day for a fête.' Rain spattered the windows looking on to St James's Park, already thinly populated with groups of tourists in transparent mackintoshes.

'The radio forecast said it would clear from the west about midday, Secretary of State.'

'Ah, the wireless . . . Well, I suppose we'd better be off. It'll take us two hours at least without allowing for jams on the motorway.' He added a little reluctantly: 'Anything new in this morning?'

'No, nothing in particular. The most urgent overnight telegrams and submissions will be in the car with you in case you have time to deal with them on the way down. And there's one message from News Department.' The private secretary hunted on his desk.

'Here it is. Enterprise Television have asked if you'd give a short interview this afternoon at the fête to Richard Herbert, the man they're sending to cover your speech. Only two or three minutes.'

'That sounds all right.' Like most people with little experience of television Sir John Pastmaster was sure he was very good at it.

It was Jack Mellon who asked the cautionary questions. As Parliamentary Private Secretary he found that this was often his role.

'Richard Herbert's pretty left-wing, isn't he?'

44

'Well, of course, that's not something News Department can answer, but I did have a quiet word with Central Office. They say they regard him as a straightforward interviewer. And Enterprise have said he'll confine himself to the subjects raised in your speech, Secretary of State.'

'Well, that's safe enough. Let's get going, shall we? No point in hanging about here.'

On his way down in the lift the Foreign Secretary had a further thought, which he communicated to the doorman at the park door.

'Get them to ring up my wife at Dorneywood, will you, and tell her I'll be on the Enterprise News tonight? She always likes to look in if she can.'

5

The rain began to ease as Richard drove on the motorway through Berkshire, and by the time he was among the downs it had stopped completely. On the whole he was glad. Wet tents and the bedraggled figures of the Tory faithful would make good satirical television, particularly on a day when they had done badly in the opinion polls. But if being Chairman of the Fête Committee meant anything he supposed that on a wet day Anne would be a general coping with defeat, taking urgent and depressing decisions, hardly in the mood to look at the whole pattern of her life afresh.

For this was what he was determined to ask for. The first enthusiasm of the day before had faded by the time he telephoned Ridingley, but the way Anne responded had delighted him. He had weighed several times each sentence she had spoken, trying to discount his own state of mind, and each time the answer came out the same. She had been eager to see and talk to him. He must come to lunch; he must stay to dinner; nothing could have been more welcoming. For a second or two the years had been swallowed up; they had spoken to each other as if they were still meeting and talking every day. If they could start from that base, then everything was possible.

He had thought of course what 'everything' should mean. They could find a flat or a little house, in London of course, and if she insisted on divorce and remarriage then he would agree, though it would be easier the other way. He would not talk about money today, though at a fairly early stage he would need to find out how much she had of her own.

As he turned off the motorway, his mind bubbling with such thoughts, Richard knew that he was racing ahead dangerously fast. To keep his mind from pushing beyond the frontiers of good sense he concentrated on his physical surroundings. It was one of the many parts of England of which he knew little. The tops of the downs were bright now with wheat and barley, only the steepest part of their sides keeping the duller green of the original turf. The road wound mostly beneath the downs through a string of villages with elaborate names. Richard reminded himself that sociologically these villages were a mess. He had read articles about them in *New Society*. The farm-workers had been pushed into the council houses on the outskirts by the middle-class elderly who had bought up and rethatched the old cottages by the stream. The pub was a tied house, the Georgian manor up the lime avenue belonged to a Eurodollar magnate, and the church could be sure of neither vicar nor congregation.

46

But now he saw the Downshire villages, not in print but on a June morning with the rain stopped, the sun out, the soft brick and stone matched once again with the performance of an English summer. Faced with roses round every corner and the towering splendour of the chestnut trees, Richard began to drive rather faster than was safe on a narrow road. For reasons not clear to himself he felt uncomfortable, as if he had ventured by mistake into alien territory.

He soon began to notice the election posters. On the motorway of course they were not allowed, and in London they were very rare. But here they sprouted on trees, at farm gates, in cottage windows. Overwhelmingly blue, with a sprinkling of red on the outskirts of some villages – names of candidates wholly unknown to Richard, until he crossed a boundary line and the message became 'Charteris again for Central Downshire'. 'Election fête and rally – Sir John Pastmaster – Ridingley Hall.' In Richard's world the general election was a mixture between a joke and a sporting event, an occasion above all for more interviews, more gossip, more guineas. The idea that to others far from the centre of events an election was something of real importance was again slightly disturbing.

The posters advertising the fête grew thicker and Richard's map showed that he was almost at Ridingley. Eleven-thirty – he had three hours before the camera crew arrived, four hours before Pastmaster's speech. For he had decided that he must make his attempt on Anne early rather than late. After the speech he imagined a chaos of homemade marmalade and buried treasure, from which it would be impossible to detach her for any coherent length of time. And he himself would have to interview Pastmaster, which might well prove a time-consuming operation.

He drew in to the side of the road where a cart track led into a field. From the carefully painted gate and the trim hedgerow he guessed that he might already be on the Ridingley estate, where there was no lack of money for such niceties. He switched off the engine and tried to think exactly how he should speak to Anne.

After lunch Charteris and Pastmaster would probably go off to brood over their speeches. There might be a calm space then in which to catch her. There would be no time to talk about the last fifteen years; they must be swallowed up as they had been over the telephone the day before. But the right words for this would not form in Richard's mind.

As an only child he had sometimes been forced to go to Cambridge tea parties where he knew no one. The remedy had been not to hang about outside the strange front door while his courage ebbed, but to go straight in and start radiating the Herbert charm while it was still fully charged. Richard restarted the engine, and within a few minutes was inside the lodge gates of Ridingley.

The drive was flanked with limes and ran level through parkland for almost a mile before rising gently, not too steep a pull for carriage horses, to the northern portico of Ridingley Hall. Sections of the park were neatly marked out with flags for charabancs and private cars. Beyond the cattle grid where the ground began to rise two old men with big blue rosettes sat at a table in charge of fat coils of entrance tickets. When they saw Richard's press sticker they waved him in with a smile.

As he swung round to park on the gravel he could see on the lawns behind the house a cluster of small tents, and one big marquee. Small groups of people were moving purposefully about the encampment carrying lists, like non-commissioned officers before an eighteenth-century battle. No doubt on some suitable eminence the Chairman of the Fête Committee herself could be found, one hand on the reins of her charger, the other flourishing a plumed hat in the direction of the nearest polling booth.

There was a side door leading through a brick wall into the main garden, and Richard was tempted to go and find Anne at once. But before the decision was made, he heard a friendly voice.

'Is your name Herbert?'

He had no difficulty in recognising the man who had opened the front door and now stood under the portico. Not from that smudged wedding photograph of many years ago, but because you must own the place if you stood under its Ionic pillars looking so unimpressive and speaking with such authority. James Charteris had not yet changed for lunch. The baggy grey flannel trousers, the long nose, fair moustache, and gently receding chin fitted exactly one of the stereotypes which lived in the back of Richard Herbert's mind – stereotypes which he trotted out as a substitute for knowledge of his fellow citizens. A not-so-young Tory backbencher, not bright enough for office, ten years away from thinking about a knighthood. They shook hands.

'Glad you could come. Message from your office in London ten minutes ago. Would you ring a fellow called Tyrrell straight away?'

The telephone was in the study, looking modern among the college and regimental photographs and the yearbooks of the Downshire Agricultural Society. Richard wondered if there was a horsewhip behind the door. He found Tyrrell in a furious temper, suavity blown away by bad news.

'What the hell are you doing down among the hayseeds so early? Your blasted meeting doesn't start till 2.30.'

'I'm having lunch with Pastmaster and the nobs.' Normally Tyrrell would have been impressed, and hidden the fact in a blaze of abuse. But he was preoccupied by his troubles.

'That bloody Joe has let us down. Got himself locked up in Teheran.'

'Teheran?'

'That's what I said. T-E-H-, the rest of it. Stupid airport brawl. He spat on a portrait of the Empress. Three months at least, the consul thinks.'

'You're going to leave him there?'

'Dry those crocodile tears, Richard. We'll try to get him expelled as soon as we can. But it won't be in time to save our programme.'

'What does Wantzner say?' Wantzner, with the wispy beard, was after all the editor of 'Our Life'.

'He's sulking, and won't hear of anything to do with Rajnaya. With luck he'll resign before the week is out. So I'm ringing you.'

'I don't quite see why.'

'Hell, Richard, you thought up this Rajnaya jape. You've heard of the place, you can find it on the map, you talked us into it. Now I want to know from you how we are going to do it. The *TV Times* for next week goes to press first thing tomorrow and they need the answer.'

'Send up Cochrane from Singapore.'

Bill Cochrane, the resident Enterprise man in the Far East, had been moved farther and farther eastwards as his natural laziness came to dominate his life. So long as Cochrane was in Singapore, twelve million people in Britain would hear next to nothing of the affairs of that region. This was probably a good thing for all concerned except those who had to find his salary.

'Cochrane, you say? Look, the idea was for our ratings to go up, not through the floor. He'd send us a still of the local temple and three sentences saying everything was quiet.'

'Why not scrap the whole idea?'

'No, I like it, and what's more, I've told everyone I like it. There's only one answer. You'll just have time if you catch the early plane tomorrow.'

'But I . . .' Looking at a photograph of a racehorse on Charteris' desk, Richard hesitated between two excuses for not going. Either he was worried in case his wife had a miscarriage, or he was about to resume an old love affair. Which would work better? Tyrrell's private life offered no clues as to the best tactic. He played safe.

'No, it's not that at all,' he said. 'It's Roberta. She thinks she's coming up to another miscarriage and her nerves are in pieces. I particularly don't want to leave her for any length of time just now.'

There was a pause. He could almost hear Tyrrell testing this piece of news against his knowledge that the Herberts were on bad terms with each other.

'O.K.,' he said finally. 'I'll go find a bomb big enough to put under Cochrane.' A pause. 'Finding the fête congenial?'

'I'm just heading for the first cocktail.'

'Remember Ramsay Mac, by the end all champagne and duchesses. I'll bet he started in a small way with sherry and an Honourable.'

Within two minutes Richard had sherry but the wrong Honourable, across the hall in the big drawing room.

'Sorry, Anne's busy somewhere out there. There's a lot of

work in a fête, you know. But then I expect in your job you go to a great many.'

'It's my first ever, as a matter of fact.' There seemed no way of bridging that particular gulf, but James Charteris found a new topic.

'Knew Anne at Cambridge, didn't you?'

'Yes, I did, quite well.'

'She was a clever girl,' then, realising this sounded odd, 'Still is, of course.'

'Of course.' Unless her brain has been addled by your company.

'She had a letter today from . . .' Anne entered the room and Richard held his breath at the pleasure of it. An inch or two shorter than he remembered, in a green silk dress which showed off her sunburnt skin. She had always managed, even in the middle of winter, to look as if she had just spent a week on a scorching beach. But it was the dark blue eyes which caught him back into the past more surely than any daydream. They were a little larger than the other features would justify, and their setting of tiny horizontal wrinkles was a little deeper than before. He must succeed; now it seemed more important than ever.

He stood up and she came quickly over and kissed him, for a moment holding both his arms in the beginnings of a embrace. Her husband turned to pour her a drink.

'Off you go, James,' she said. 'You haven't changed yet, and Sir John will be here any minute.'

When he had gone: 'Any minute means twenty minutes. Not enough for all I want to ask you. Give yourself some more sherry. I am very, very glad to see you again, Richard, and for a particular reason.'

So far so good. No use waiting till after lunch; he must

make his strike now. Anne sat down on the end of the sofa next to his chair.

'So am I glad to see you, Anne. And I've got a special reason too.'

'Fine, but let's start with mine. Please tell me all about politics in Rajnaya.'

'But how did you know . . . ?' Of course that was wrong. She didn't know anything about Tyrrell and Enterprise; it must be something to do with Francis.

'It's Francis – have you heard from him lately? I know he writes to you.'

'Yes, I had a letter this week. He's in charge of the High Commission at the moment, and he expects a flare-up between the communities any time.'

How on earth was he going to turn the subject? It wouldn't be easy. Twelve-fifteen, and old Pastmaster, hungry and thirsty, might be on them any minute. Or James come back with a suit on and a fresh supply of small talk. Richard turned half out of the armchair in what he hoped was an impulsive gesture.

'Anne, my sweetheart, I know Rajnaya is fascinating, but I didn't come here to talk about politics of any kind.'

She didn't seem to notice any of this. She took a cigarette from the silver box on the table between them. He lit it in such a way that their fingers just touched.

'I'm worried that Francis is too mixed up in it all,' she went on. 'What I want to know, Richard, is if there's any chance of us getting involved if there's fighting?'

'Well, of course, there's the Treaty, but no chance at all of that being used. For one thing it doesn't apply to trouble in Rajnaya unless the trouble-makers are getting help from out-side. But even more important, the trouble's expected next week. Not even the Tories are so dim as to commit British troops to a jungly island no one's ever heard of, bang in the middle of an election campaign. And anyway Francis wouldn't be in any danger whatever happened.'

'That's what James says.' She got up and began to walk up and down the drawing room, the ash growing longer on her cigarette. 'But it's not the point. I thought you might understand, knowing him so much better of course. I'm not really worrying about him getting shot or anything. But if he's really involved in all this, you know what I mean, then he may get badly upset.' She stopped short of his chair. 'He looks so ordinary and dull, especially now, but you know that inside he . . .'

An idea came to Richard so brilliant that it passed straight through his mind into words. 'Then why don't you come with me?' He jumped up and put his hands on her shoulders.

'I'm going to Rajnaya tomorrow to make a programme. I'll see Francis, we can both see him and we can help him. You must come, Anne – not just come with me but stay with me afterwards.'

She stood still, amazed at his touch. In the moment of surprise she seemed to him to lose the certainties which her surroundings gave her – the portraits, the big furniture, the bustle of activity, the spread of the lawn down to the lake. She looked younger. Richard tightened his grip and almost shook her. 'You know perfectly well this Ridingley charade is nonsense, Anne. You've given yourself all this to do, all these hideous people, this terrible fête, you've buried yourself in another age. It just doesn't mean anything any more. And I've made a hash of my choice too, in a different way. Francis needs your help, but by God, so do I. Won't you come out of this dug-out and help us both?'

He pulled her into his arms and her face slipped to one side of his so that their hair and cheeks touched. She did not resist. There were two clocks in the drawing room, the French carriage clock on the mantelpiece and the mahogany grandfather in the corner. Their ticking, not quite in unison, seemed to Richard to last forever.

He must crown the argument with the old pull between those particular two bodies. He was sure it was still there. Three more seconds and he would kiss her in such a way there would be no going back, and damn James and the horsewhip and the Foreign Secretary and as many Humbersful of red boxes as they could pump out of Whitehall on a Saturday morning.

But before that happened she pushed him away, not roughly, but disentangling herself from his arms.

'Richard, I'm so sorry it's a hash,' she said.

'But you too . . .'

'No, Richard, that's where you're wrong.'

'How can you say that when you used to see things so clearly? All this . . .' he waved around him.

'I know we used to lay down a lot of rules for other people. Perhaps you still do. But I've grown up, Richard. People like James, or the others out there on the lawn, are more real than you and I ever used to be when we talked so loud.'

'And exciting?'

'Ah – exciting, if that's the test . . .'

'Of course it's the test.' Richard would have been angry anyway because he had misread her, and there was perhaps a chance that anger would still find a weak spot. 'You live down here in this dim irrelevant world, no one ever hears of you, you've let your brain run to rot. It's a prison, this place,

55

and when I show you how to walk out, you say you'd rather live behind bars. For God's sake, Anne, you've got more imagination in your little finger than that husband of yours will have in his whole life. You like interesting people, you like keeping up to date . . .'

Then she laughed at him. No one had done this for many years. Sitting down again on the sofa, smoothing the green silk dress against her brown neck, she actually giggled.

'Up to date, oh, Richard, that's it . . . you'll be talking about this day and age soon, or the spirit of the seventies. It's just like the stuff you churn out on the telly, and your chums in the high-class papers. It's always a challenge or a crisis or a gap, day after day. Ordinary people outside London don't take much notice, you know, they go on living their own lives and thinking their own way. It's you who get trapped in your own platitudes, and then you're surprised and shocked when once in a while you look round and the rest of us aren't following.'

'Why the hell are you reading me a lecture? All I'm saying is that I still love you.'

'No, Richard.' Damn her, she was genuinely amused. 'That's not in the least what you've been saying – Oh, here they are.'

Sir John Pastmaster was in the room, Jack Mellon behind him, two labradors and Charteris bringing up the rear. The Foreign Secretary had taken a nap in the car, and was in the highest spirits. A good lunch with a pretty woman in a fine house, get the speech over and wander round the stalls chatting and signing autographs in the sunshine; to him these, not power and office, were the real pleasures of politics.

'Sorry we're a few minutes late, Mrs Charteris. Caught a glimpse of your rose garden coming through the hall –

magnificent, much better than ours at Lynde. You must tell me how you manage it. How d'you do — your face is familiar, surely we've met somewhere before. Of course yes, on the box. You're the chap from Enterprise?' But the plunge back to ordinary civility was too sudden for Richard's system.

'I'm sorry, Anne,' he said rather loudly. 'The camera team is coming rather earlier than I had thought, and there are some technical points I must go and settle.' He gave a composite nod to the rest of the company, and left the room.

'I thought he was staying to lunch,' he could hear James Charteris's surprised voice behind the closing door.

At least he would have upset the placement.

6

It was two before the Enterprise outside broadcast camera team arrived in the usual smart green van. Richard had found a stall which sold chicken sandwiches and sausage rolls so flaky as to be unmanageable. He took them with a paper cup of orange squash to a clump of Irish yews on a knoll just beyond the two main lawns. There he brooded over his own thoughts, noticing, without being able to place exactly, occasional movements in the first floor room just to the left of the south portico which he took to be the dining room. Probably the butler plying the hock, or perhaps on democratic occasions Charteris did this himself.

The lawns were filling up fast now, and he could see that a queue of vehicles had formed on the drive in front of the entrance table. Buses from Oxford and Cheltenham as well as Swindon, people of all shapes, ages and income groups, children and dogs, chatter in a dozen accents. The produce stalls were under siege, in the side paddock (rides 3p) the first pair of donkeys had already been relieved. The band, encamped in blue and silver uniforms under the portico itself, ranged across that segment of musical achievement which stretches from *Aida* to *Mary Poppins*. The loudest laughter came from the stand where by throwing a tennis ball straight you could empty a bucket over a man dressed in a London suit and made up with the sombre features of the Leader of the Opposition.

Richard sat in the shade of his yews, worlds apart from the scene before him. Normally a worrier about clothes, he did not notice the effect of the damp grass on his best suit. He was fighting again sentence by sentence the battle of the drawing room. Perhaps he should have said earlier on that he loved her; but there had never been an opening. Perhaps he should have concentrated on getting her to Rajnaya without any further implications; but that would have been hideously expensive for so uncertain a gain. Perhaps he should have – but on the whole it was a relief to walk down to the newly arrived van and involve himself in easy familiar decisions.

The camera team had been given the press handout of Pastmaster's speech, a thickish slab of paper under the blue Central Office heading. As usual Central Office had marked in pencil a few pages which they suggested might be the extract taken by television. It was just a suggestion and as usual Richard looked for something better. But it was a lifeless hopeless speech, no spark, no news value. The marked passage was a careful piece about the forthcoming European Security Conference, designed to build up Sir John's electoral image as a world statesman. All this Richard understood, but a plan was forming in his mind which made Sir John's speech eminently dispensable.

'Take one minute then, beginning of the marked passage.'

'It'll hardly make sense, just that much.'

'Ten minutes wouldn't make any more.'

Deferential chuckles. Richard as a visiting performer from the prestige programme 'Our Life' was half-disliked, half-envied by the regular news unit.

'You'd better get plenty of stuff on film from the fête itself. He'll be going round the stalls; follow him close with the mike and get odds and ends of vox pop. Did he agree to do an interview straight to camera?'

'Yes, the message came through just after you left.'

'Fine, we'll go alongside fairly soon after the speech. There's a study in the house, I expect we can do it there, good Tory setting.'

'But won't we have too much with all that? Extract from the speech, fête scenes and vox pop, plus your interview to camera. We're only a news bulletin, you know.'

'I know. Let's take it all, and see at the end what's best.'

The stalls and sideshows were beginning to close temporarily, and young Conservatives in big rosettes were shepherding as many people as they could persuade through the gap in a copper-beech hedge on to the double grass tennis courts, where seats had been placed for nearly a thousand people. A wooden dais at the end by the rosebeds was set with a pair of microphones and chairs under a canopy for the platform party. The Enterprise camera was already well-placed, forward and to one side.

Richard walked away from it all. By the edge of the lake was a tiny Grecian temple, asymmetrical to the axis of the house, and far enough from the activities of the fête to be deserted. From there, on a stone bench shared with ants and earwigs, Richard watched the scene. As the people streamed cheerfully across the bright turf into the enclosure under the chivvying of the stewards, the band tuned to 'Colonel Bogey.' From Richard's position the musicians were virtually concealed behind the pillars of the portico. It seemed that Ridingley Hall itself, honey-coloured stone resplendent against trees and grass, was pumping out the well-worn tunes from its heart. The sun, the house, the happy people, the occasion, the jaunty imperial music – all were alien to Richard, but for a few minutes, sitting apart in the summerhouse, he felt the power of their combination.

Then the music stopped and the spell was broken. He watched trim little figures take their places on the distant platform. A few words from the chairman, and Sir John Pastmaster was in full flow. The speech came to Richard over the microphone like the noise of the sea, an ebb and flood of general upper-class sound. At the fringes of the crowd, where the microphones failed to carry, children yelped and played and dogs wandered. A gardener crossed the deserted lawn among the tents, filling a basket with sticky litter. Richard could just see two female figures on the platform; it was too far to distinguish faces, but the slim one without a hat must be Anne. The Honourable Mrs Anne Charteris, wife of the Member of Parliament for Central Downshire, sister of the Acting High Commissioner in Rajnaya, hostess on this occasion to Her Majesty's Principal Secretary of State for Foreign and Commonwealth Affairs. Writing slowly in his notebook, he began to work out the first stage of their destruction.

*

Although Pastmaster was enjoying himself doing the round of the stalls it was not difficult to persuade him that the time had come for a little television. He beamed with anticipation as he came into James Charteris's study, where the cameras and microphone had already been installed.

'An excellent speech, sir,' said Richard.

'Oh, thank you, it seemed to go down all right.' He did not refer to the incident before lunch. 'Don't want anything too heavy for an occasion like this. Ready to start, are we?' Sir John sat in the more comfortable of the two chairs which had been set at an angle to each other in front of the desk. Mellon and Charteris stood behind the camera, their backs to the bookshelves. It was rather crowded in the small room.

'Could we have ordinary conversation to test voice levels?' said the production engineer.

Richard sat down on his chair. At this critical moment he could not think of any small talk, but Pastmaster broke the slight pause. 'Mrs Charteris tells me you were a friend of her brother. I mean the one working for us out in Rajnaya.'

'I hope I still am.' But Pastmaster was not conscious of any prickliness.

'A very able chap, going a long way.' He had only met Francis once, and finding him hard to talk to, had put this down as a proof of ability.

'Voice levels O.K.'

Mellon intervened from behind the camera.

'How much are you going to take? As you know, we don't like editing.'

'About three minutes, no editing. We'll use it all,' said Richard quickly. Then he turned to Pastmaster and put on the rather deeper knowledgeable tone which he had chosen from several variants as his interviewing voice.

'Foreign Secretary, you spoke here this afternoon about your hopes for a European Security Conference. Do you expect there to be a meeting of the Western Foreign Ministers to discuss this fairly soon?'

A full toss, to put the man at his ease. 'Well, of course, a Conference of this kind would need careful preparation, very careful preparation indeed.' Sir John cleared his throat; there was nothing to this TV business, it was simply a matter of keeping your head. 'It might well be that as part of this preparation my colleagues and I may decide to hold a meeting. You won't expect me to give away any secrets this afternoon, Richard,' he understood these fellows liked to be called by their Christian names, 'but I can say that we are having exchanges with our Western partners at the present time about exactly such a meeting.'

Richard moved a little closer to his prey.

'Would you say, Sir John, that foreign affairs are playing a major part in this election?'

'Well, no, not much difference between the parties, you might say, I wouldn't think so . . .' incoherent, casting about for inspiration, finding it, 'but I have found everywhere great satisfaction at the worthy and . . . er . . . statesmanlike part which our country has played in world affairs under this administration. It is fair to say, I think, that we have sought, and indeed achieved, peace with . . . er . . . honour.'

'Quite so, Sir John, I think you also touched on that point this afternoon. But there is one subject which you did not mention at all in your speech. There have been disturbing reports lately of serious trouble in Rajnaya, a country with which Britain is of course linked by treaty. Do you foresee Britain having to intervene in Rajnaya with armed force in the immediate future?'

As he put the question Richard heard a slight movement behind him. It was Mellon making up his mind to intervene. But, as Richard had hoped, Pastmaster was by now feeling fluent and as a result rushed happily into trouble.

'Well, I think quite frankly you're painting a rather gloomy picture. You're quite right, there were troubles there not so long ago, and it is a very difficult and delicate situation they have to cope with, with all the racial implications and so forth. But I have the utmost confidence in the President out there, Mr . . . er . . . a proved statesman and a good friend of Britain.'

Richard abandoned professional Voice No. 1 (humane resonant man of the world) for No. 2 (People's Prosecutor, to be sparingly used): 'With respect, Foreign Secretary, you have not given me a direct answer to a direct question which could closely affect the lives of thousands of British servicemen and their families. If the need arises, do you mean to use British troops in Rajnaya or not?'

Sir John Pastmaster by great effort kept his temper just at the moment when he should have lost it.

'Well, it hasn't really come to that at least so far, as I've been trying to point out . . . but if you're asking me if Britain will carry out her obligations under our Treaty, well then in those circumstances, which haven't arisen yet mind you, the answer would be, yes, of course we would.'

Back to Voice No. 1.

'Foreign Secretary, thank you very much.'

The interview over, Richard leapt in with politeness, trying to wipe out as completely as possible the memory of Voice No. 2.

'Thank you very much indeed, sir, I think our people will be very pleased indeed with that . . .'

'Well, ours won't.' Jack Mellon was kicking himself for not having broken in earlier. The job of a P.P.S. was full of those split-second decisions. 'If you think you're going to be able to use that interview, you can bloody well think again. It was clearly understood between Enterprise and the Foreign Office that the interview was to cover points raised in the speech, and nothing else. So all that crap about Rajnaya was out of bounds, and you know it.'

Richard continued to speak to Sir John Pastmaster. The camera crew listened intently, an audience awaiting a new actor's rendering of a well-known part.

'I'm so sorry, Foreign Secretary, if there has been some kind of misunderstanding. I certainly wasn't aware of any such agreement, nor could I have consented to it . . .'

Sir John found himself acting as peacemaker. He couldn't for the life of him make out what the fuss was about. The interview had really gone rather well, one tough question, but he'd handled it adroitly and he was looking forward to seeing it later in the evening.

'Well, Jack, I think you're standing too much on the letter of the law . . .'

But Jack Mellon was now angry and sure he was right. Half a lifetime farming in Devon had not given him quick responses, but he knew deception when it hit him hard enough.

'The point is, Secretary of State, that he led you on without warning, to make a statement about something which hasn't happened and probably will never happen. That's dangerous and contrary to what was agreed, and I must let the Chief Whip know at once what has been done. It's for him to carry the matter on as he thinks best. But,' turning to Richard savagely, 'I'll lay you ten to one there's not a word about Rajnaya on the bulletin tonight. James, I suppose there's another extension to this telephone of yours?' And he was out of the door, moving fast for a man of his bulk.

Richard disengaged from Pastmaster as quickly as he could, with a mutual mutter of apologies. Then he got the van to drive him to the telephone booth which he had seen not far from the lodge gates. Using his credit card he found Tyrrell without delay.

'. . . So now there'll be a hell of a stink, and the Government Chief Whip will be on to the Chairman.'

'Well, what d'you want me to do? Perjure myself the way you've already done?'

'Will the Chairman give way?'

'The man's a jelly.'

'Well, please do nothing to stiffen him. I'd much rather not have the Rajnaya interview in tonight's bulletins.'

Tyrrell snorted. 'Cold feet bring home no bacon, you know. You stand there wasting good new pence to tell me your interview's no good.'

'It's good as it stands, but it'll be much, much better once we've got some hard news from Rajnaya, to run with it.'

'So?'

'So, the Chairman can give way gracefully as far as tonight is concerned, provided he doesn't promise never to show the interview at all. They can show the fête and the speech on the news tonight, and we can keep the interview for 'Our Life' next week.'

'Very ingenious, there's only one snag.'

'What's that?'

'Cochrane's sick in Singapore, sounds pretty bad. So we've had it. There'll be no hard news from Rajnaya.'

'I'll fly there myself tomorrow morning.'

It was a pleasure to feel Tyrrell's surprise. It was an even greater pleasure to surprise himself.

One final detail, and he would be free of Ridingley. He scribbled a note and asked the lodgekeeper to deliver it to Mrs Charteris.

Thank you for your hospitality. I will give your love to Francis. But it is time that he, like the rest of us, learnt to solve his own problems.

R.

As he drove round the first corner of the road back to the motorway, Ridingley Hall came fully into view for the last time. The last charabancs were extricating themselves from the muddy verges of the drive and the shadows of the trees and of the house had met across the lawn. The fête had raised £1,100 and been judged by all a great success.

7

Priority

Rajnaya telegram No. 613 of 7th June to Foreign and Commonwealth Office repeated for information to Washington, Moscow, New Delhi, Cairo.

Your telegram No. 963 (of 5th June: Internal situation).

In accordance with your instructions I sought an interview with the President. There was some delay in making the arrangements but Mr Lall received me in his private residence this evening. He was as usual friendly and asked me to convey to you his personal good wishes for success in your election campaign.

2. I spoke on the lines of paragraphs 2–7 of your telegram under reference. I emphasised that Her Majesty's Government had no desire to intervene in any way in the internal affairs of Rajnaya, the full sovereignty of which they had always respected since independence was achieved four years ago. They were actuated solely by a desire to help a friendly Commonwealth country. They had watched with admiration the work of President Lall and his colleagues in consolidating the independence of Rajnaya, particularly in the economic field. It was a source of regret to them that these achievements had not been matched by greater progress towards racial harmony. I had been instructed to express the hope that the recent disturbances in the city of Rajnaya would not deter the Government from carrying through its legislation against racial discrimination in the field of employment and its plans to hold the next political elections on the basis of universal suffrage. An announcement to this effect would in the view of H.M.G. have a steadying effect if made at once before the forthcoming independence celebrations.

3. President Lall said that he was always glad to listen to advice from the British Government, but he must add that we seemed to be increasingly out of touch with the realities of the situation in Rajnaya. He quite understood that British public opinion was always sensitive to stories of oppression and discrimination however unsubstantial. But the fact was that the majority of the inhabitants of Rajnaya were of Indian origin, and no government could survive in Rajnaya which undermined the position of that majority. The Government was doing its best to give technical training to young Arabs

but it would be many years before there would be enough qualified Arabs to occupy the senior positions in commerce and industry which Revani and his friends were claiming for them as of right.

4. The President said he would speak to me with utter frankness. Rajnaya as a thriving modern state was a product of British rule and Indian business enterprise. If it had been left to the original Arab population it would still be a desert island with half a dozen villages remarkable only for disease and ignorance. The Government was not prepared to put at risk the prosperity which had been achieved. The recent riot had been a serious setback and they must think seriously before making any further political concessions. In particular direct elections in the village would undermine the authority of the tribal sheikhs who were the one factor for stability in the Arab community.

5. I said I knew that you would be disappointed by the negative tone of his response. I asked if he was satisfied with the security aspect of next Monday's independence celebrations. Mr Lall said that on the whole it was less risky to proceed with the celebrations than to cancel them. I pressed him on the point, saying that my military attaché had received reports of sizeable movements of Arabs from the villages into the outskirts of the city during the last seventy-two hours. Mr Lall did not comment directly, but said that it was always a comfort to him to feel that in the last resort the British would intervene to prevent the collapse of what they had achieved in Rajnaya. I thought it right to take him up fairly sharply on this, pointing out that under the revised Treaty of 1969 the only British obligation was to consult with the Rajnayan Government in the event of an external threat to the security of the island. Mr Lall commented that

there could be no doubt about the external support for Revani and the extremists. He then invited his daughter into the room to serve refreshments and there was no opportunity for further confidential conversation.

6. For comments on this conversation please see my immediately following telegram.

TRENNION

8

On most Sunday mornings about a dozen British businessmen came for a drink at the British Club in the Inter Ocean Hotel, Rajnaya. The royal Annigoni above the bar reassured them weekly amid the vicissitudes of Eastern life that their house was built upon the rock.

'Where's the bloody High Commissioner then? Still chasing the fish in Galway Bay?' The very young man from I.C.I. sought acceptance in this strange world by criticising everyone except his immediate audience.

'He's got another fortnight's leave to go. But I don't know where Trennion's hiding. He should make a point of turning up when H.E.'s away.'

'Probably so busy learning Arabic that he overslept.' They all laughed. It was a belief, universally accepted and wholly untrue, that Francis Trennion, a self-contained bachelor, had an affair with the young Palestinian professor from the University who taught him Arabic.

'No, not this time.' John Katrakis, sleek-haired and thirty-five, ran his own business downtown near the refinery. Before independence he had called himself a private detective. Now he was a public relations consultant, but his way of life had in no way changed. 'I saw the Rolls heading west down the Albert Road just before eleven, with the flag flying.'

'He's no right to fly the standard as Chargé d'Affaires. It's presumptuous and improper.'

'I suppose he was going to see Lall.'

'On a Sunday – whatever for?'

From their steel and canvas tubular chairs they gazed out over modern Rajnaya. Of the group old Paton alone remembered the old British Club which had stood upon the site. The Club – deep veranda and dark furniture, big slow fans turning on the high ceiling of the dining room, tiffin and pink gins, full length portraits of the Viceroys of India, the lawn stretching down to the harbour, watered and clipped daily with scissors by an army of gardeners, the green-domed bandstand slowly falling into disrepair.

In the old Sultan's time the Club had been the only place where Europeans could by established custom break the law and get a drink. In Paton's first year the Sultan had come to the Club to celebrate the Queen's Coronation, carried in a litter by huge slaves, and they had all drunk orange juice until he left. After His Highness had gone they had emptied ten bottles of Scotch and the Vice-Consul had fallen into the harbour. Soon after independence the Club had been forced to sell the site to Inter Ocean Hotels for a fraction of its worth, being able to stipulate only for a rent-free room on the sixteenth floor of the new building.

As Paton remembered, the conversation flowed past him. 'Perhaps Lall is getting scared about the parade next Monday.'

'What's he got to be scared about? Forster will take care of it all for him.' Colonel Forster was the Chief of Police. 'They say Arabs are streaming in from the villages.'

'They always say that, but nothing ever happens.'

'Perhaps it's Trennion who's scared.'

'That's far more likely. He's too new to understand that we've seen it all before.'

'Well, now we can ask him, can't we?' John Katrakis got to his feet with a politeness which showed his foreign origin. 'Good morning, Mr Acting High Commissioner. We do not often see you here at the Club.'

Francis Trennion said good morning to each of them. At Cambridge he had looked old for his age, now at thirty-eight he looked much the same; short and slight in a brown suit now somewhat crumpled by contact with President Lall's furniture. Stiff and rather curly black hair, eyebrows together in concentration, lines spreading outwards from eyes and mouth, he looked undistinguished and straightforward.

After six months in Rajnaya he knew all the faces in front of him, most of their surnames and a sprinkling of Christian names which he did not find easy to use. Of all his duties in his various posts Francis found mingling with the British community the most difficult. He drew up a chair alongside Paton.

'How's business with you, then?' To ask that question in the Club on a Sunday morning was itself the sign of an outsider. Francis half-realised this, but did not know how otherwise to get on terms.

'Not bad, not bad at all. It looks as if the Dermajan mill will get built after all.'

'Your board finally agreed to put in their sixty per cent?' Although his work was basically political, Francis made it a point to know the details of the main deals in the offing.

'Well, subject of course to a last minute visit by the Chairman's son. It wouldn't do to leave the local representative

71

to assess the local situation.' Paton grimaced and they all knew what he meant. In theory visits by board members were admirable evidence of keenness; in practice they were usually an expensive pain in the neck.

'When's he coming? I'd like to give him a drink.' Francis was entitled to spend a slice of the High Commissioner's entertainment allowance during the latter's leave.

'Tomorrow night. Guy Winter's his name, he's all of twenty-eight and I've booked him in here.' Paton's bungalow had seven bedrooms but nowadays he didn't give hospitality to his company's executives. It was too much bother to conceal for a day or two the fact that he lived with his Indian housekeeper.

'I'll give him a ring. How long will he be staying?' Francis took from his inside pocket the white card on which he jotted things he had to do. He was the only one present who had kept his coat on.

'As short as I can make it. He's got full powers to sign the financial agreement with the National Bank. With any luck we'll have the gold pens out Tuesday evening and pack him home on Wednesday.'

'Before the dramas on independence day. I see, I see, very neat.' They frowned at the young man from I.C.I. for this remark. It was an article of faith for the business community that nothing would happen the Monday after next. The confidence factor was written on their hearts. Paton turned the conversation.

'How is Lall, by the way? We hear you saw him this morning.

Francis laughed; he was beginning to feel more at ease.

'Oh, it was just some details about the Treaty he wanted to clear up.'

'On Sunday morning?' But Paton knew they would not get any more. He launched into a familiar lecture on the Treaty, and the outer fringe of the group round the window melted away in the direction of the bar.

'. . . the Germans, Italians and Japs get on perfectly well without a Treaty, look at their export graph compared to ours. No one really believes that British troops will ever be seen here again, external threat or not. It's just a myth, a husk which lost its content years ago, and it doesn't do us any good with the young, whether they're Indian or Arab. We'd do much better to forget the past and throw the Treaty out of the window.'

'There may be something in what you say,' said Francis flatly. He sat quiet in his chair, looking out of the window through which Paton wanted to throw the Anglo-Rajnayan Treaty.

Across the harbour he could see the big squat storage tanks which held the oil pumped in from the refinery and then fed it along the specially constructed pier into the huge tankers which carried it round the world to Yokohama, Rotterdam and Milford Haven. Below him were the downtown offices and the commercial centre, springing up to ten or twelve stories of tinted glass, flashing even during the day with vivid neon. To the West the new residential suburb, a grid of neat bungalows for the Indian middle class, civil servants and businessmen, self-conscious little swimming pools beside the bigger buildings.

Between the oil terminal and downtown Rajnaya lay the old city, a huddled confusion of grey and brown buildings shrinking month by month, a minaret, the spire of the Anglican cathedral and by the water's edge, separated from the other buildings by a glacis, the jagged white walls of the old Palace. Colonel Forster used the Palace to drill and instruct the police force of the Republic of Rajnaya.

Gripping the town in an untidy embrace were the Arab shanty towns on its outskirts, brown splodges stretching up into the foothills; and behind them in turn the hills which formed the spine of the island, sometimes blue and sharp, more often grey and dusty. In the old days Europeans used to walk through the hills in the spring in search of wild orchids. For some years the hills had not been safe and in any case the botanists had been expatriates, teachers and colonial officers now dead or old and poor in England.

'Pretty well sums it up, doesn't it?' Katrakis had watched Francis switch from the conversation to the city below them.

'What does?'

'The view from this window. Indians, Arabs, money, poverty. The pattern shifts a bit from month to month. That shanty town above the ravine wasn't there last winter.'

'Another couple of thousand votes for Revani.'

'Votes, hell,' Katrakis turned his chair so that he and Francis were separated by its back from the others. 'Votes come too slow. It'll take too long to breed back an Arab majority in Rajnaya. What Revani wants from the R.L.F. in the shanty towns is a lot of noise when the right time comes. Plus of course a few hundred Arabs who can shoot straight.'

'How well do you know him?'

'We used to have some business dealings. I don't see much of him now.' Katrakis knew that Francis knew that Katrakis ran Johnnie Revani's fund raising for the R.L.F. (Rajnaya Liberation Front). It was a tidy little network of protection rackets plus some hefty remittances from overseas.

'You were at Cambridge with him, weren't you?' he asked.

'Yes, I knew him quite well then. But in a way that makes him harder to know now.'

'I must try to get hold of him today to ask if he'll see Richard Herbert.'

'Richard Herbert?'

Katrakis enjoyed the obvious astonishment on Francis's face. 'D'you mean to say they haven't warned you from London? That really is rather hard. Richard Herbert's coming here to do a big programme on the politics of Rajnaya, with special reference to the British commitment. A rush job and no expense spared. They're obviously timing it with the British election in mind.'

Francis was not often confused, and he hated the feeling when it happened. He sorted out his reactions as tidily as he could. Item, the Foreign Office had let him down by not warning him of this. Item, Richard had let him down ditto. Item, he would be glad to see Richard. Item, Lall would be upset and suspicious about this new complication. He would never believe that H.M.G. were not behind it. Item, should he ask Richard to stay at the Residence? Item, Katrakis was a shrewd and disagreeable man.

'I don't understand how you come into it.'

'Oh, the Enterprise man cabled me from Singapore. He's on his back, and can't come here to make the arrangements. As you know, I've just started up a P.R. agency and they asked me to bearlead the TV team, fix the appointments, that sort of thing.'

Katrakis saw that all this was unwelcome and was glad. He knew that however successful and respectable he became there would always be something about his hair, his shoes and his voice which would cut him off from people like Francis Trennion.

Francis got up and began to say goodbye all round, muttering about a telegram he had to send. When he came back to Katrakis he said: 'When exactly do they come?'

'By the B.O.A.C. flight tomorrow night. Shall I give Herbert a message? He'll be staying here of course.'

'No, no. I'll get in touch with him direct.'

'Just as you like.'

When Francis was out of the door the mood of the gathering relaxed again.

'What's biting him then?'

'Oh, I told him about the TV team that's turning up tomorrow. Poor chap, nothing scares a British diplomat more than the thought of a British television camera.'

9

My immediately preceding telegram: Internal situation.

It is clear from this conversation that President Lall has no intention of making special concessions to appease the Arab minority. He is conscious of his own reasonable record as a reformer and of the difficulties which measures in favour of the Arabs would create for him among his own supporters. He can reasonably argue that the prosperity which has been his main achievement would be seriously at risk if he moved too fast and that this prosperity benefits all races.

2. He appeared unmoved by any suggestion that in the absence of any political concessions there could be serious trouble next Monday during the independence parade. This confidence must result from advice received from Forster

who as Chief of Police reports to him direct on security matters. In conversation with me Forster has always minimised the threat of Arab violence on the grounds that the villages are badly organised, and incurably divided among themselves. This analysis does not take into account the rapid spread of the shanty towns in recent months and the growing cohesion of these urbanised Arabs under the extremist leadership of Revani and the R.L.F. (see my despatch No. 63 of 31st May).

3. In my judgement there is a serious risk next week of a trial of strength between the R.L.F. and the security forces of which the outcome can only be uncertain.

4. If such a conflict put Lall and his Government in serious danger he would probably appeal to Her Majesty's Government for armed support. I have frequently warned him against assuming that H.M.G. would interpret their obligations under the Treaty as meaning that we must accede to such an appeal. I have explained that H.M.G. would have to be satisfied that there was a clear external threat to the security of Rajnaya and that even in those circumstances our obligation is simply to consult with the Rajnayan Government with a view to concerting joint measures. I am not confident that these warnings have had any effect. Lall gives every sign of believing that in the last resort Britain will not let him down. It is thus possible that within weeks, possibly days, we may be faced with an exceptionally difficult decision.

5. I have just learned that a British television team with Richard Herbert is due here tomorrow night to make a programme on the current political situation. I should have welcomed advance notice of this development which is frankly an unwelcome complication. I assume it is too late to

dissuade them from the expedition. I should welcome urgent guidance about the status of this team and the extent to which I should comply with any requests for assistance which they may make.

TRENNION

10

Richard had been determined to avoid a quarrel. In, pack the small suitcase which he kept at the top of his wardrobe, answer as few questions as possible, and out to Heathrow in the minicab which he had just ordered from a call box.

But Roberta had the envelope, the fat envelope with the Enterprise flash on it and inside his passport, air ticket and a bundle of Rajnayan dollars. Tyrrell had sent it round by messenger an hour before. She had opened it, as was her habit, and he found her sitting on the bed, crouched over the contents which she had spread out on the white bedspread. She wore a blue quilted dressing gown with coffee stains. It was seven in the evening, and she looked exhausted.

'You're going after all then?'

'I have to, darling, Steel's been arrested and Cochrane's ill, there's no one else.'

'And what about me?' She was still quiet.

'You'll be all right. I'll ring Dr Street now and ask him to give you a ring every evening till I get back.'

He put out a hand to touch her thin fingers. She moved quickly away.

'Well, you'd better hurry then. I can't drive you to the airport. The baby seat in the car has broken.'

'No, that's fine, I've ordered a cab.' He was amazed; she had not been so gentle since she became pregnant again. 'You don't mind, then?'

'Not much use minding, is there?' She got up and he noticed that her cheeks were puffy. 'You've just got time for a bath before you go. I'll run it for you.'

A few minutes later he lay in the water, tepid as he preferred it, green and bubbly with Pine Essence from Boots in East Sheen. Was it possible to make something of his life with Roberta after all? He looked down the bath at his own body and thought of Anne, slim with the cool brown skin, and of Roberta, plump and pale. No doubt which was the more desirable property, but she had said no and he doubted if she would change.

The hot tap was still on, but through the noise of the water he heard the key turn in the lock. He was out of the bath at once; but it was too late.

'Roberta!'

'Turn that tap off. I want to talk to you.' He knew she had won and he did as he was told. His clothes were in the dressing room across the passage.

'You're not going to Rajnaya tonight. You're going to stay there in the bathroom until the plane has gone. After that you can leave or stay, I don't care a bloody damn what you do. But someone's got to teach you a lesson and it's going to be me.'

'But Roberta, you don't understand . . .'

'It's you that don't understand. I gave you up long ago. You're not a husband, you're not a father, you think of nothing except television. The great Richard Herbert, always so suave, so good-looking, hobnobbing with the politicians, so much better company than that sick dull wife of his.'

79

He had heard all this before. The water on his legs and shoulders was turning cold. He rubbed himself with a towel from the rail and rattled the door handle.

'That won't do you any good. In an hour exactly I'll ring up Tyrrell and tell him the whole story. He'll laugh like a drain.'

Of course, she was right, Tyrrell would laugh and tell everyone else too. It was a joke that would last all his life.

'Goodbye now. I'm going to take Robert out in the pram before he goes to bed, but don't worry, I'll be back within the hour. And you can't reach the drainpipe from the window, I've looked.'

He heard her go along the corridor to wake up the baby, then a pause while she changed him, down the stairs, out the front door, a pause, and then the noise of the pram wheels out across the gravel. He had not felt so humiliated since he saw Anne stand in the cottage doorway with Revani that wet night before he drove Simbury-Smith back to Cambridge station.

Five minutes of silence, and the door bell rang. Thank God, the minicab man must have come early. Richard tucked the towel round his waist and climbed on to the lavatory seat, and then up on to the ledge inside the window. The thick green leaves of the wistaria blocked his view, but he could see that it wasn't the minicab man. A young man and a girl stood expectantly on the gravel by the front door; the girl held a notebook.

'Hi there.'

'Oh, hallo.'

'Who are you?'

'I'm sorry to bother you on a Sunday, but we're getting behind hand. We've come about the election.'

No need to ask where they came from. Only one party took the trouble to canvass these particular streets. Now that they had turned towards him he could see the blue rosettes.

'Do me a favour, will you? In the garage you'll find a long ladder with an extension. I've somehow locked myself in and I've got a plane to catch. Could you put it against the wall under here? With the extension, I think I could just manage to reach it.'

They trotted off, and soon the ladder was in position beneath him. Richard began to squeeze himself through the window, feet first with his stomach on the sill. The towel rucked up round his buttocks and he stuck. He swore, thinking of the two young Conservatives at the foot of the ladder. But there was only one way. He unwound the towel, threw it on to the bathroom floor and began to back through the window again. This time he stuck at the shoulders, but with a twist sideways he managed to get through. For a few seconds he hung naked, from the sill, feeling with his toes for the top of the ladder. He heard the girl giggle.

'It's only a foot or so, sir,' said the boy. 'We'll hold the ladder firm.' There was laughter in his voice too. Join the Young Conservatives and see the world.

Richard looked down, saw the top rung and let go. A sharp spur from the main branch of the wistaria caught him under the rib and his feet missed the top rung. He grabbed at the foliage to steady himself and his toes connected with the third rung. An agonising downward slither, his hands full of leaves and he was safe on the ladder. The blood from the graze was trickling across his stomach. He went down very fast.

Roberta was pushing the pram in through the garden

gate. She had been joined by an old lady with a peke. Outside the gate was the minicab, the driver leaning out of the window. Two small boys carrying a football were staring over the fence.

Without a word to his rescuers Richard ran round the house and in at the back door, upstairs and into his dressing-room. He threw on his clothes and filled his suitcase.

At the foot of the stairs there was a friendly gathering to meet him. Roberta had asked the two canvassers and the old lady in for a cup of tea, she said. She was in high good humour. 'Must you go so soon, dear? Here are these nice Young Conservatives who've been working so hard.'

He saw that she didn't really mind now if he went to Rajnaya or not. For the first time in her married life she had scored off him, completely, before a considerable public.

After he'd gone Roberta put the kettle on as if nothing had happened.

'He often gets excited like that, you know. I suppose it's the artistic temperament, but it wears off quite quickly,' and then, with a chuckle, 'What a pity none of us had a camera when he jumped on to the ladder.'

For the first time in weeks she forgot that she was pregnant.

11

Outside on the tennis courts in the gardens of Pembroke Square white figures ebbed and flowed and the shadow of the chestnut leaves flickered over the red asphalt. The windows of Sir John Pastmaster's drawing room were open, and from Kensington High Street they could hear the steady grumble of returning traffic. The blue and red Persian carpet was untidy with open red boxes and empty tea cups.

'Bloody election,' said Sir John, and Jack Mellon knew exactly what he meant. If it hadn't been for the election neither the Foreign Secretary nor his Parliamentary Private Secretary would have been cooped up in London on a perfect June Sunday.

'Not a bad press for yesterday's speech, Secretary of State,' said the third man in the room. Donald Pringle, a civil servant, meant by this that the speech, though barely reported, had passed off without complication or scandal.

'A lousy press, I call it,' said Jack Mellon. 'Just a paragraph or two tucked on an inside page of the qualities.'

'But then it was a damned dull speech,' said Sir John. He had his moments of half-irritable self-criticism, and that was why Jack Mellon had agreed to work for him.

The old gentleman was sitting in an upright chair with his back to the summer evening, cream shirt open at the collar, showing thick white hairs on his chest.

'At least we managed to stop that television interview on Rajnaya,' said Mellon. He went over to the silver tray on the sofa table, poured three whiskies, added a little water and handed them round. 'That fellow Herbert must be sick as mud. His boss caved in as soon as the Chief Whip spoke to him.'

'You thought I made a hash of that,' said Sir John, swirling the liquid in his glass.

Mellon did not bother to deny it. A flatterer was no good as a P.P.S.

Pringle's trained mind was clicking ahead of the others. 'If that's the Richard Herbert who works for Enterprise Television, he's going off to Rajnaya in person. There are a couple of telegrams here from Trennion, Secretary of State, which I've been keeping until you'd dealt with the others.'

Sir John worked slowly through the two pink pieces of paper, then handed them to Mellon.

'Well?' Sir John asked.

Donald Pringle had been hot driving in from Roehampton in his Austin 1100 and he could still feel the dampness of his vest. But the discomfort, the unmown lawn, the neglected children were worth it for the moment when he was asked for advice which he had pondered and prepared.

'As regards the last paragraph of Trennion's telegram, I've asked News Department to check up with Enterprise television about their team,' he said. 'We'll get any information we can off to him tonight.'

'Funny that chap Herbert didn't say anything yesterday about galloping straight off to Rajnaya.'

'They're an underhand lot,' said Mellon.

'I think there's an explanation,' Pringle was almost purring. This was going to be a bumper evening. 'They sent out another man to do the job, but he became involved in an incident at Teheran airport, and is still being held there.'

'A woman, I suppose?'

'In a way,' Pringle permitted himself a thin smile. 'The man in question is alleged to have assaulted a photograph of the Empress.'

But he did not get the chuckle from the Secretary of State for which he had angled. Sir John had abstracted himself to worry about a different point.

'Where the hell's the High Commissioner then?'

'He's got four weeks of home leave still to go. As a matter

84

of fact I gather he's fishing somewhere in the west of Ireland.'

Jack Mellon chipped in, 'Of course he must go back at once. You can't leave young Trennion there more or less alone if there's a real crisis blowing up.'

'You are thinking of the political impression which might be received here?' Pringle implied a slight reproach that such matters should be openly discussed.

'I certainly am. The opposition will flay us, and they'd be right. Can't you see the photographs in the *Mirror* – side by side, the High Commissioner catching trout in County Limerick and the Shell terminal in Rajnaya going up in flames?'

'The refinery is in no immediate danger. And there are perhaps other considerations which need to be taken into account,' said Pringle. 'In the first place, a sudden interruption of the High Commissioner's plans would suggest that we were seriously worried by the situation, and this would add to the general tension. Secondly, his leave has already been postponed once at our request. Thirdly, Francis Trennion is one of the ablest . . .'

'Yes, yes, yes,' said Sir John. Pringle must somehow learn not to talk as if he were dictating a minute. 'We'll talk it over with the Permanent Under-Secretary in the morning. But how do we stop this fellow Lall appealing to us for help under the Treaty?'

'Trennion has done his best to warn him not to expect us to bail him out,' Pringle was not easily deterred. 'And there are, of course, wider implications outside Trennion's particular sphere. The Planning Group did a paper on this exact hypothesis at the beginning of last year.' He whipped the pale green document out of his black-leather pouch with a practised movement. 'The Arab world would bitterly resent any action by us in Rajnaya, and there might be reprisals against British citizens and British property throughout the Middle East. At the U.N. we could expect a condemnatory resolution in the Security Council which we might have to veto. And then of course, there are the difficulties of timing here at home.' He paused and smiled coyly. For Pringle British politics had the charm of a forbidden fruit.

'What exactly d'you mean?' asked Mellon.

'Well, it's not for me to say of course – but I hardly suppose the Cabinet would want to commit British troops to such a difficult and controversial operation between now and polling day.' He looked to Sir John for support.

'You're right, it's not for you to say.' Jack Mellon was getting cross: a summer evening drifting away, and nothing done.

'But it's true, you know,' said Sir John. When he first came into Parliament he had been filled with firm convictions. During twenty-five years on the back benches they had ebbed away, and promotion had come too late to turn the tide. Now he thought of the Prime Minister, who had been sent Trennion's telegrams in the usual way. It was perhaps surprising that he had not reacted. At the best of times the P.M. was uninterested in foreign affairs, but now he was in the middle of an evenly balanced election campaign which an outside storm could ruin. An outside storm such as was brewing at that moment in the dust and stink of Rajnaya. Sir John did not know the P.M. well, but well enough to be certain that he would not be pleased.

'The P.M. would not be pleased,' said Jack Mellon. 'And the experts at Conservative Central Office would say it was madness. And so would the opinion-formers, and the students, and of course the bishops. But isn't there a chance that if we really had to go in, as a matter of honour, I mean . . . ?' He broke off. The thought was so unfashionable that the words would not come.

'Honour?' said Sir John. Slowly he got up from the armchair and went out on to the little balcony with the trim wrought iron railing. In the square the shadows had lengthened across the tennis court, and a young girl with tousled hair was winding up the net. In the street below them a family was unloading the weekend paraphernalia from an estate car. From an open window two doors down came the sugary theme tune of a television serial.

'D'you really suppose that anyone out there cares a damn about Rajnaya?' asked Sir John. 'D'you think they could find Rajnaya on the map? D'you think any single one of them could imagine any conceivable circumstance in which they would approve of British troops going back to Rajnaya?'

Pringle smiled discreetly. He thought he knew now how the land lay. This would be useful if Rajnaya did in fact come to the crunch.

'I'm not sure we can carry this much further this evening, Secretary of State . . .'

12

Who in his strength setteth fast the mountains:
  and is girded about with power.
Who stilleth the raging of the sea: and the noise of his
  waves, and the madness of the people.

The psalm had a melancholy chant, and the young Indian voices of the choir lingered over it with obvious pleasure. At evensong the high west doors of the Cathedral were left open, and the strong sunlight poured in upon the floor and the columns of the nave. The strong light and the two rows of electric fans, suspended from the ceiling and revolving slowly in a ritual of their own, reminded the worshippers that they were not in England.

Francis Trennion. enjoyed evensong at St John's. The congregation, scattered in ones or twos among hundreds of empty bamboo chairs, was usually outnumbered by the choir. Even in June without benefit of airconditioner the church remained cool, achieving a quiet privacy which easily absorbed the street noises coming through the west door. It was heresy, he knew, but for him the attraction of the Church of England had always been the distance it kept from the madness of the people. In St John's Rajnaya there was fortunately no question of anything except the Authorised Version and the 1662 Prayerbook.

As Acting High Commissioner he sat at the front on the right in what before independence had been the Governor's pew. The mahogany pew end was carved in the shape of a lion, and a Governor's lady had embroidered the hassocks with haphazard impressions of various regimental coats of arms.

Thou crownest the year with thy goodness: and thy clouds drop fatness

For Francis the 65th psalm meant harvest festivals in a tiny Cornish church, marrows at the base of the font, red apples crowded on the narrow windowsills, sheaves of oats and barley round the pulpit. He knew the words by heart –

and realised with a start that the psalm was coming to an end. He looked behind him and across the aisle; Colonel Forster, Chief of Police, was not there to read the lesson. He himself was primed as usual for the second lesson, the Chief of Police having a rooted preference for the Old Testament.

> *They shall drop upon the dwellings of the wilderness:*
> *and the little hills shall rejoice on every side.*

There was an approaching clatter of boots on the black and white tiles; Francis looked round again, in time to see a tall bony Englishman sink briefly to his knees in the church-warden's pew. Instead of the usual light suit Forster wore his police tunic and shorts, and as he stalked to the lectern Francis could see a patch of sweat between his shoulder blades. His sunburnt forehead carried the red mark made by the hard rim of his cap. An Indian sergeant followed him more quietly up to the brass eagle with the big Bible on it, and stood with his back to the altar, hands fingering his sub-machine gun, eyes searching each section of the Church in turn. This had never happened before at St John's. The scattered congregation, half English, half Indian, most elderly, shifted pleasurably on the hard chairs.

'Here beginneth the twentieth verse of the thirty-sixth chapter of the book of the prophet Ezekiel . . .'

The voice of the Chief of Police, rising through the white Gothic arches built by Indian convict labour a hundred years before, was controlled but not quite steady.

The least important of the many roads which led down from the mountains into Rajnaya followed the course of a dried up ravine through the shanty town of El Atassi. The houses of El Atassi were made of mud and oil drums with roofs of rough matting, and the ravine stank of refuse.

Usually it was a town of children and dogs. The women stayed indoors, on weekdays the men were away in the textile factories or the oil terminal, and on Sundays they slept. It was one of the grievances of the Arabs in Rajnaya that the rest day was Sunday even though most of the manual workers were Moslems. But on this Sunday there were plenty of men out of doors. They lounged by the entrances to their houses or sat on benches in the shade by the single municipal tap and the stall which sold bright fizzy drinks.

It was evening now. Through the day at intervals of about an hour they had seen a cloud of dust appear on the road as it twisted in and out of their sight down the slope of the mountain. Half an hour later and the cloud of dust was a group of men, some on bicycles, some on donkeys, but most walking. When each group reached the little square with the trees and the drinkstall they were given water by a fat man with a red armband. He ticked the name of their village in a notebook and handed each man over to the care of one of a troop of small boys. The boy escorted him through the narrow twisting lanes to whichever house had been allocated for his stay for the next few days. Johnnie Revani had taught the Rajnaya Liberation Front meticulous staff work.

Just before dawn the usual lorries would wheeze slowly into the city loaded with vegetables for the market. But for the next few mornings the housewives would go short, forced to content themselves with the top layer of cabbages and onions which covered the rifles and sub-machine guns of the R.L.F. Forster had for weeks been asking permission to search the vegetable lorries, but Lall, anxious to avoid provocation, had always refused. Forster's other, more important request had however just been granted.

The police sub-station at the end of the square was also made of mud, but whitewashed and neat, with oleander in straggly pink flower by the door. The flag of Rajnaya, red, white and black stripes with a gold crescent and a sprinkling of stars in one corner, drooped from its flagstaff. Inside the Indian lieutenant and his sixteen men, twelve Indians, four Arabs, were uncomfortably hot, and weary after a day of doing nothing. The normal complement of the sub-station was a sergeant plus three – all Indian, on the usual principle that each sector of the city was policed so far as possible by men of a different race from its inhabitants. The lieutenant and the extra men had come in one by one during the night, and on Forster's strict instructions had not stirred out the whole day. He had been with them half an hour earlier to make absolutely sure that they understood their instructions.

On the table in front of the lieutenant was spread a large-scale sketch map of the district. One lane had a red cross marked in chalk half-way down it. Sweat ran down the inside of the lieutenant's forearm on to the map. He was young and passionately keen that his first big job should be a success. His black belt was highly polished and the creases stood out sharply on his shorts. He looked at his big metal watch.

'In five minutes they will hear that Colonel Forster is in the church. They will be sure that nothing is to be done tonight. At that moment precisely the jeeps will come. That is the moment at which we are to act.' He spoke in English, which by history and convenience was the working language of the Rajnaya Police Force. He said what they already knew, as much to reassure himself as his men. Somehow when Forster had been with them it had seemed easier. The big fan turned slowly on the ceiling, but they felt no relief.

'You see exactly where the house is. And you see where each of you is to stand. You must take up the exact position indicated.' Forster had left with them a second sketch, a rough drawing of a house with ten dots encircling it and six dots at the door. By each dot was one of their own names. For the success of this operation no detail was too small.

At six-thirty exactly the two jeeps swept through the clearing and jammed to a halt in front of the police station. The man who sold fizzy drinks began to pack up his stall. The fat man snatched off his armband and shouted to his cohort of small boys, who scattered in all directions, but not haphazardly. Much thought had been given to the warning system of the R.L.F.

But Forster had calculated that the two jeeps could overtake the swiftest messenger on the way to that particular house. They had practised over and over again on the playing fields of the police training college, hidden by a high wall from prying eyes. Now they leapt into the jeeps, five inside each, the others on the special running-boards which Forster had had fitted. Back across the little square, first right, second left, and sure enough there was a twelve-year-old sprinting in front of them as if his life depended on it.

It did, for his body was found in a ditch three days later. The R.L.F. were never interested in the reasons for failure.

The first jeep stopped in front of the house door and the lieutenant jumped out, the warrant in his hand. His cap was jammed down over his eyes, as he had seen in a hundred films. The second jeep stopped short, and the nine men kicked their way through skinny chickens and debris. They fanned out round to the back to where the house hung over a shallow ravine. Here there was one big unglazed window almost down to ground level. The Arab corporal and a grizzled Indian constable trained their sub-machine guns on the easy oblong of black. Both in their different ways were excited. A man escaping through that space would be easy to recognise, easier to kill.

The lieutenant had to get his men to kick the front door down, but this did not take long. Inside, a big dark room full of protesting women, a ragged old man smoking in a corner, and two men apparently asleep on mattresses. The lieutenant's Arab orderly shouted a name at each of them, but all shook their heads. The other constables pulled the men up from the mattresses and bound their hands; but neither was the one. The lieutenant pulled his revolver from his belt and sent three men up the bamboo ladder which led up into a loft. The only outcome was a further flurry of chickens.

The lieutenant pushed through the women to a small door in the inside wall of the main room. One of the women struck him in the face as he passed, and her broken nails drew blood on his cheek. The inner door was open. It led into a small room belonging to a different world from the rest of the house. There was an Anglepoise lamp and a typewriter on a table and on the wall a calendar of Cambridge views and an oil portrait of the old Sultan in his turban. Two bookshelves of English paperbacks, a wash basin with a jug of still steaming water, and a truckle bed with crumpled sheets and a dented pillow. Opposite the door was the oblong unglazed window looking out on to the ravine.

The lieutenant sprang on to the window sill from which he could see the banks of the ravine. The only living object in sight was the grizzled Indian constable, and he hardly counted, having only two minutes to live. He lay in the dust just below the top of the near bank, knifed in the back. He had served the British Empire for forty years, and the Republic of Rajnaya for four.

Of the man they were hunting there was no sign. Of the Arab corporal there was no sign either. A few days later the corporal broadcast a denunciation of British neo-colonialism on Aden radio.

> *The day thou gavest, Lord, is ended,*
> *The darkness falls at thy behest.*

The choir at St John's enjoyed this hymn more than any other, and in order to humour them it was sung at evensong at least once a month while Francis Trennion and Colonel Forster took the collection round. There were five verses, but the two men always managed to get round the scanty congregation in three. This gave time for a whispered word or two in the nave, as they clutched the embroidered green bags.

> *As o'er each continent and island*
> *The dawn leads on another day,*
> *The voice of prayer is never silent*
> *Nor dies the strain of praise away.*

'How are things?' The two men were not intimate, but Francis found it easier to talk with Forster than with most Englishmen in Rajnaya.

'Not so bad. Pretty busy.' Forster turned away from the hymn and the quiet dimness of the church towards the glare of the street beyond the west door. News ought to come any minute now.

Francis looked at the faded banners which hung in the northern aisle, big brass plaques of departed governors, smaller plaques for chaplains, colonial secretaries and station commanders. In the old days Rajnaya had been notorious for a quick and fatal fever which had been no respecter of uniforms. In three months of 1875 it had carried off more than half the crew of the frigate *Bellerophon*, whose exploits in suppressing the slave trade were sculpted in stone behind the font.

> *So be it, Lord: thy Throne shall never*
> *Like earth's proud empires, pass away.*
> *Thy kingdom stands and grows for ever*

The despatch rider in smart khaki breeches was there at last. Three sentences were enough to tell Forster what had happened. Francis could not tell from his face if the news was good or bad. Side by side they walked up the long aisle and placed the green bags on the salver which the dean held out for them. Stiffly they stood together as he turned and raised a total sum of thirty-eight Rajnayan rupees towards the altar.

'All things come of thee, O Lord; and of thine own have we given thee.'

As they turned to go down the aisle, Forster plucked at Francis's sleeve.

'Where's your car?'

'Outside.'

'Yes, but where?'

'Usual place, by the south porch.'

'Let's go.'

Forster pulled Francis out of the main aisle towards the south door.

'Why on earth?'

'Come on.'

The dean, poised for the blessing, watched amazed as the two most distinguished members of his congregation sprinted unblessed from his service. But he was not more surprised than Francis.

In the car Francis said crossly, 'What the hell's going on?'

'My jeep's parked outside the west door. There's an Arab crowd gathering there, and they might have lynched me.'

'Why today?'

Forster laughed, but the news was too bad for the laugh to last.

'The fat's in the fire. I tried to arrest Revani thirty minutes ago. He got away.'

13

The young man had Guy Winter stamped in full in gold on his despatch case, and he had pinched the window seat. Seat D1 was clearly marked on Richard Herbert's boarding pass. As soon as he had boarded the elderly Air Rajnaya Comet a smiling stewardess with a purple sari had explained that there had been a misunderstanding and Richard's seat was D2. It was the sort of trick Richard played on other people, and he knew how it was done. He drew the girl into the alcove where her colleague was putting dollops of caviar on salty biscuits.

'How much did he give you?' he asked, moving his hand towards his wallet.

'Oh, no it wasn't that.' The girl didn't mind being accused by so good looking an Englishman. 'You see, he is Mr Guy Winter, and we have instructions to treat him as a V.I.P. I think he is going to build some big factory in Rajnaya for our people. So you will not mind if we are a little nice to him?' She smiled at Richard, and he thought of Roberta, so sullen and hostile and English in S.W.13. It was good to be on the road again. And good to be travelling alone like a gentleman, with all the clutter of the camera crew gone ahead.

Installed in D2 he set himself to sum up Guy Winter. Twenty-eight he guessed, but the flesh already straining against the waistband of his light fawn suit, and premature streaks of grey in the straight dark hair. A regular dull face, pink English cheeks and full lips. He was reading an article in *The Times* Business News of ten days before. When he had read the article once the young man read it again, sidelining occasional passages with a gold pencil. Richard was good at reading over the shoulders of other people, but the young man noticed.

'Care to look at it? It's a thing I did myself.'

The article by 'Managing Director' was entitled 'Race relations and modern management in Britain.' It started with a long anecdote of how the writer had sacked on the spot a foreman who had sworn at a Pakistani for being late on the night shift. Richard only pretended to read the rest of the article while he rummaged in his memory for the facts about Guy Winter. He found quite quickly what he was trying to remember. Sir George Winter, rumbustious Yorkshire tycoon, was still Chairman of his group of textile companies, but now comfortably chewing over the conquests of earlier years, content to leave affairs more and more in the hands of his son. Harrow, Stanford, the Harvard Business School, marriage to a pretty pop-eyed blonde as rich as himself, and now pushed by father straight in at the top of the Winter group. What more could life offer young Guy Winter?

'. . . determined that we shall carry the same ethical standards into our work overseas.'

'Of course,' said Richard, realising that this had been going on for some time. 'But you'll find real problems in Rajnaya, you know. The Arabs and Indians hate each other's guts.'

'That's nonsense, you know,' said Winter, sipping champagne from a plastic cup. 'You talk just like old Paton, the man we've got there at the moment. A sour chap with no grasp of modern realities. I had a long discussion with the Rajnayan High Commissioner in London only this week. The British of course tried to divide and rule in their time, and that's left some bitter after effects. But basically the communities in Rajnaya are working more and more closely together. They're all determined to catch up with the rest of the world now that they've escaped from colonialism.' He carefully retrieved his article from Richard. 'After all they're all coloured, you know,' he added, 'and that must make a difference.'

Richard concentrated on Winter's profile before coming to his decision. The Comet began its downward approach towards Athens and the stewardess handed sweets. Yes, Winter would look better on film than in the flesh. And his outlook was obviously as fashionable as anyone could wish. He was long winded and would need editing; but on the whole quite a catch.

'I am a television reporter. My name is Richard Herbert,

and I am going to Rajnaya to make a film for the "Our Life" programme next week. I would very much like to interview you in three days' time to ask you about your impressions of Rajnaya as an up-to-date British businessman with a lively interest in social matters.'

14

The big conference room at Conservative Central Office was already full, but half-way through the Prime Minister's morning press conference there was a sudden jostling at the door as a fresh cohort of journalists forced their way in. This had happened every morning during the election campaign. It meant that at the other side of Smith Square the leader of the Labour Party had just finished his press conference. The new arrivals carried in their notebooks his latest challenges, just ten minutes old, with which to harass the Prime Minister. In anticipation the vast army of technicians manning the television cameras stepped back to their machines. The Prime Minister waited for it, fingering his tie. He sat alone on a dais, behind him a blown-up photograph of the whole Cabinet, The Team You Know. He watched the faces upturned in front of him, trying to guess from which quarter the trouble would come.

It came from the back, a tall greying man. The Prime Minister's memory for faces was famous, but it took him four seconds to place this one. The campaign must be tiring him already. But he noticed that as soon as the question started the Enterprise cameras began to whirr.

'The situation in Rajnaya is getting desperate, and there is likely to be bad trouble at the parade next Monday. What plans have you for intervention by British troops?'

Barney Tyrrell of course, head of the Enterprise Current Affairs Division. Not strictly entitled to come to the press conference at all, but it wouldn't do to make a point of that. Meanwhile play for time.

'Good morning, Barney, what brings you to a respectable gathering like this? Did you get all that stuff from the other side of the Square?'

'No, it's based on my own information.'

'Good for you, then.' Rajnaya, Rajnaya, Rajnaya. The tired brain raced round the subject. A race riot some days ago, soon over and never made the front pages. A garrulous little President who had sent him a carved cigarette box six months before. And some telegrams lying unread at the bottom of a red box; he had noticed them in the sleeper at Glasgow just before he turned the light out. It had been more important to get five hours' sleep. Ah well, take the plunge.

'Rajnaya is a sovereign independent state which runs its own affairs. I am quite satisfied that there is nothing in the situation there which would give rise to a call for intervention by British troops. I think everyone in this room would like to wish the Government of Rajnaya well in their constructive efforts to solve the island's problems.'

Afterwards he did not reproach anyone for failing to brief him on Rajnaya. There was no point. Those around him were intelligent enough to see that they had let him down. But he called at once for the unread telegrams and as he read them his face set hard. The smell of danger was unmistakable.

'Ask the Foreign Secretary to be good enough to come over at once.'

He looked again at the telegrams. Trennion, Trennion – his mind and memory attacked the danger from another angle.

'Trennion's sister married James Charteris, didn't she? And they live in the constituency. That can't be far from Swindon – look it up on the map will you?'

15

'How's the election going, then?'

'Touch and go, I'd say. There's still a week to go, and I think Labour will pull ahead.'

'I see.'

There was a pause. An Indian servant appeared and offered cigarettes from a silver box engraved with many signatures. When Richard and Francis both refused, he retired to his position just outside the pool of light where the two men sat in the centre of the drawing room. In the glimmer it was hard to distinguish the white of his jacket from the pillar by which he stood.

There was a short pause.

'James Charteris will get in again, I suppose?'

'Oh, yes, that's a safe enough seat. And of course Anne's a great help to him.'

'Of course.'

The conversation was stilted, between two Englishmen who long ago had known each other well.

'D'you think Lall will see me?' Richard was tired after the flight and was thinking of the neat little bed waiting for him in the Inter Ocean Hotel. There was a neat little chambermaid too, but that must wait till tomorrow. He was quite willing to spend an hour with Francis in the High Commission talking about the situation in Rajnaya and his programme, or alternatively about Anne. He sensed that neither was what Francis wanted, but that was just too bad. Later, a good deal later, there might be time to listen to Francis talking about Francis, but first he must catch up on his sleep and work out his programme with Katrakis.

'Yes, certainly Lall will see you. He fancies himself on television, and we've told him your programme is important.'

'What sort of man is he? I mean, underneath the facts in my briefcase and that smooth facade.'

Francis had no doubt of the true answer. Lall was an honest skilful man; now also a frightened man because he knew that the skills which he possessed were not those which would soon be needed in Rajnaya. But Richard was now asking him professional questions, and Francis felt the defensive reflexes of the diplomat confronted with a journalist.

'He's a decent chap, who's done his best.'

'You mean, for his Indian supporters.' Richard's knowing worldly laugh was effective everywhere except in his own home. 'Well let it pass, who else should I see?'

'Well, on the business side, there's Paton, who's this year's President of the Anglo-Rajnayan Chamber of Commerce . . .'

'You mean the dried stick in the lounge this afternoon? No, no, I've got a much brighter idea than that. In a day or two I'll interview his managing director, Guy Winter. That's the plump sweaty young article I sat next to all the way from Heathrow.'

'But he's never been to Rajnaya before.'

'That's why I'm going to leave him for a day or two. By then he'll have more opinions about Rajnaya than old Paton could achieve in a lifetime. He's a natural for television, that young man.'

There was a pause. The High Commissioner's house stood on a foothill of the mountains. The drawing room was framed on three sides by high white wooden pillars, beyond which were open verandas. From the sofa they looked out through the pillars south on to the city glittering two hundred feet below them. The Inter Ocean Hotel was the tallest of several pillars of light: beyond lay the black of the harbour across which a tanker was slowly moving. By first light she would be ready at the terminal to start unloading her cargo of crude.

On the other two sides the verandas gave on to the foothills and the suburbs, a scatter of winking lights without landmarks. The dark mountains were at their back. Francis had ordered that the insect screens should not be put up that night, so that Richard should see the view unspoiled. There was a buzz of tiny insects around the chandelier.

'What about the Chief of Police? He's English, isn't he?'

In Richard's experience Chiefs of Police were easy game, inarticulate and unattractive. In Argentina once a provincial Chief of Police had been so enraged in argument that he had drawn a gun on Richard in the middle of the programme. That interview more than any other had advanced Richard's career. Then the gun had not been loaded; but weeks later the man shot himself with it.

'I don't think Colonel Forster would see you.'

'But you could help me persuade him?'

'I doubt if it'd be any good.' Francis knew that Forster had done his damnedest to prevent Richard getting a visa.

'Then what about Johnnie Revani?'

Francis looked away from Richard's flushed weary face across the city. One of those pinpoints of light must be the house where Revani would sleep that night. The police had failed to get him yesterday, and today the town had been full of rumours. Forster's informers would have picked up perhaps too many signals for there to be any certainty. But tonight they would undoubtedly try again . . .

'He's wanted by the police. Lall signed a warrant for his arrest yesterday morning.'

'All the more reason for my wanting to see him. With a price on his head he'd be the making of the programme.'

'But it means he's no longer just the head of an opposition party. He's pulled out of ordinary politics and is trying to smash the government by force. You can hardly give him the run of your programme if that's his aim.' For the first time Francis spoke as if he had something real to say.

'Quite right, my dear Trennion. But Richard will do it even so, won't you, Richard?'

Richard had not seen Johnnie Revani since that misty October evening when they had shouted at each other in the cottage sitting room about the fate of Simbury-Smith. Now he stepped out of the dark veranda into the drawing room and sat in the armchair opposite the big sofa, directly under a full-length portrait of the Queen. His face was older and deeply lined. His slim erect figure seemed out of place in the comfortable European contours of the armchair. The servant hovering at the end of the room gaped, slammed down the brandy decanter and ran from the room as though from a ghost.

'How the hell did you get in?' In the High Commissioner's absence Francis had been much bothered with unfamiliar questions of the mission's security. It did not look as if he had solved them.

'Aren't you going to give me a drink?' Johnnie Revani got up and helped himself from the tray. 'I talked to the police sergeant at your gate.'

'But he's an Indian with twenty years' service.'

'You're too simple by half, Trennion,' Revani laughed. 'He's an Indian, but his brother-in-law is the third biggest smuggler of gold into Rajnaya out of Bombay. A fact which Forster does not know. And when the matter was explained to the man he thought it only reasonable that I should come and collect one old friend from the house of another.'

'Collect?' Richard forgot that he was tired.

'Yes, I thought the two of us might go for a nightcap to a little Arab club I know just on the edge of the city.'

'But Katrakis is expecting me back at the hotel to work out tomorrow's programme.'

Revani looked at his watch, which was large and gold.

'On the contrary, Katrakis is at this moment picking up your camera team and will join us at the club in twenty-five minutes.' He turned to Francis. 'And of course it would be delightful if you could join us – but I'm afraid you may feel somewhat . . . er, circumscribed, if that's the right word, by your official position.'

Francis was nettled. He shifted round in the corner of the sofa to face Revani.

'You really are ridiculous, you refuse all kinds of suggestions that we should meet, you deliberately keep out of my way – and now when there's a price on your head and you know we can't have any dealings you break into my house in the middle of the night and ask me out for a drink.'

'Don't worry, don't worry.' Revani spurted soda into his glass. He wore what was in effect a uniform, dark blue and buttoned up to the neck, but without insignia of any kind. 'We shall have many opportunities later on. When I become President of Rajnaya, there will be a small commotion in Whitehall because their puppet has been thrown out. They will find Lall a little house in Surrey near a golf course, they will withdraw the High Commissioner and there will be many rude adjectives about me in the House of Commons. Then after a few months, when they find other countries are beginning to get the big contracts, they will quietly make you High Commissioner, and we shall have many cosy talks down there in my uncle the Sultan's palace.'

He gestured towards the harbour. The tanker was now alongside the terminal, and the semicircle of black water was empty.

Revani turned to Richard. 'But for you, poor Richard, it is a different story. It is sad that this will be your last visit to Rajnaya.'

'But when you are President you will invite me often.' Richard wished he had the cameras with him.

'No, no, you understand nothing about it. I would never dream of letting you in.'

'Why on earth not?'

'I saw a repeat the other night of a British television programme on North Vietnam. They had not sent a professional reporter, but a left wing trade unionist. He asked no questions at all, he trailed round the collective farms like an old sheep, bleating every now and then to show that he was still swallowing the party line. Now why did the television company send such a man to North Vietnam? Why, of course, because they knew they couldn't get a visa for anyone else.

106

That is exactly the principle on which I shall operate. And I don't think you will be quite committed enough for the new Rajnaya.'

'You'll be very unpopular with the opinion formers in England.' Richard realised that this was a feeble remark as soon as he had made it. Revani laughed in genuine amusement. He had lit a small cigar and sat in a wicker armchair far too big for him.

'Not at all, not at all, you know your own profession better than that. They admire a dictator, provided he's a thorough-going one like Mao or Ho Chi Minh, with complete censorship and no nonsense about human rights. It's the half-dictators, the semi-Fascists, who get the stick. Take poor little Lall for example, a nice decent man, he's hardly a dictator at all. A fairly free press, a free judiciary, only a couple of dozen political prisoners, a parliament, foreigners coming and going at will – the man's almost a liberal. And yet by the time he's through his name will stink from Fleet Street to Shepherd's Bush, just because he's fool enough to let people like you come into Rajnaya and poke about the dungheaps which every country has.'

'Couldn't you ever work with Lall, under any circumstances?' This was a question Francis had despaired of ever being able to ask. Revani answered it seriously.

'He is an Indian and a capitalist. I am going to make this country Arab again, and revolutionary. That is your answer. Personal likes and dislikes don't come into it.' He looked again at his watch. 'Richard, I don't wish to hurry you, but if we are going to my little club, we ought to go soon. They put on a little performance at midnight; nothing special, but it would be a pity to miss it.'

Richard was on his feet.

'Good night, Francis, and very many thanks. I'll give you a ring.'

They shook hands, a thing they would never have done in former days.

'Please don't see us out,' said Revani. 'The same sentry is still on duty, and my car is in the wood two hundred yards from your gate.'

And so they were gone, and Francis was left alone, nursing his whisky, looking at the imprint on the cushions where they had sat. He could just hear a chorus of dogs barking in the village nearest the foothills. Perhaps it was the police looking for Revani. He had often sat watching that view of the city at night, thinking of the calm prosperity which the last decades had so suddenly brought to Rajnaya. Now it was all shifting again. The old Sultan would have chuckled in his white beard.

The Indian butler scurried in as if he had only been absent five minutes.

'You are not hurt, Mr Trennion?'

'I am not hurt . . .'

'You will have another whisky? As soon as I saw that wicked man I ran to summon the assistance of the police. It was my sad misfortune that the instrument was temporarily out of order.'

'Indeed.'

'It is working again now. It is my belief that he had the wires cut and then repaired them again on his way out. They say he is a very clever man, sir.'

'They do,' said Francis. So clever that already men like you would rather invent fairy stories than do anything to lay him by the heels. Yet there would be no life for an Indian servant in Arab revolutionary Rajnaya. Then he smiled at his own illogicality. For he knew that he himself had no intention of telephoning Forster about Revani's visit.

'I'm going to bed – Good night.'

'Good night, sir, and sleep well.'

On the staircase he caught the eye of the first British Governor of Rajnaya, Sir Stratford Roebuck. That evening Sir Stratford's expression was particularly sombre as he stared from his gold frame.

16

'Why on earth is he coming?' Anne Charteris was circling the big drawing room at Ridingley in the opposite direction to her husband. They exchanged a few words when they crossed. He carried a bottle of champagne, she a plate of sandwiches. The room also contained about seventy Conservatives sipping and munching expectantly.

'He's later than he said, anyway,' said James. 'I hope to God he's not going to let us down after all the commotion.'

It had not been easy to lay on a gathering of this size at a few hours' notice, but by much telephoning they had managed it. The Prime Minister's Political Secretary had rung up after breakfast, just as they were about to set off in different directions for the day's canvassing. He had been quite specific: the Prime Minister wished to have an opportunity to meet the workers in the Central Downshire constituency and thank them for their efforts. For this purpose he was ready to leave the train at Swindon after his afternoon rally in Cardiff and drive to Ridingley, arriving about 9 p.m. and staying an hour before continuing his journey to Chequers.

He hoped there would also be an opportunity of a quiet word with Mr and Mrs Charteris.

'I can only think he's had some terrible report of how we're doing,' said James. It had been clearly laid down at the beginning of the campaign that the Prime Minister would only visit marginal seats. The Conservative majority in Central Downshire had never been less than 2,000 since the dawn of universal suffrage. But in each campaign on the evening of polling day James Charteris spent a few hours convinced that he had lost.

'Nonsense darling, it can only be that he means to offer you a job, after the election.' But she did not really believe it.

'He can't do that till he's won. And anyway, for God's sake, Anne, pull yourself together and stop talking nonsense.' She had married him for his modesty, and it was a constant refreshment.

They went their ways round the room, trying to hearten people who were looking at their watches.

'That train is often late, I believe. I'm sure they'd have rung us if there's been any hitch.'

The stiff green brocade curtains were still open, for the light was only now fading across the park. Anne loved the shape of summer trees against an evening light, and sometimes sat for as long as an hour at that window, when James had to spend the night in London. Stopping there for a moment, the plate of sandwiches still in her hand, she could hear sheep bells despite the chatter inside the room. They often grazed right alongside the garden fence. What hell elections were.

There at last were the two cars, headlights on and moving faster up the lime avenue than was safe. The cars and buses from the fête had churned up a new series of ruts and bumps.

'Here he is,' she said, turning into the room.

They crowded on to the staircase, and clapped the Prime Minister as he came into the hall. In his neat dark city suit he looked out of place among the antlers and lithographs of prize pigs and oxen. He looked up and waved and smiled, and a current of sentiment passed through them all at that moment. Here in the flesh was their standard bearer. It was for the cause, for the Party, not for any one man that they were working. But at this election and the one before he had been their leader, and they knew that he had not stinted himself. The old ladies and the young men were the ones who clapped loudest as he climbed the stairs.

In the full light of the drawing room, though he did not know him well, James Charteris could see that his guest was dead tired. As he took him through the throng introducing his constituency faithful, he tried to hurry through each encounter. But the Prime Minister would not be rushed. He had always been exceptionally good at these gatherings and he had a professional pride in his ease of manner. Tonight the performance was entirely mechanical; the smile, the deft personal question, the extra pressure of the hand, the slight modification of his upper-class accent when required – all these made no demands on his mind. He was trying to shake off his physical tiredness and the impact of a lacklustre meeting at Cardiff. He must concentrate on the next day's needs, the morning press conference, the party political broadcast to be recorded, the flight to Newcastle, the evening rally. And the immediate need was to talk to these Charterises. It was a minor matter, a small cloud as yet, but he saw clearly how it could fill and blacken the sky. It was a long shot, but they might be able to help.

At last the voyage round the room was complete. Charteris

steered him to cleared space in front of the fireplace stacked with neat unlit logs, and called for quiet.

'. . . I have been in Wales today and my journey home brought me through Downshire so I thought I ought not to go home to my bed without coming here to Central Downshire to thank you all for the splendid effort which you are making to return James Charteris once again to Westminster. You have chosen an excellent candidate and yours is the credit for that . . . he has chosen a most beautiful wife, and I suppose he must get the credit for that . . . ten days now to go . . . coming into the straight . . . vital to put forward all our strength . . . the only poll that matters is the one on polling day . . . I know that I can rely on you . . . not only for your candidate, not only for our Party, but for the future of our country . . . God bless you all and good night.'

They clapped enthusiastically and except for the Charterises saw no need for any further explanation of the sudden visit. They were reluctant to go till James Charteris explained that the Prime Minister had some boxes to deal with before he went to Chequers. It took a long time for them all to file out; but finally, an hour after his arrival, the Prime Minister was alone with his hosts among the empty plates and full ashtrays.

'That was very good of you, sir, and it will have helped a lot.' James Charteris at forty-eight was five years older than the Prime Minister, but his deference came naturally.

'Not at all, not at all, I enjoyed it.' The Prime Minister looked at his watch, and refused another glass of champagne. At this stage after such an exhausting day most men would have wanted to relax. But Anne could feel that for this man the mingling with the old ladies and the young men had been the relaxation. Now he was tightening himself up for a new bout of serious action. Thank God that James after fifteen years in politics showed no signs of becoming a politician.

'I believe your brother is at present in charge of the High Commission in Rajnaya?' he said to Anne. His tone was not conversational, and she began to concentrate hard.

'That's right, the High Commissioner is still on leave.'

'Does your brother enjoy himself out there?' These were obviously ranging shots but Anne could not imagine what the target might be. Some special job for Francis perhaps, but surely this was an odd way of offering it.

'Yes, I suppose so,' she said. 'He writes fairly often, and the people there have obviously caught his imagination.'

'My brother-in-law is a very serious person,' James Charteris tried to draw the questioning on to himself, but the Prime Minister took no notice at all.

'What sort of people out there does he, as you say, take a fancy to, and what does he write about them?' Then he realised that he was pushing too hard. A pretty woman, beautiful even with that brown skin and dark blue eyes; up to now a face to be nodded at from a distance, seen at Westminster dinner parties, but not important enough to be placed next to him. Now conceivably she could be important.

'I'm sorry to cross-examine you in this way,' the Prime Minister underlined the apology with a thin smile. 'Before I ask you to answer any more questions I certainly owe you some explanation of what this is all about.' He filled his glass, deliberately slowing himself down.

'You see, we have a difficult situation building up in Rajnaya. It's not got into the newspapers yet, but when it does it could be serious. You probably know from your brother's letters about the racial tension out there and the way it's come to a head in the last few weeks. Next Monday the country is celebrating its independence day. Your brother's telegrams suggest rather strongly that it may do so by tearing itself apart.'

Anne felt no wiser. Her shoes were pinching slightly, and there was a great deal to do in the house before they could in good conscience go to bed.

'But there's much more to it than that.' The Prime Minister had now achieved that smooth flow of exposition which could have earned him a noble living at the Bar. 'If there is an explosion on Monday leading to some kind of racial war, then there could be a serious risk of Britain being asked by the President of Rajnaya to intervene under our treaty with them. He would need to show that the Arab extremist movement was receiving help and inspiration from outside. I have been reading your brother's reports in the train, and I understand that Lall could make out a substantial case to this effect. Any such appeal would obviously be a very serious embarrassment.' He sipped his champagne as a sign that he was getting to the central point.

'Now in such a situation your brother, Mrs Charteris, has a key role. His up-to-date assessment of the local position would be circulated to the Cabinet before they took their decision. It is fair to say that not many of my colleagues have followed these matters with particular attention. Because of their relative ignorance the views of Her Majesty's Chargé d'Affaires will carry the more weight.'

James Charteris had remembered something.

'But Anne that was what that old flame of yours was asking Pastmaster about on Saturday afternoon after the fête. Herbert, or whatever his name is. You remember, that long interview which never appeared on the news after all. That was about Rajnaya, and poor old Jack Mellon got very worked up for no good reason that I could see.'

And so the Prime Minister learnt for the first time that Enterprise Television had in the can a wholly unauthorised and unprepared interview with the Foreign Secretary on Rajnaya. He showed no surprise, but now the whiff of danger was unmistakable. 'This makes it all the more interesting to know how you think your brother would react. Of course his telegrams and despatches do not deal with the purely hypothetical situation of an appeal for British help which has not been made. But possibly in his private letters . . . or perhaps you speak to him sometimes on the telephone . . .'

Anne still did not understand, and thought the time had come to say so.

'I am still not quite sure what this is all about.' Her face was still flushed by the exertions of the evening and she sat rather untidily in her chair. The Prime Minister could tell from her tone that she had decided to dislike him; but that in itself did not matter. 'You and your colleagues have to decide difficult and important things every week, many of them far more tricky than this one. But I can't suppose that each time you ferret about among the families of your different advisers, trying to find out what their advice will be when it comes to the crunch. I may be stupid, but it seems to me an extraordinary thing to do.'

James Charteris made an embarrassed gesture, and for a moment the Prime Minister hoped that he would do the explaining. After all, Charteris was supposed to be a Member of Parliament. But nothing happened, and he had to do it himself.

'The campaign is going well,' he said, and for a moment Anne thought he was changing the subject. 'The polls are exaggerating Labour's position, as I hoped they might. Their organisation is bad, the trade union base is eroded, and they've lost the young. Provided nothing surprising happens meanwhile, we should win quite handsomely on Thursday week. *Provided nothing surprising happens.* But I'm afraid a crisis involving the use of British troops would count as something surprising. You can guess what the opposition would make of it. We'd be in trouble whether we answered the appeal or not; and if we accepted it, as we might have to, we would probably lose.'

He paused. 'You will understand then how interested I am in your brother's position.'

'Well, I know he respects Lall and thinks he's a genuine patriot. We both used to know Johnnie Revani at Cambridge, but Francis hasn't been able to make contact with him lately. So far as I can remember he's never mentioned the idea of having to use British troops . . .' Anne broke off, as another thought struck her. She was suddenly angry.

'But of course I see now what you're really up to. You don't care a fig what Francis thinks, you want *us* to warn him not to upset your applecart. That's why you switched your plans and came here. That's what all this palaver is about. You want me to ring up and make sure that nothing embarrassing reached your desk till after Thursday week. Well you are making a mistake if you think Francis . . .'

Both James Charteris and the Prime Minister were on their feet, but the Prime Minister got in first. His tone was very dry.

'I am making no such mistake, Mrs Charteris. Your

116

brother is a distinguished member of the Diplomatic Service. As such I would expect him to make his report and recommendation with complete objectivity. As Prime Minister I have to keep myself informed and sometimes I choose to do this by unorthodox as well as orthodox means. I had hoped that you could give me some useful background tonight. That was my mistake, and I apologise for troubling you. And now, as it is rather late . . .' and then to Anne '. . . please do not bother to come down.'

But she did, half-angry, half-ashamed. On the landing half-way down the staircase he paused. They were just under the main pediment of the house, and the big arched window looked out over the park. There was still an edge of departing light in the west, but it was the full moon which gave a glimmer to the grouped trees and the clocktower on the stable roof.

'There is a lot to spoil,' the Prime Minister said quietly, 'if things go wrong.'

17

Johnnie Revani avoided the centre of the town and his battered Pontiac was almost as wide as the unlit pot-holed alleys through which he drove. The cool breeze from the sea made Richard realise that he was more than a little drunk. The *tête à tête* with Francis over dinner had been a strain, and to ease it he had let the servant fill his glass too often. As an undergraduate he had learned the trick, in this condition, of gripping solid metal and thinking of something specific. In this way the mind could keep nausea at bay. Clutching the window lever tightly he thought hard about the club for which they were heading.

Johnnie had given no details, and Richard had no idea of what to expect. His only experience in these matters had been in Europe and the United States. He had a hazy expectation of belly dancers in a low-ceilinged cellar, lots of smoke and strange liqueurs and afterwards a long corridor with little rooms on each side, furnished only with a divan. Richard did not feel up to anything in the way of a strenuous programme. He tried to summon up from Cambridge days some scrap of evidence about Johnnie Revani's sex life.

A vivid picture forced itself to the front of his mind. Himself squelching to his car late that October night to drive Anne and Simbury-Smith back to Cambridge; Anne twisting herself free and running back across the muddy ruts to the lighted doorway of the cottage; the silhouette of Johnnie Revani standing in the doorway to receive her. The lintel was so low that Richard used to have to stoop to go in; but for an instant that evening, before the door shut, Anne and Johnnie had stood upright and close together.

'Did you sleep with Anne that night at the cottage?' The question escaped, without a conscious decision to ask it.

Johnnie laughed and stepped on the accelerator. They were heading towards the hills, and the houses were thinning out. 'I tried, Richard, I tried. You will remember that I was very angry with you, and you seemed to regard her as your property. So I tried as soon as the noise of your noisy car had died away.'

'And what happened?'

Johnnie laughed again, but the note was harsh.

'She kissed me on the forehead and then burst into tears.'

She stood in the middle of that little sitting room weeping very hard. She would not be kissed, she would not sit down. After a little she asked if she could borrow the handkerchief from my blazer. She blew her nose several times and said she was going to bed. She slept on the sofa with all her clothes on, and I slept on the sacks upstairs.'

'And in the morning?'

'She cooked me bacon and eggs, and we drove back to Cambridge, talking about politics. In those days, you see, I was still a gentleman.'

So the old question was answered. Last week he would have been delighted to hear this answer, but now he was not sure. The woman had patronised him only two days before. She was surrounded by comfort and convention now and from these high walls had repulsed him. It would have been soothing to suppose that once in a moment of anger she had fallen to an Arab on the sofa of a damp Cambridgeshire cottage.

'We've arrived.' Revani did not seem in the least put out by Richard's questioning. He looked at his watch, which showed five to twelve. 'We're just in time.'

It was not at all what Richard had expected; indeed it was not really anything at all. A mud house, perhaps a little more solidly built than its neighbours, but with the same whitewashed wall on to the street, the same single door leading into a small courtyard in front of the house itself. As soon as Richard and Revani got out of the car a shadow detached itself from the opposite wall and the Pontiac was driven away.

The door was not locked, and Revani crossed the court-yard with a stride as if he had been there many times before. It was very dark; Richard could just see the outline of a single fig tree against the sky. He tried to follow Revani, but caught his shin painfully against something hard. He felt forward with his hands to find the obstacle, and then stepped back in shock. But his eyes, accustomed now to the darkness, confirmed what his fingers had found. Lying on the ground just outside the inner door was a television camera tripod. The camera itself loomed just beyond; he did not doubt that it was one of his own.

'What the hell is my equipment doing out here?' Revani had already knocked on the inner door.

'I told you, Katrakis thought it would be a nice idea to invite your crew over here too. They would not have a very amusing evening at the hotel.'

'But why the equipment?'

'Well, you might find some local colour, I suppose. As I said, there's quite an interesting performance here a little later. And anyway, the equipment is safer here than in the Inter Ocean Hotel. The staff there are all Indians, and a terrible collection of thieves.'

And once they were inside, there indeed sitting round a table looking sweaty and sheepish were the two Enterprise electricians, the two cameramen and the sound man. Katrakis was with them, the neat creases on his biscuit-coloured suit and the sleekness of his hair standing out like a declaration of independence from his surroundings. For the rest it was a roomful of about a hundred Arabs sitting in groups at bare round tables and on hard benches against the wall. All men, mostly young, almost all in cheap western-style suits. Three older dirtier men were circulating among the tables pouring coffee from big burnished pots with long spouts. Katrakis had provided the television crew with glasses of light fizzy beer. Vivid posters decorated the places on the walls where the dark orange paint was flaking away. Though Richard could not read the Arabic captions, he saw that one of them represented a youthful Revani kicking a cringing Indian figure off the map of Rajnaya. The buzz of Arabic hushed suddenly when Revani appeared in the doorway, then resumed. Richard had the impression that most of the people in the room were concentrating on not looking at them. Revani crossed the room and slipped through a door in the far side.

'No personality cult, you see.' Katrakis offered Richard some beer, and motioned him to an empty seat at the table.

'What kind of a night club is this then?' asked Richard.

'Bloody lousy, I would say,' cut in the sound man. 'We've been here twenty minutes and not a bird in sight.'

'I am afraid that to your colleagues a club means striptease and nothing else,' said Katrakis. He had obviously had an uncongenial evening with the camera crew, and meant to take it out on Richard.

'What is this place, then?'

'It's the North West City district headquarters of the R.L.F.'

'But Johnnie Revani talked about a performance.'

'It will begin in a few minutes. I will give you plenty of notice so that you can set up your ingenious equipment.'

Revani was not to be seen, and Richard had no choice but to settle down beside Katrakis.

'Oh, by the way, your late travelling companion asked me to give you this.'

Katrakis took a carefully folded notice from his black crocodile wallet. It was printed in blue on stiff white paper.

Mr Guy Winter

(Managing Director Winter Group, London, England)
invites you to a press conference at 11.30 a.m. sharp.
Wednesday June 12.
In the Conference room at the Inter Ocean Hotel prior to
his return to the United Kingdom.
All accredited journalists welcome. TV facilities available.
Champagne.
R.S.V.P. Mr J. Katrakis,
          New Era Projects Ltd,
          23 Nehru Avenue
          TEL: 633–078.

'Mr Winter told me that you had said you would like to
interview him. He would be glad to see you immediately
after the press conference, before he leaves for the airport.'

'I thought Paton was looking after Guy Winter. Surely
he's their representative here?'

'Yes, indeed, poor Paton, he deals with the commercial
aspects of the visit.' Katrakis spoke as if he had never seen
money in his life. 'But Guy decided he needed someone
with, shall we say, a little more delicacy, to handle his public
relations.'

'I see. What's he going to say tomorrow, then?'

'Oh, you can hardly expect me to tell you that in advance.
Even if I knew.' The grin was even more disagreeable.
Katrakis recognised in Richard a more successful version of
himself.

Suddenly there was a hush, and the sound of glasses
returning to the tables. Johnnie Revani stood on a small
one-step stage which jutted out from the side of the room
which faced the courtyard. He had taken off the jacket of his

122

uniform and wore a white shirt open at the neck over the dark blue trousers. He looked twenty years younger, and the intensity which Richard remembered from earlier days had returned to his face.

He began to speak in Arabic, softly so that they strained to hear, and after the first few sentences everyone turned to laugh at Richard and his crew.

'He is telling them to behave well, as they are about to be seen by ten million English people,' said Katrakis. 'I would advise you to get your equipment ready.'

'What's the point of taking a political speech in Arabic?' The cameraman's glass of beer was empty, and the sweat was prickling on his forearms. He was beginning to feel the effects of the long flight from London.

'Better set it up,' said Richard, and the two men pushed their way clumsily between the crowded tables to the door which led to the courtyard.

'He is saying, only a few days more, a final heroic effort and the Indians will be thrown into the sea,' said Katrakis. There was another laugh round the tables. 'The wise ones will take their wives away on ships, the foolish ones will go to the sharks. And Rajnaya will join the brotherhood of Arab nations as the youngest, most socialist and most glorious member.'

'Don't bother to translate it all,' said Richard. 'I get the gist.'

Johnnie Revani was getting into his stride. They had turned out the lights except for two naked bulbs on the stage. The skin of his throat and neck looked darker against the white of his shirt, and his hips swayed slightly as he spoke. The gold of the watch flashed as his long slim arm forced home a point. They had shifted round their chairs to

123

face him, fans at the only festival they knew, waiting for the moment when he would ask them to applaud.

'What makes you go along with him?' said Richard. 'There wouldn't be much room for your kind in a Socialist Rajnaya.'

'That shows how little you know,' said Katrakis. 'In a capitalist Rajnaya there are many businessmen, they all compete and they all complain. In a socialist Rajnaya there will be two or three only, each with a monopoly, no competition, no complaints. And of the two or three, I shall be the first. It will last only three years or so, but they will be good.'

'I'm not sure Johnnie is like that.'

'He will have no choice. It is life that is like that.'

Johnnie was warming up now. He did not flinch when the camera lights suddenly switched on. The humour had gone from his voice as its volume increased. The old man who was still hovering among the tables with a big copper beaker of coffee was motioned to sit down.

Johnnie looked for a moment at his watch, and then sharpened his voice still further. Katrakis began to translate again in an undertone.

'Lall is counting on the British to come and save him. He remembers how they pushed out the Sultan and paved the way for the Indians to exploit us and rule over us. But he has forgotten one thing. The English have changed, they have grown old, grown soft. Old Atif there can remember when you could stand on the mountain and watch the ships of the King's Navy in the harbour, all grey and gleaming brass, so many that you could not count. The King's Statue was in Roebuck Place and his tune was played in the cinema each night. At every corner there were English soldiers and English policemen, pushing us off our own pavements.

'Where have they gone now? Gone home of course, grown fat, fit only to watch football and take drugs, not men any more, caring for nothing outside their little island.

'They will not come back, the English; little Lall will weep and sigh for them in vain. But if they do wake up and come across the seas, when Lall calls, if that miracle happens, then I, Johnnie Revani, will be glad. For then we can show the stuff of which we are made.' A murmur of approval round the room. 'It is too easy to kick the Indians out of their offices and little villas. We can leave that for our schoolboys to do on a half holiday. I pray to God that we may have a nobler destiny. Do not forget how the great Gamal Abdel Nasser triumphed over the English at the time of Suez. I shall not be happy until you and I, fighting side by side, have done the same as he.'

Katrakis was an accomplished interpreter, and he brought out the last words only three seconds after Revani had stopped. He had to shout them against the growing surge of applause. As the clapping rose the television camera swivelled from speaker to audience. Richard noticed Revani glance again at his watch. Although he had hurled the final challenge at his audience with an emotion too rough to be faked, he was already back in full control of himself. There was no doubt that he also controlled every Arab in the room.

An old man at the next table to Richard was slobbering into his coffee with excitement. A boy in the corner jumped on to the table in front of him and stamped about on it, clapping his hands above his head. He set up a rhythm which others began to copy, and the naked electric bulbs hanging from the ceiling began to vibrate.

Suddenly there was a scuffle at the door, the sound of a whistle, and several things happened at once. Johnnie Revani laughed. The lights went out. Captain Kaul, of the Rajnaya police, shouted into the darkness in English, 'Everyone stand exactly where they are.' His voice rose shrilly as he added: 'Or I shoot.' It was an odd phrase from the cinema not the police manual: but after the failure to catch Revani two evenings before Kaul was tense. On Sunday the young lieutenant and his men had let Colonel Forster down. Forster had given them another chance, and this time he would justify that trust.

The lights went on again. Police stood round the room sixteen in all, their backs to the wall. The captain carried a revolver in his hand, two sergeants held sub-machine guns at the ready; the rest were armed only with long wooden lathis. The Arabs sat quiet by their tables, as though they too were following a long-practised drill.

The little stage was empty, and of Johnnie Revani there was no sign.

For the first time Kaul noticed Richard and the camera crew. He was nonplussed for a second, but an Englishman would surely help the law.

'Revani was here?'

'He was here.'

'Don't worry.' Captain Kaul smiled like a schoolboy. His father had been a district officer in Punjab in the last days of the Raj and afterwards had bought a small printing business in Rajnaya with his pension. 'We have another whole platoon surrounding the house, and this time they are all picked men.'

One of the sergeants shoved his way through the tables towards them.

'Sir, they have found a tunnel.'

'What sort of tunnel?'

126

'It leads for two hundred yards and then there is an iron gate, which has been locked.'

'Why do you come and tell me these things?' Kaul's voice shot up again. 'He will be halfway across the city by now. Shoot at the lock and smash it.'

'Yes, sir.'

Tears of rage stood in the captain's eyes. He turned to Katrakis.

'You are his jackal. Colonel Forster has some questions to ask you.'

He motioned to one of the sergeants, and three men moved to arrest Katrakis. As they closed in the young man who, ten minutes before, had jumped on to the table hurled himself at the captain with one hand, pushed aside the chairs which separated them. The other hand he kept inside his shirt, and it was not until he was within three paces that they could see what it held. The grizzled sergeant who had been moving on Katrakis jerked the barrel of his sub-machine gun sideways and upwards. It caught the young man's wrist as he brought it out of his shirt and the knife spun to the floor.

The weapon, gleaming in the harsh light of the naked bulbs, acted on the police like a word of command. Within seconds the small stuffy room was a battlefield. The lathis rose and fell on the heads and shoulders of the Arabs as they scrambled from their tables. The old sergeant, swearing hard in Punjabi, struck the young man a blow across his face with the gun barrel, and at the same time placed his boot carefully on the knife. Kaul stood stock still, as if dazed by the danger which he had escaped.

Richard did not need to say anything to his cameraman and engineer. Several months later, when they collected the

Enterprise Television Award of the Year at a reception in the Hilton Hotel, they explained that the lighting had been absurdly bad; but everyone agreed that it was a remarkable piece of film.

It did not last long. The Arabs, who outnumbered the police three to one, made virtually no resistance. They jostled towards the narrow door which led out into the courtyard. Each waited his turn to escape and the police did not try to stop them. The beating went on, but after a minute or two it became less violent, and the constables began to look inquiringly towards the captain. He made no move to stop or to encourage them; there was no expression on his face.

The tall young ringleader was the last to reach the door. Blood was pouring from a cut just below his cheekbone. As he stooped into the doorway one of the constables struck him a final blow which sliced open the shirt across his back. Then he too was out in the quiet darkness.

'We can go back to the hotel now,' said Katrakis.

The police made no further move to arrest him or to stop them taking the car in which Johnnie Revani and Richard had arrived. Katrakis drove, and there was just room for the camera in the boot without its tripod.

'Bloody good evening,' said the sound engineer, forgetting his earlier boredom.

'I hope you too found it worthwhile,' said Katrakis to Richard.

Richard thought of Johnnie insisting so hard that he should come; of Katrakis bringing the crew and the equipment, of Johnnie looking at his watch in the middle of the speech; of the young man's single act of provocation; of the Arabs so meek and strangely passive under the police.

Did Johnnie take him for a total fool? For a moment he was angry. He thought of lashing out at Katrakis, sitting so smugly beside him. The anger passed. He had every intention of using the film, and in a way it was a compliment that such trouble had been taken to set it up for him.

'Double agents?' he asked. Katrakis laughed.

'Johnnie said you were not stupid in your own profession.'

'But how was it done?'

'Double agents is a dramatic term for a simple thing. Colonel Forster is proud of the number of his informants. He pays well, but not quite enough. It is a profession where it is easy for a man of intelligence to have more than one employer.'

In the club room the sergeants and constables had become policemen once again. They were searching the whole house and the tunnel for traces of Revani. It was a futile task, and they knew it.

Captain Kaul sat at one of the tables, staring at but not noticing the disorder of broken coffee cups and upturned chairs.

Ten years before when he was still a small boy his father had taken him as a special treat to Delhi for the Republic Day Parade. He had seen the elephants, the guns, the scarlet lancers, the domes and columns of the great palace which the British had built for their viceroys. On the final morning as they drove out of Delhi they had passed a squadron of cavalry exercising in a cantonment on the outskirts. Long lines of khaki troopers, motionless at first, then trotting and wheeling in perfect formation under the trees, the straight line of barracks behind them, the morning mist white between their hooves. It had been a marvel of order, a message so strong that the small boy from the Punjab had received it as a vocation. But in this moment of disorder among the broken cups even that memory brought no comfort.

18

FLASH   *Secret*

Foreign and Commonwealth Office telegram No. 793 of 13th June to Rajnaya repeated for information to Washington, Islamabad, New Delhi, Kuala Lumpur, Colombo, Singapore.

Your telegram No. 863: Independence Day Parade. The arguments in your telegram under reference against making representations to the Rajnayan Government on this subject have been carefully considered. It is recognised that our advice may be resented and that Lall and his colleagues have limited room for manoeuvre. Nevertheless the risks inherent in the present situation are so grave that it would be wrong to neglect any means of averting a possible catastrophe.

2. You should therefore seek another interview with the President at the earliest opportunity and speak to him on the following lines:

a. My colleagues and I have watched with admiration the statesmanlike way with which he has confronted the difficult situation of recent weeks.

b. We have received alarming reports about possible disturbances inspired by the R.L.F. during the Independence Day parade on Monday. The parade might provide Revani and the extremists with the pretext which they have been seeking for bringing the mass of the Arab population on to the streets.

c. The consequences of a major outburst of racial violence on Monday would be incalculable. It might prove a fatal setback to the policy of gradual reform which the Rajnayan Government has been pursuing with the full encouragement of H.M.G.

d. In these circumstances, while recognising the difficulty of changing plans at such short notice, we feel bound as old friends of Rajnaya to suggest an indefinite postponement of the parade. Possibly it might be held in a modified form at a later date.

3. If Lall should ask you whether this demarche means that H.M.G. would refuse any request for help under the 1969 treaty to deal with disturbances arising out of a parade on Monday, you should say that your instructions do not cover this point, but that obviously such a request would place H.M.G. in a considerable difficulty. It would hardly be possible in the circumstances to disguise the fact that advice which they had offered had been ignored.

4. You are authorised to speak informally to Colonel Forster on the same lines if you think it advisable.

In the flat of the Resident Clerk at the top of the Foreign Office a brandy glass standing on the dressing table picked a fight with the tumbler on the floor by his bed. The tumbler, which was white with the dregs of Alka-Seltzer, had the worst of the battle. Just as the tumbler was about to be smashed it began to scream rhythmically. The Resident

Clerk, who had only been asleep one hour, fought his way to consciousness and lifted the receiver.

'Resident Clerk.'

'Duty Clerk No. 10. You know the telegram you sent off to Rajnaya at midnight?'

'Of course.' It had been the last outward telegram of the evening, and the flimsy lay on the dressing table to which the brandy glass had now returned.

'The P.M. wants to send a follow up. I can read it you over the telephone. It's very short.'

The Resident Clerk found a ballpoint pen with his diary between the blanket and the sheets and began to scribble.

'It's not exactly Foreign Office language,' said the Resident Clerk after two minutes.

'It's not meant to be,' said the Duty Clerk. 'It was written by the P.M. on the back of a B.E.A. menu on the flight back from Newcastle.'

'Has the Secretary of State seen it?'

'They talked earlier on the phone. It's O.K.'

'O.K. it is.'

The Resident Clerk wrote out the telegram tidily on a blue telegram form, put the form in a red box, locked the box and buzzed for a messenger to take it down to the Communications Department for despatch.

'My immediately preceding telegram. Following strictly personal for Chargé d'Affaires. A smash in Rajnaya must at all costs be avoided during the coming week. It would throw the Rajnayan question into the thick of the British election campaign. This would be disastrous for both countries. If necessary you can tell Lall this.'

19

It was natural that Guy Winter's suite should be the best in the Inter Ocean Hotel, since he had agreed to pay a rate normally charged only to visiting Japanese. It was on the same floor as the British Club, but its windows faced inland. They looked immediately on to a ragged little roundabout, watered by an Arab urchin throughout the day, waiting for the traffic which never quite came thick enough to justify its existence.

The press conference was scheduled for four and by twenty past Guy Winter was muttering impatiently to Katrakis.

'I relied on you to make proper arrangements. There's only a seven-hour time differential, you know. At this rate we shall miss the evening papers at home.'

Katrakis knew enough to know that on a Saturday the London evenings didn't matter a damn; but it would not do to contradict so new and so rich a patron.

'The man from the *Sunday Messenger* said clearly that he would come. Of course if you'd rather start without him, Mr Winter . . .'

'No, no, no.' There was an irritable flash of the expensive watch. Guy Winter was wearing a green suit over a pink shirt. His dark hair was carefully sleeked over the bald patch, and he was reasonably certain that he looked every inch the progressive young British businessman.

'Here he is, I think.' Katrakis by the window was looking straight down ten floors to the point where two magnificently turbaned Sikhs administered the comings and goings of the hotel. Richard Herbert, glass of whisky in hand, looked down through the same panel of glass. A tiny blue Volkswagen drove up the ramp, the first Sikh stepped forward to open the door, and Richard had a distinct shock. For the brown shock of hair and gross figure which emerged from the car could only belong to one man, whom he believed to be locked up in a Persian prison.

Richard put down his glass and hurried out through the open door of the suite and down the corridor to the lift shaft. A green arrow rose unsteadily on the indicator in front of him, then halted. There was a dribble of canned music as the lift doors opened and he was right. It was Joe Steel, whom he had last seen in the Enterprise board room, two weeks before. Steel charged out of the lift like a penned bull. He wore an orange bush shirt open at the neck and dirty khaki slacks. He stopped in his tracks when he saw Richard.

'At it already?' he said, grimacing at the whisky glass in Richard's hand. Richard had once had a row with Steel about the latter's habitual drunkenness.

'What the hell are you doing here?'

'Sent out to take over from you, of course.' Steel waited for the glint of uncertainty in Richard's eyes, then laughed. 'You can relax. The *Messenger* got hold of me in Teheran. They asked me to come on here as a special. Tabloid on weekday, quality on Sunday.'

'But they've got a man here already.'

'Yes, indeed, poor guy, but he's only good for local politics. This time they smell race in the air. You know what a good race story does for circulation in North Oxford, North London and other seats of learning.'

'You don't know anything about race relations.'

'No one knows anything about race relations. That's why everyone's always writing about them. But when I'm sober

I'm a better moralist than anyone in Fleet Street. And a moralist who was already halfway to Rajnaya at someone else's expense was too good to miss. Even if it meant getting me out of prison first.'

'How did they manage that?'

'For God's sake, where's the press conference?' Steel pushed down the corridor towards the clink of glasses and buzz of chat through the open door of Winter's suite.

'Ah, you must be Steel. The drinks are on the side, help yourself. We're complete now, Mr Winter.' Despite the vehement air conditioning there was sweat on Katrakis's forehead. He had never supposed that the job of handling the British press would be easy, and it wasn't.

Guy Winter sat on a gilt chair of spindly hotel elegance with his back to the window. Katrakis was on his right, and on his left a grey man whom Richard recognised from a brief meeting at the airport as Paton, the local manager of Winter Textiles. A long, low table separated them from the journalists, carrying a glass of water for each, though Richard noticed that for some reason Paton had two.

'Gentlemen, there is no need for me to introduce Mr Guy Winter.' Katrakis was on his feet, a lock of greased black hair across his forehead. Uncertain of himself in this new role, he talked too long. Richard could see that Guy Winter's plump buttocks were squeezed uncomfortably in the confines of the silly chair.

At last Winter was on his feet. Richard had told his team not to start shooting until he gave the signal. Winter, though promising, was not certain material, and he did not want to run short of film.

'I had come here with the certain intention of signing a firm agreement to build a £20 million rayon plant.' The tone was brisk and businesslike. 'Winter Textiles has always been proud of its record of helping developing countries such as Rajnaya with their plans for industrialisation. We had been able to reach agreement with the Government-owned Rajnaya Development Corporation on a 60–40 partnership, with the possibility of doubling capacity after four years. You will find details of the proposals and an illustrated brochure on the desk on your way out. The Board in Bradford went into the scheme very carefully with our financial advisers and were entirely satisfied with it. I came out here with full powers to sign a binding agreement.'

Guy Winter poured himself a glass of water and flicked the dark red handkerchief an inch higher in his breast pocket. He nodded to Richard, and then nodded again. Richard signed to the camera and Winter raised his voice very slightly to compete with its whirr. He spoke now in a different voice, richer and more liquid, as if lubricated by the workings of a good conscience.

'But at Winters' there have always been some things which are more important than money. In recent years we have prided ourselves in particular on the excellence of our race relations. As you may know, we employ upwards of 2,000 Pakistanis in our Yorkshire mills and have three years running won the Community Relations Commission's Award for outstanding codes of industrial conduct. It is twenty years since we had any dealings with South Africa. I am determined that Winters' will never condone or be associated with any form of racial discrimination. We cannot and must not betray the ideals for which our company has stood.'

Another pause to twitch at the handkerchief, and a waiter moved round refilling glasses of whisky.

'And that is why, ladies and gentlemen, I have refused to sign the agreement for the new plant. That is why I am returning to England to recommend that the whole project should be dropped and forgotten. For I have discovered that it would be impossible to construct and operate the new mill here without conniving at a system of racial discrimination which is wholly repugnant. To be precise, I have found that under the rules applied in practice by the Indian-dominated trade unions in Rajnaya most of the main clerical and other salaried jobs would have to go to Indians. And that is something I am simply not prepared to tolerate.'

Winter paused, obviously expecting a murmur of approval, but it did not come. Richard and Joe Steel were the only journalists who had so far arrived from Britain. There was the political editor of the *Times of Rajnaya*, an Indian-run paper of high repute and small circulation. There were three Arabs from the cheap violent papers which circulated along the dockside and in the shanty towns. The rest were stringers for British papers, familiar enough with Rajnaya and its ways, but with no particular nose for the kind of story which would match the tastes of the British market.

Winter changed his tone to one of wheedling reasonableness.

'I can't pretend it was an easy decision. My fellow-directors and I have been keen on this project for a long time now. As I said, we've been into it very thoroughly, and it looked good. What is more, when I explained my difficulty to the Rajnaya Development Corporation this morning, they offered even more favourable financial terms. But I told them there was only one thing I wanted, an assurance that every job in that mill, from the top to the bottom, could be awarded by my company on merit, without regard to racial origin. And that assurance they could not give.'

He paused for the last time, then his voice went deep, and acquired a distinct American accent in tune with a slight shift in his vocabulary. 'I would like to speak to you, gentlemen of the press, entirely openly and frankly about this. There comes a time in every young man's life when he has to come to terms with his own nature. Know thyself, the Greeks said, and they were right. In the last few days I have had to face a harsh reality. I had to choose between, on the one hand, a satisfactory contract which would have brought me personally a good deal of credit, and a good deal of profit; and on the other hand the good name and moral reputation of my family and our firm. When it came to the point I found that I had no doubt. I hope that my decision will be a major and perhaps a decisive blow to a system of discrimination which would at any period have been evil, but which in this day and age I can only describe as intolerable.'

Joe Steel led off with a handclap so loud that Richard thought for one moment that it was sincere. The others followed with a ripple of applause.

'Mr Winter has kindly consented to answer questions.' Katrakis still looked uneasy, and Richard could guess why. A man who by instinct and training lived by playing both sides saw the moment of choice approaching and did not relish it.

The youngest of the Arabs chipped in first.

'Will you return to England, Mr Winter, and rouse the whole British people against this monstrous system of discrimination? Will you ensure that the U.N. intervenes to give justice to the Arabs?'

'Well, I'm not a politician, just a plain simple business-man running a family firm. But I've always found that actions speak louder than words, and I certainly hope that my decision may make people realise that something needs to be done.'

The political editor of the *Times of Rajnaya* began to extri-cate himself from his armchair, with the help of a knotted stick. He was a silvery Indian of extraordinary thinness, the oldest man present except for Paton. Seeing him move, Guy Winter tried to neutralise his question before it was asked.

'I should perhaps say that I feel nothing but friendship for all the Indians I have met in Rajnaya. I am full of admiration for everything which has been achieved here since indepen-dence. Your progress has been remarkable – I had read about it of course, but it goes beyond anything I had imagined.'

'Quite so, Mr Winter, quite so.' The frail figure of the editor was erect now, and the stick quivered slightly under his weight. 'We are indebted to you for your kind words. As regards the new mill your statement is entirely clear. But you have an existing factory which has operated here for many years at Langrisalam in accordance with the customs and practices of our country, imperfect though these may be. Is it your intention to close that mill and if not how will it operate in the future?'

'That's thrown him,' said Joe Steel.

'Why didn't you ask him yourself?' said Richard.

'And kill the goose which has just laid such a beautiful egg?'

Winter was thinking on his feet, but Paton got in first. He shoved his chair so violently behind him that it fell over. Grey hair, and moustache, grey-white face, grey suit, he looked exactly what he was – a safe prudent Briton some years beyond his best. The climate was draining the colour out of his face and the energy out of his mind. Such men were to be found by the dozen in every big city of the East.

He swayed very slightly as he stood behind the table, and Richard knew that at least one of the two tumblers in front of him had contained neat gin.

'With your permission, Managing Director, perhaps I could sum up in one sentence the policy of our company.' Paton spoke with quiet precision and for a moment Richard thought he must have been wrong. Winter nodded graciously, twitching up his trouser leg comfortably to show an inch of smooth calf. There was a tiny pause, Paton gripped the edge of the table, and leant over it towards them. His voice suddenly rose into a cracked shout as the anger reached it.

'Yes, one sentence will do it, I think, and from the New Testament too. D'you remember the first man who went up into the temple and what he said? "I thank thee, Lord, that I am not as other men are." It's a special tone of voice you need to say that and we heard it loud and clear this morning, didn't we? Or have we all got to such a pitch that we can't spot a Pharisee when we see one?'

Winter and Katrakis were both on their feet and they could hear a confused duet of conciliatory phrases:

'. . . strain of the last few days.'

'. . . not been at all well.'

'. . . natural disappointment.'

But these were only a muffled background to Paton's fury. He swung round and pointed out of the window, with a dramatic gesture dredged perhaps from some ancient film shown at the British Club.

'D'you see that grey blur over there on the edge of the

city? That's Langrisalam, the shanty town where our factory is. We employ 2,500 men, and they get a fair wage. But I reckon there are 6,000 men at least, and every man of them an Arab, in Langrisalam today. For six months now they've been swarming in over the mountain from the villages, waiting for work to start on the new mill. They've left their families for the moment, they're using up their savings waiting for us to start taking on new labour. There's a queue outside my foreman's office every morning and he tells them to come back in three weeks. Tomorrow he'll have to tell them not to come back at all.' He paused. 'Maybe they'll break the place up. Or maybe they'll shuffle over the hill again, back into malnutrition, ignorance, dirt and illness, forever and ever Amen. It's a half-life they live in the villages, and they thought Winters would show them a way out of it.'

'But you don't understand, there's a principle at stake . . .'

Winter made the mistake of arguing with the avalanche.

'Of course, there's a beautiful principle at stake.' In his exaltation Paton was reverting to the eloquence of the manse where he was born. 'The beautiful principle comes in a jet and stays in a rich man's hotel. The beautiful principle says that there must be no new mill because if there were a new mill the clerks would be Indian. It's too easy now for the Indian unions, you couldn't find a dozen Arabs in the whole city you could safely hire in a staff job. But if we built the mill Arabs who are hungry now would know what it is to have a full belly. And what's more, their children would be educated. Once that happened and factories were going up all round the island, the unions could huff and puff as much as they liked. Give capitalism its head, and these silly restrictions would be unworkable in three or four years. But the beautiful principle says no. The beautiful principle gives a press conference and

141

puts the clock back for these children, back to trachoma and starvation and rifles hidden in the roof.'

There was silence. Paton turned his back on them all and stood slouched by the window. His moment passed, and once more he looked grey, trim and second rate.

'He's a self-confessed racist,' said one of the Arab journalists, loudly.

Winter had the gift of reinflating himself quickly. He took no notice of the last remark.

'I must apologise to you all for this untimely incident,' he said. 'Mr Paton is an old friend of all of us, and we know how much he has done for Rajnaya during his time here.' He glanced behind him, but Paton was not reacting, so he gained courage. 'We all know too the strain which he has been suffering and the disappointment he must feel. I am confident that on more mature reflection he will come to the conclusion that . . .'

Paton laughed. There was no strength of feeling in the noise, it was simply the laugh of a drunken man who wishes to share a thought.

'It's crazy,' he said, and laughed again. 'Here am I, a racist they call me, but I've got an Indian woman in my bungalow and I do my duty by her Tuesdays and Fridays God willing. Whereas, whereas . . .' he advanced towards Winter and held out a hand as if to pluck him by the cheek, '. . . But – can anyone imagine him shacking up with anyone who wasn't very rich and very white?'

Editorial Sunday Messenger
All men of good will must welcome the decision reported on our front page by the Winter Group to abandon their plan to

build a new mill in Rajnaya. We have often expressed our disquiet in these columns at the slow progress being made in overcoming racial prejudice in that troubled island. History has imposed its burdens on Rajnaya, but that is no reason why the rest of the world should turn a blind eye to blatant discrimination. In view of our past connections Britain has a clear duty to give a moral lead, and it is a healthy sign that calculating profit has been given second place and that the conscience of Britain on this occasion should be expressed so eloquently by one of our youngest and most progressive business leaders . . .'

20

It had rained heavily during the night, scattering twigs and leaves on to the succulent little lawn in front of President Lall's bungalow. At one point a rivulet had washed a deposit of gravel on to the grass from the path which led tortuously up from the white gate to the steps of the veranda. These small untidinesses were being quickly put to rights by three ragged men and a boy.

'I see I have a new gardener today,' said Lall. The sitting room was cooled only by a small electric fan on one of the many occasional tables, but Lall wore a waistcoat and little gold chain with his grey suit.

'Your life is important. We cannot afford to take any risks,' said Colonel Forster.

'As long as he is not allowed to prune my roses,' Lall smiled for a second, and this showed more clearly the tiredness round his eyes. 'But things have been fairly quiet this week. After you failed to catch Revani you told me there would be serious trouble.'

'He has his people well in hand. He is waiting.'

'For the parade?'

'Perhaps.'

'You are not sure?'

'I cannot be sure.'

Of many things Forster was sure, for many people gave him information. He knew how many men had come into the shanty towns over the last three weeks. His men had picked up five dozen sub-machine guns and he knew there were several hundred more, maybe thousands, well hidden by now. He knew the names of the R.L.F. commanders in each district, two of them being intermittently in his pay. He knew that Revani changed his hiding place each night. He knew that Lall was an honest man with air-conditioning only in his bedroom, as allowed for in Ministry of Works regulations. He knew that Lall's nephew the Chairman of the Development Corporation enjoyed a lavish penthouse and an Italian mistress out of public funds. There was not much that Colonel Forster did not know, but it did him little good.

'I want your latest assessment of the security situation if we hold the parade.'

'I have brought you a report.' He had it in the buttoned down left pocket of his khaki shirt.

'Thank you. But tell me yourself.' Lall rang a tiny brass bell in the shape of an elephant and a servant brought cups of tea and a plate of very sweet cakes. Lall motioned him to the table by the window overlooking the garden.

'I'd rather you didn't work there, sir.' Forster spoke more formally than before. He looked out towards the white gate leading on to the road. 'Farther away from the window, if you don't mind.'

Lall made no comment, and the tea was served at another table in the centre of the room, by a green glass tank of tropical fish. Forster had always thought of Lall as a fussy little man, tiresome over details like all politicians, wrapped up in his own trivial manoeuvres, likely to be unreliable when the crunch came. Now the crunch was here, and they would see.

Lall took off his spectacles and wiped them on the edge of the tablecloth. The servant had left the room.

'Well, then?'

'Well sir, I am of course directly only responsible for the police. But as you instructed I have kept in close touch with the Army, and this is our joint assessment. We think we can deal with any insurrection that the R.L.F. can mount – provided that all limitations on our action are removed.'

'Limitations?'

'It would mean putting operation Dragon into action at the first sign of trouble – martial law, preventive arrest, house searches, immediate deportations and so on. It would almost certainly mean heavy street fighting and probably the demolition of at least four of the shanty towns.'

'And how long would this take – assuming that Revani used his full strength?'

'Perhaps a fortnight, perhaps three weeks.'

'That's far longer than you said when Dragon was first discussed.'

Forster shrugged his shoulders. 'That was a year ago. The R.L.F. is much stronger now.' He paused. 'There's one thing which could shorten the fighting. If you invoked the Treaty . . .'

'Ah, the Treaty,' Lall dropped cake-crumbs into the tank. A scarlet fish with a bulbous snout plopped to the surface.

'Of course there are no joint contingency plans, but I've followed carefully the British force movements in and out of Cyprus. Two companies of infantry, plus one of the R.A.F. Regiment, with plenty of military police – Near East Command could spare that easily enough, and it would make all the difference here.'

'What makes you think the British would come?'

'Of course they would, sir. You'd have no trouble proving external support for Revani.'

'No, indeed.' Another pause while the fish fought each other for the crumbs. 'Well, Colonel Forster, one last question: if you were in my position, would you cancel the independence day parade?'

Forster was tired of this little room, crammed with knick-nacks and fussy furniture like his mother's house at Leatherhead, sick of Lall and his crew of ministers, not a man of them over five foot five, sick and tired of the heat, the soft handshakes, corruption, flies on the food and equivocal orders. He was forty-eight, and felt seventy. But his advice had been asked.

'No, sir. I would carry on.'

'Thank you, Colonel Forster.'

Standing exactly at the spot against which he had been warned, Lall watched Forster stride down the garden path. He slashed at the low hedge at the bottom with his cane, like an overgrown boy released from school.

Forster would have to go. Of course it had always been easier at any given moment to keep him on for a few months more than to choose an Indian successor who at first would be less competent and at last might prove less loyal. But now it would have to happen.

It was intolerable to have a Chief of Police who could

seriously talk of two or three weeks' fighting in the streets of Rajnaya. Lall thought of factories destroyed, houses burning, the pall of smoke, bodies sprawled at each crossroads. An Indian Chief of Police would have told him three days; neither of them would have believed it, but both would have felt better.

He tinkled the brass elephant again.

'What time does the British Acting High Commissioner come?'

'In five minutes, sir.'

It was certain that Francis Trennion would be punctual. And it was almost certain that he would advise Lall to cancel the parade. It was difficult to think why else he should once again ask so urgently for an interview at a weekend. He would give him a vague answer, of course; no point in taking this decision, any decision, before the last possible moment. He would ask two or three of his colleagues round after supper for a final whisky or orange juice; then he would ring Forster with the decision before going to bed. For a moment he was comforted because he had sorted out a timetable in his mind; he had always been good at procedures.

Then the weight of doubt fell on him again, and his shoulders slumped in the weary gesture which he could never afford in public. He thought of Francis Trennion, coming to speak on instructions worked out thousands of miles away: Trennion had nothing to worry about. He thought of Revani, slipping in and out of the shanty towns; Revani would never have a doubt until the moment of his death, and perhaps not then. He thought of the parade broken up by violence, tanks and snipers in desolate streets, the prosperity of Rajnaya dissolving in an afternoon. He thought of the parade cancelled, the jeers and accusations of

147

his own people, the rapid ebb of his authority, of any authority through the island.

Lall's ugly dark sitting room was packed with the story of his political career – signed photographs of Presidents and Prime Ministers, framed election manifestos, cigarette boxes and ashtrays inscribed for particular successes, *Who's Who*, collected speeches and bound volumes of the *Economist* and *Foreign Affairs*. In one neglected corner was a small revolving bookcase of medical textbooks from his student days in London. He picked out one of his own notebooks and blew the dust from its sides; it was full of diagrams of the lungs and stomach, vivid in blue and red, annotated at the side in the precise handwriting of his youth. Lall put the book back. The care of the human body seemed an easy and predictable profession.

21

It was only when she saw Anne for the second time that Roberta Herbert realised who she must be. At the morning's briefing session for Conservative workers in London she had seen Anne Charteris on the platform, round fur hat perched on smooth dark hair, listening with attention born of long practice to James prosing away from the lectern about agricultural policy. At that stage she had simply noticed that Anne's legs were good, that she was the best-looking wife on the platform, and that this was not saying much.

Now in the coffee break between sessions she saw Anne again, and this time the name clicked in her mind. She was bored and knew no one in the room except her fellow workers from Barnes. So she nudged and shoved her way through the bulky chattering crowd over to Anne.

'I enjoyed your husband's speech.'

'Oh, thank you very much. I don't think it was too bad, considering he was asked to stand in for the Minister at a day's notice.'

'No, indeed, I learnt a lot.' Roberta took a tomato sandwich from a passing Young Conservative. 'I'm sorry, I'd better introduce myself. My name's Roberta Herbert.' A slight pause. 'My husband's Richard Herbert. He's with Enterprise Television and I think he came down to your house last week for a fête or something.'

'Yes, of course, he came to lunch.' Anne was fascinated, and then found herself feeling sorry for Richard, for reasons which she had to admit were bad. To be landed as a wife with this large messy-looking creature was bound to be a strain. She wondered whether Roberta looked better when she was not pregnant. 'I must say I would never have thought Richard would marry a Conservative.'

'You'd met him before somewhere, then?'

'Oh yes, didn't he tell you, we knew each other quite well at Cambridge. But that was years ago.'

'No, he didn't mention it.' Roberta knew little and cared less about Richard's Cambridge days. She assumed that he had slept with a lot of easy girls, but it would not have occurred to her that this fastidious looking woman could be one of them. She felt badly dressed and frumpish in front of Anne. Her hands were red and scaly from the sink. At such moments of discomfort Roberta usually behaved badly.

'I'm not really a very keen Conservative myself. I only got involved so as to annoy Richard.'

To Roberta's surprise Anne followed her without hesitation into this thicket.

'You like to spite him then?'

'If I didn't I'd fade out of existence altogether.'

'I don't remember him as such a dominant person.'

'It's not exactly that.' Roberta wanted to explain that she too had once been slim and pretty and socially superior to Richard. But the right words did not come.

'You mean that he takes everything for granted except his career?'

'Something like that, I suppose.' Roberta was mumbling now, already sorry that she had said so much to this stranger.

Anne was swept by a desire to talk to Richard again. Last time had ended so unsatisfactorily that it spoiled the earlier chapter. Anne liked her memories to be tidy, and she wanted that earlier chapter to remain a happy one, though of course tucked away comfortably in the past.

'Richard said something about going off to Rajnaya, but it didn't sound too certain. Did he go in the end?'

'Yes, he's there now, God knows what for. They're always making films about blacks, aren't they? And if I'm going to have another miscarriage my husband would rather be in Rajnaya than Roehampton.'

'You should be sitting down.' Anne spoke perfunctorily, trying to push down her feelings of alarm. An insignificant island, a routine diplomatic situation – why was everyone in such a fuss?

Suddenly, and without any logical process, Anne wished that she had gone with Richard Herbert to Rajnaya.

The Indian chauffeur who had driven Francis Trennion to see Lall hovered round the Rolls. He flicked a speck of dust off the bonnet with his gloves, turned the radio on, then off again, gazed over the hedge at the lawn of the bungalow where the gardeners were still busy picking up non existent leaves. He looked in every direction except at the small group of about thirty Arab men and boys clustered on the dusty pavement outside. They were penned into a smallish space by half a dozen police constables, but this still gave them room to hoist and wave their placards. These were inscribed in English and Arabic:

> *Death to the British imperialists!*
> *Down with the racist Lall!*
> *The Indians into the sea!*
> *Cancel the fascist parade!*

Each theme was vividly illustrated; the picture of plump little Lall (black face) being pitchforked into the sea by a handsome young Arab (white face) was particularly vivid. At intervals of about two minutes, despite the heat, they jumped up and down and chanted the same slogans.

'Small beer,' said Richard. 'I'm glad I didn't bring the cameras out in advance.'

'You were wrong,' said Joe Steel. 'There's plenty enough here if it's organised right. And with luck it'll catch everything except the first edition.'

They had shared a taxi from the hotel. Richard found

that he liked Steel a good deal more now that they worked for different organisations.

'I'm more fussed about Monday,' said Steel. 'I bet young Trennion's on his knees in there among the antimacassars, and he'll be pitching it fairly strong. If he gets his way, bang goes our nice little parade. I'd been looking forward to that Pulitzer Prize.'

'Depends who wrote the instructions, I suppose,' said Richard. 'Perhaps Pastmaster got his way after all.'

'What d'you mean?'

'Oh, it's nothing, just gossip.' For a moment Richard had forgotten that Steel was no longer part of the Enterprise current affairs team. So he knew nothing of the interview with Pastmaster at Ridingley.

'Gossip, hell.' Steel pulled in his anger with an effort. 'For Christ's sake, Richard, I know you hated my guts when we were dear colleagues united by the team spirit. But now we're just simple straightforward competitors, we ought to do better. None of the others here is worth a row of beans, you and I have got the whole Rajnaya story sewn up. And we'll make a better job of it, if we do it together.'

The dandruff had fallen thickly from Steel's jungle of brown hair on to the collar of his suit and his face was the colour of dough. Richard believed him to be a man without a tie or a scruple in the world. But to Steel the story, not the truth but the story, was a glorious end in itself, and not just a rung in the ladder of advancement, as it was to Richard.

And so, standing alongside the rioters in the hot suburban road, Richard sealed an alliance by telling the story of the Pastmaster interview.

'You mean Pastmaster definitely undertook to send British troops in under the Treaty?'

152

'Certainly he did. It's all in the can at home.'

'Then you must tell Lall.'

'What on earth for?'

'How do you English manage to think so slowly and stay alive?' There was a glow in Steel's dark eyes which Richard remembered from moments of skulduggery in earlier years. 'We don't want Lall to cancel the parade, do we? No parade, no story – no story, no glory for Steel and Herbert. Got that far, or shall I repeat it? O.K. The one thing that would screw up Lall's courage would be certain knowledge that if he whistled the right tune under the Treaty the British Army would come running. Well, you can give him that knowledge. It's as simple as that.'

'But old Pastmaster was talking out of the top of his head. He was full of champagne and home-baked cake and making no sense at all. The P.M. would never let the Tories go in for that sort of ancient nonsense, even after polling day.'

'It's no good explaining all that to Lall. It's your simple duty to tell him what happened at your goddam fête. It will give the poor man great pleasure, it will lead him to fall off the fence the way we want, and what's more it happens to be true.'

Before Richard could reply there was a bustle around them, caused by the appearance at the gate of Lall's major-domo, splendid in white-coat, turban and moustaches. He spoke to the driver of the waiting car and the little crowd of Arabs took this as a signal for renewed jumping and shouting. They were tired by now, and their output of noise had slumped.

'This is tame stuff,' said Steel. 'I'll see what I can do.'

He wandered across the road, looking like a malevolent dormouse, and began to chat. Expecting Francis to appear at any minute, the driver had taken the cover off the little Union Jack with the royal arms which fluttered over the right wing of the elderly Rolls. Steel apparently asked the driver a question about the flag, and bent over to inspect it. The next moment he was lolloping back across the road, the flag in his right hand. He tossed it to the nearest of the demonstrators, gave him something else from his own pocket, and shouted in Arabic. The driver also shouted, and began to follow in pursuit, but halfway across the road, faced with the small jeering group, he shrugged his shoulders and turned back to pick a quarrel with the major-domo. The police constables looked on and did nothing.

Francis appeared behind them, walking quickly down the garden path towards the gate. His head was down, and he did not seem to notice the handful of demonstrators. The driver started to explain something to him volubly, but he took no notice and opened the door of the Rolls himself.

As the car began to move off, the placards were hoisted again, and the slogans shouted. The tallest Arab boy took something shining from his jacket and lit the Union Jack. It took a couple of seconds for the stiff cloth to catch fire. The flag flared and crumbled, and the demonstrators scorched their fingers snatching happily at the fragments. Francis by then was halfway down the street to the main avenue at its end. He had seen nothing.

Steel had his notebook out. 'British Envoy watches Flag Burn. Fights Way through Jeering Mob' he said. 'Always imagine the headline before you start the story, that's the secret of journalism, I'm told. My God, I'm making a success of this profession.' He was scribbling fast. 'White-faced Francis Trennion, Britain's man in Rajnaya, today struggled through a shouting mob of several hundred Arabs after a key talk with Premier Lall about latest developments in this race-torn, oil-rich island. Bachelor Trennion (38), Winchester and Cambridge, saw the Union Jack torn and burnt before his eyes as speculation reached fever-pitch on Lall's eleventh-hour bid to keep power with British help . . . don't you wish now you had got your camera here ahead of time?'

'It's not oil-rich,' said Richard. 'The oil is only refined here. It comes in tankers from the Gulf.'

'A quibble, a pedantry fit for television. A current affairs programme lasts forty minutes, God help us, and you get the little things right so that you can go on getting the big things wrong. My story last four seconds if I'm lucky, jostling in a train from Beckenham to the Bank, and it's got to be noise and colour all the way. When's your interview with Lall?'

'In five minutes time. Here's the camera truck now.'

'Can I come in with you?'

'No.'

'I thought not. But remember what I said. Oh, thanks kid, I'd forgotten all about it.'

For the tallest Arab boy had returned his cigarette lighter.

23

In Lall's student days in London, being solitary and poor, he had fallen into the habit of walking back to his lodgings at lunchtime and boiling himself some plain rice or the weekly ration of eggs. He ate this with a piece of thinly spread bread and butter on one side of the plate, and a medical textbook on the other. Some of the books in the revolving case in the corner of the sitting room still bore the thirty-year-old mark of buttery fingers. The habit had remained, for he liked the clean taste and the light feeling through the afternoon, and the touch of hunger just before the evening meal.

As he sat alone at the table covered with papers – Forster's security report, Trennion's aide-memoire, the detailed programme of the parade – the arguments crowded back in his mind. There were more of them on either side than there had been when he and Forster had talked that morning. Trennion had spoken well, quietly but using strong words. At the end he had just about told Lall that because of the elections in Britain he could expect no help under the Treaty however strong his case. Then at the end of the TV interview Herbert had told him exactly the opposite, quoting something Sir John Pastmaster had said at something called a fête.

Lall had long since given up trying to understand the British. His father, a loyal servant of the Raj, had taught him that they were a handful of honourable and invincible men who knew everything and kept their word. At medical school in London just after independence the received doctrine among Indian students was that they were infinitely mean and deceiving. He had tested both theories and proved them wrong without being able to put another in their place. It was profoundly unsatisfactory to deal with people who were so unpredictable.

As he completed his second egg Lall saw that the arguments for and against holding tomorrow's parade were so evenly balanced that it was not worth weighing them any further. The decision did not depend any longer on the arguments. It depended on what sort of man he was. He, Atma Lall, grey, Anglicised and stout, doctor of medicine, shortsighted and liable to indigestion, a man adept at patient compromise and slow manoeuvre.

Lall got up and unlocked a little upper drawer of his desk. The only object in the drawer was a small photograph, still sticky at the edges where it had been torn from a police report. Johnnie Revani was smiling at the camera, a hard young clear face, conveying the charm of total determination. Lall looked at it for almost a minute, then returned it to the drawer.

They all expected him to give way. That distant Prime Minister in London whom he had never seen. Francis Trennion, and the soft many-tentacled machine of British diplomacy; Herbert and the flock of journalists, drawn to Rajnaya by the scent of carrion. Forster the dour and cynical mercenary. His colleagues in the Government, nonentities now doubtless in search of cover. Revani, dodging the police among the shanty towns, the face a little harder now but the smile certain as ever. He, Atma Lall, was to all of these a slightly ridiculous man of peace and manoeuvre. They believed that faced with such risks he would certainly give way.

Lall decided to wait no longer and lifted the telephone.

24

'No, I haven't heard anything since I saw him just before you did this morning . . . No, I haven't the slightest idea which way it'll go . . . Glad that little demonstration didn't bother you too much. I'm sure he'll ring you direct, but in any case I will as soon as I hear.' Colonel Forster put down the phone.

'Trennion's got the wind up,' he said. Even two years before it would have been unthinkable that he should discuss other Britons with his Indian subordinates.

Captain Kaul sat upright behind the smaller of the two metal desks which the room contained. His desk was new and shiny, whereas Forster's was shabby and scratched. Unlike his superior, Kaul wore his police jacket and tie. The Chief of Police's room in the former Sultan's palace was reasonably cool by any standard in Rajnaya except that of air-conditioning. The walls were thick, and the only window a narrow slit through which the Sultan had watched the dhows arrive in the bay with their cargoes of slaves from the African coast. Two years before, during the first racial troubles in Rajnaya, an ingenious Arab had lobbed a grenade at that window from a fishing boat below. His aim had been excellent, but the slit was too narrow for the grenade. It had smashed harmlessly against the outside masonry.

'I am surprised you told the Acting High Commissioner so little, sir,' said Kaul.

'What d'you mean, so little?' Forster pulled open the bottom drawer of the desk on its runners and began to grope for the bottle which lay at the back. 'I wish to hell I knew any more myself.'

'But the President couldn't possibly cancel the parade. You must know that, sir.'

Forster poured three fingers of neat whisky; duty-free Scotch was the only perk which he allowed himself. There was one tumbler on the desk, for Forster knew that his Adjutant would not drink on duty. Kaul disliked alcohol and only drank a whisky and soda on occasions when Anglo-Saxon convention required it. 'Why on earth not?'

'It would be entirely subversive of the whole authority

158

of the government to yield in the face of terrorist threats,'
Forster had noticed before that when Kaul's conversation
verged on politics he drew his vocabulary from leading
articles.

'Stranger things have happened.'

'I can assure you, sir, that it would be inconceivable. He
might just as well . . .' Kaul broke off, but Forster knew how
the sentence would have ended.

'He might just as well make young Johnnie dictator right
away – that's what you mean, isn't it? I tell you something,
Kaul, you've got that bloody man Revani too much on your
mind.'

Opposite Kaul's desk on the whitewashed wall, where
the old Sultan had displayed the most famous of his Isfahan
carpets, there now hung a large-scale map of the city. It had
originally been put there for general police work, but during
the last few days it had been used only for the hunt of
Johnnie Revani. Kaul had pinned a sheet of talc on to it, and
marked with red chalk crosses the houses of known R.L.F.
sympathisers. Black circles marked the area of the raids
which had failed. As reports came in about new hiding
places they were carefully tested against existing information
and if they stood up were marked on the talc in green as possible targets for the next raid. Big blue lines showed the
boundaries of the R.L.F. ward organisation.

The map was a competent and meticulous piece of work,
and Kaul had once got up in the middle of the night and
driven two miles to the office simply to look at it again.
Forster understood that for Kaul the map was a temporary
substitute for Revani dead or Revani in prison.

'With your permission, sir, I propose to raid the V.M.S.
again tonight. I am sure Revani is in touch with them, and

159

even if there's no sign of him, there will probably be arms and ammunition.'

The Vegetable Marketing Syndicate was a group of rich Arabs who used their virtual monopoly to extort money for the R.L.F. They also acted as the Front's communications link between the city and the farmers in the hills and along the northern coast.

'No raids tonight,' said Forster. 'And above all no more chasing around after Revani.'

'We've got plenty of men for Monday morning, sir,' said Kaul. 'Those who work tonight will be perfectly fit by then.'

'That's not the point. Whatever Lall decides, I don't want to stir anything up.'

He caught the glint of disapproval in Kaul's eyes, and was in turn annoyed.

'And what's more I'll have a bet with you. I'll lay you two hundred rupees that he lets you down and calls the parade off.'

'I never bet, Colonel Forster, and certainly not on so serious a matter.' Kaul was now alarmed and angry, and to hide these emotions he walked stiffly to the slit window and looked out over the harbour.

Poor chap, thought Forster, looking at the straight back. I can chuck it in, go home, grow runner beans in Leatherhead, and grumble in the pub to the neighbours. He's stuck here in this bloody hopeless little island, brimful with ideas of ours about discipline and losing face. They suited fine when we were ruling India with a handful of men but are going to be no damned use to him from now on. Whereas young Johnnie Revani has done just the opposite – grabbed all the knowledge he wanted from England and has now gone back to bribing and lying and killing as merrily as any of the old Sultans.

Kaul turned from the window. He was still angry. When he had joined the Rajnaya Police he had thought of Forster as a model of courage and wisdom.

'May I ask a question, Colonel Forster?'

'Go ahead.'

'Did you advise the President to cancel the parade?'

'I told him that if there was trouble Operation Dragon would mean maybe three weeks of fighting. I dodged the main question as long as I could, but when he put it to me direct I said if I were in his place I'd carry on. But I'm not in his place, and he won't. And what's more, when he doesn't, he'll get rid of me.'

'What d'you mean?' This was a subject on which Kaul had not so far sorted out his feelings.

'If he cancels, he won't want me hanging round like the ghost of Christmas past. It'll be a political struggle then, and I'm too old and rusty to be a political weapon.' Forster put his not-so-highly-polished brown shoes on the surface of the desk and sipped his whisky. He would pay Kaul back for that disillusioned look. 'Oh yes. I reckon Colonel Chowdhry will be at this desk in a week's time.'

'That's impossible,' Kaul was duly provoked.

Colonel Chowdhry, who was related to the Minister of Development, had been suddenly transferred to the police from the customs service six months earlier, and promoted at once to second in command. A fortnight later substantial peculation had come to light at the No. 8 go-down where imported consumer goods were stored. Three junior customs officers were convicted, and all the witnesses were at pains to point out that Chowdhry was in no way involved. He was just over sixty, and fat.

'Why impossible?'

'You know perfectly well, sir, he has no real police experience.'

'I know perfectly well he's proved he's a good politician . . .'

The telephone rang, and Forster slipped his feet quickly off the desk. Routine calls came through to the orderly room next door and the caller waited until a constable had established if Forster would speak to him. Only a handful of people knew the number by which they could call him direct.

The conversation was short, and on Forster's side a mixture of 'Yes' and 'I see'. Over years of talking to his superiors he had learnt to keep expression out of his voice.

'Two hundred rupees wouldn't have been bad for a policeman's bet,' he said when it was over.

'That was the President, then? What did he say?'

'The parade is on, definitely on. And that means there's a lot to do.' He got up briskly, pleased to have been wrong. 'Get out the Dragon orders will you? I want the D-I posts in position throughout the city by midnight with double issue of ammunition. Reliefs every twelve hours till the parade starts to muster at 06.00 Monday morning. Make sure they know the special orders and warn them I'll be coming round . . .'

The telephone rang again and Forster snatched at it. 'Forster here . . .' then 'it's for you,' in a surprised tone.

Kaul crossed to the desk to take the receiver, and he too answered little but 'Yes, sir.' He stood to attention while he listened.

'Well?' asked Forster eventually. 'What had he got for your ears that weren't fit for mine?'

Kaul was stiff and embarrassed. This was a moment for which he had never prepared.

'President Lall said that he had appointed me to succeed you as Chief of Police. On promotion to full Colonel. With effect from the end of the parade Monday night.'

Forster gaped for five seconds, laughed, swore, then laughed again.

'Well, it had to come. Better to die at the job, but that's too much to hope. But why the bloody hell didn't he tell me himself ?'

'There is an old Punjab saying: "The wise man is one who gives the first news of a death to the heir".' And then Kaul added rather solemnly, 'But I am not sure that I am glad.'

'Of course you're glad. It's a desperate job, and I've enjoyed every minute of it.' Forster pulled another glass out of the drawer and tilted the whisky. 'I'll give a toast which even you will drink.' He stood up. 'To the confounding of Colonel Chowdhry,' then Foster broke off.

'Well, you've got to put up with me for another twenty-four hours. Better get a move on with those postings.'

As they drank their eyes met.

25

They clustered round with congratulations, but the Prime Minister knew it had been a bad meeting, indeed the worst of the campaign. The audience had been elderly, the seats soft, the acoustics of the modern concert hall too perfect. There had been none of the resonance and tension needed for a really successful meeting. No hecklers either, despite the tickets on sale at the entrance at a knock down price.

The text of his speech had been flat, with too many statistics, and when in despair he had launched away from it to capture the audience with oratory, he had gained no more than a dim and dutiful round of applause. Why the hell hadn't the meeting been held in the old Guildhall, where the hard chairs and dark soaring Victorian arches made the right atmosphere before the first word was spoken?

Now, forty-five minutes in the Conservative Club, working his way round a crowded room of supporters. These were the real guts of the Party, and with four days to go it was essential that they should not relax. There were two marginals in this city to be clung to, plus a Labour seat which might be won against the swing because of a big influx of owner-occupiers.

The Prime Minister was so tired that the exhortations which he gave them were mechanical, but he knew that by now the message hardly mattered. It was his face, his smile, his handshake which would keep them on their tired feet, spur them to that extra evening of canvassing, that final stint in the committee rooms which might make the difference on the day.

He kept just enough beer at the bottom of his tankard to prevent anyone filling it up. The room was hot, and the tobacco smoke swirled slowly beneath the yellow ceiling. One small open window next to the portrait of Churchill let in a reminder of summer air, but he had to circulate well beyond its range. He joined a new group of supporters.

'Good speech tonight, sir.'

'Thank you very much. I enjoyed the meeting myself.'

They paused for a moment to digest these untruths.

'How's it going here then?'

There was a chorus of 'Pretty well, pretty well,' and a

middle-aged man with a red face and waistcoat added, 'We should hold East and West all right the way things are going.'

'We need to win South as well this time. I'm counting on the ladies to do that.'

The two ladies in the group giggled and promised to do their best.

He saw the *Daily Express* man pushing through the groups of drinkers towards him holding a piece of paper in his hand. He knew exactly what it held. The *Express* had again bought the rights of the Lou Harris Poll and their reporters would just have got on the telephone from London the details of the poll taken for next day's paper. The Prime Minister stood very still.

The young man stumbled over the figures: Conservative 42 Labour 40 Don't know 18. For the first time in the campaign a Conservative lead; there was a buzz of happiness in the group.

'Any comments, sir?' The young man's forehead was glistening. He too had had a hard day.

'You know I never comment on polls, good or bad. It only encourages the damned things.'

A mild chuckle all round, and the Prime Minister moved towards the door. He smiled and shook hands enthusiastically, but his mind was elsewhere.

It looked as if he had done it. Just as he had intended, four days to go, four days of steadily increasing lead if the trend continued. His had been an unpopular government through almost all its life, and he had minded; but now it was coming right.

He thought quickly of the things that could still ruin it. There was the rumble of a railway strike, but they could spin that along for a week or so. There was the libel suit brought by the Lord Chancellor, but nothing really damaging had come out so far. He thought he had shaken that little man in Rajnaya out of holding his parade. What else?

He was at the door now, making his farewells, and into the Rolls Royce. Detective and driver in front, a young private secretary beside him who knew that by this time of night his role was silence.

The Prime Minister settled against the cushions and thought of Chequers, two hours in front of him in the rushing summer darkness. Another five years as its tenant seemed almost assured. Clean stiff sheets, whisky and George Eliot by the bed, his wife turning peacefully in her sleep as he came in, and tomorrow Sunday morning poached eggs and a pile of newspapers on the terrace, sunshine on massed roses, and the delight of not having a press conference at Central Office till Monday.

'There was a message from the Foreign Office,' said the young man, as they left the suburbs. 'Apparently the Rajnayan Government has decided after all to go on with that parade.'

But he had missed his moment. By his side, chin nodding on chest, the Prime Minister slept.

26

'Jesus Christ, not another regiment of schoolgirls,' said the Australian High Commissioner. 'When's the bloody thing supposed to finish?'

'Half an hour ago,' said Francis Trennion.

'How you manage in that starched-up uniform I'll never know,' said the High Commissioner.

Francis managed by wearing nothing except underpants beneath it, but he envied the Australian's grey suit. The independence parade had started an hour late and looked like lasting an hour longer than the Protocol Department had said. It was true that there was an awning over the diplomatic stand, but it only covered about a third of it, just enough to give some protection to the ladies. Flasks were being passed round, and there had even been the surreptitious rustle of a packet of sandwiches. At this rate it would be three o'clock before they were home.

Francis looked at his programme and ticked off another item.

Valley Road Secondary School (Female: fourth to sixth grade).

They were pretty, most of them, and they giggled their way cheerfully past the saluting base, not bothering to keep step to the band three sections in front of them. They wore blue pinafores over red skirts which ended well above the knee, and carried silk banners on which patriotic slogans had been worked. Some of the workers from the oil terminal marching in the section in front turned round to look, and there were a couple of whistles. Even the jaded diplomatic corps took pleasure in the sight before reverting to their chatter.

Francis raised his binoculars.

'Try the one on the left in the third row,' said the Australian High Commissioner. 'Pity they don't have phone numbers on their pinnies.'

Francis focused on the flat white roof of the Ministry of Foreign Affairs opposite. He could not see exactly what was happening behind the parapet, but it looked as if they were relieving the crew of the machine-gun post which had been visible there all morning.

'Not bad,' said the first cameraman.

'I dunno.'

'Don't excite yourself, will you?' Then, in a different key: 'Hold it, you're not going to shoot this lot, are you?'

'Why not, they look good. Better than that mile of oil workers, anyway.'

'Forget their busts and look at their faces, just for a second can't you? That's a nice procession of Arab and Indian girls walking happily along together. But it never happened, boy, it never happened. No more use to us than a Sunday school outing. So far as Enterprise Television is concerned this is a savage race-torn island, and don't you forget it.'

'This is a farce,' said Richard. Everyone in the press stand had shed coats and ties. 'What the hell's Johnnie Revani up to, lying low on a day like this?'

He felt genuinely let down. He wished he knew what other material Enterprise had collected for the 'Our Life' programme on Wednesday night. If the parade passed off quietly and they had enough general election stuff in the can, they mightn't give Rajnaya even a ten-minute slot. All his splendid film would be wasted.

'I don't care if he doesn't show,' said Joe Steel. 'There are worse things than being shoved on to page six.'

'What d'you mean?' Richard did not suppose that Joe was suddenly smitten with concern for the fate of Rajnaya.

168

'Look at this. Came with the morning tea.'

IF PARADE PROVOKES CRISIS WILL LEAD A SPECIAL GROUP REPORT
DEPTH KINDLY BOOK PROVISIONAL FOUR SINGLES BATHS FROM TUESDAY
INTER OCEAN REGARDS HARLAND JONES

'Why the hell did I ever say I'd work for a British Sunday
paper?'

Richard didn't understand.

'The *Messenger*'s Special Group has a good reputation.
They won't put your nose out of joint. Harland Jones was at
Cambridge with me.'

'And I bet his suits fit. But he's not a journalist, none of
them are. All your quality papers have got the same disease
now. These high-flown guys with Cambridge degrees don't
check their facts because they think their opinions are more
important.'

'Whereas you're as pure and objective as the *London
Gazette*? What price that gag with the Union Jack yesterday
morning?'

Joe Steel turned on him. Richard could not remember
him being genuinely angry before. There was a thick dusting
of dandruff round his collar. He had to shout to drown the
tinny noise of the Valley School band which was passing
the press stand.

'O.K. I enjoy myself playing tricks and everyone knows
I'm a bastard. But by Christ I take trouble about my facts
and I know what lies behind them. These *Sunday Messenger*
guys step off a plane into their singles with baths and within
hours they're spinning it out – a thousand words of gossip
laced with a spot of paperback learning. The next week
there's a tiny lawyer's paragraph tucked away somewhere

169

withdrawing most of it – and six months after that it's all spewed up again in a paperback. Even you, Richard Herbert, phoney though you are, earn a straighter living than they do.'

'You're getting sour in your old age,' Richard had always supposed Steel was the perfect cynic; it was odd to discover otherwise. The relationship of cheerful hostility between them seemed threatened.

'Here comes Forster's Porkers.' The last schoolgirls had filed past the white dais at the front of which President Lall stood with a metal canopy over his head. Last in the parade came the Rajnaya police, marching six abreast. Richard and Joe Steel could hear the wave of applause which passed down the pavement on each side of the street as they approached. Not that the police were particularly popular; it was simply that with their shiny black caps, black belts and polished boots they looked what they were – the most effective of all the public services of the Republic. Compared to them the tiny armed forces, which had led the parade, were a scruffy and characterless lot.

'But where's Forster? That's not him in the front jeep unless he's painted his face?'

'No, that's Chowdhry, the Number 2. Look bad to have a white man leading the independence anniversary.'

Looking at Colonel Chowdhry, Lall felt a sense of huge relief. Not that the Colonel in himself was exhilarating, hoisting himself slowly out of his seat to salute the dais, fat, corrupt and to Lall's certain knowledge fully as stupid as he looked.

But it meant that the parade was virtually over. The crowds had been thin, the organisation poor, and the heat

170

punishing. A year ago he would have been bitterly disappointed. But now none of this mattered compared with the fact that it had passed off without a shot or even a shout of anger. The R.L.F. had stayed at home, their bluff had been called, Revani was a paper tiger, and he, Lall, could now step back out of the world's limelight into the job he was good at – the job of making Rajnaya, year by year, compromise by compromise, a slightly better place for its people to live in.

At that moment Colonel Chowdhry's jeep stopped and a puff of smoke escaped from its radiator. Half a second later Lall heard the explosion. It was a small one, just enough to blow open the bonnet of the jeep and shatter the windscreen, sending glass into the driver's face and the ample flesh of Colonel Chowdhry's legs. The Colonel swung round to face the marching column behind him, and shouted unintelligibly for help before collapsing on to the seat. The column halted raggedly and broke formation, uncertain of the next move. A sergeant swung on to the back of the jeep and went to help Chowdhry, leaving the driver to shout with pain. For about thirty seconds half of the total police force of Rajnaya stood exposed and vulnerable in its principal thoroughfare.

'For Christ's sake.' Colonel Forster pushed through the dignitaries behind the saluting base. He had been watching the parade from the very back of the government stand. He wore a civilian suit, and his head was bare.

He jumped on to the saluting base and pushed Lall aside to grab the microphone which Lall had used to start the parade.

'Detachment commanders! Get your men back in formation and clear the streets!'

The whole street could see him now. It was a voice the police knew, and a manoeuvre they had practised often on the big parade ground at the edge of the city. The voices of the different commanders took up the order. The columns divided, the marching men became policemen again, sprinting to either side of the street, frisking bystanders for arms, shouting to teams to go home. Colonel Chowdhry was hauled off his jeep on to a stretcher.

'D'you have to break up the whole parade just because of an accident to a jeep?' For a moment Lall had been frightened but now he was petulant. He could see the television cameras turning.

'Yes,' said Forster. He did not speak again, for at that moment a rifle bullet entered his brain. His body fell across the microphone, without blood or fuss.

Lall knew at once what he must do, for he too had been carefully trained. He ran back through the bewildered throng of ministers and officials to the V.I.P. car parked just behind. His car had the flag of Rajnaya flying from the bonnet.

'Take the flag down,' he said to the driver. 'Then to the broadcasting station as quickly as possible. By the backstreet way, no siren.'

He heard firing behind him, but he did not stop.

The machine gun started within seconds of Forster's death. The firing came from the police post on the Foreign Ministry roof, a hundred yards up the street from the saluting base, opposite the diplomatic stand. The Valley Road secondary school contingent had halted at that point, and their band was immediately below the Ministry. The sound of 'A Life on

172

the Ocean Wave' had died raggedly into the air a few seconds before.

For a moment after the machine gun began to fire on the girls there was no other noise. The bullets hit the second row of musicians, who carried mainly percussion instruments. Before they began to scream Francis heard the jangle of cymbals hitting the ground. Then the girls scattered, rushing away from the Ministry and jumping over the low wooden paling into the diplomatic stand. There were six bodies lying in the street, some still, some thrashing about. The girl who pushed past Francis must have been sixteen. She was sobbing and pulling at her breast under the pinafore. When the cotton tore the blood poured out.

He turned to follow her, but felt a tug at his binoculars.

'Let me have a look through those,' said a fat scruffy panting American whom he had never seen before. Behind him came Richard.

'This is Joe Steel from the *Messenger*. We ran from the press stand, what the hell do those police butchers think they're up to?'

'I must help that girl.'

'Off you go, then, Sir Galahad, but leave me these.' Joe Steel yanked so hard at the binoculars that he broke the strap. Something in his manner prevented Francis from grabbing them back. He turned to follow the wounded girl.

Richard was deeply upset. He had never seen civilians deliberately killed before.

'The bastards won't get away with it,' he muttered. 'We'll see to that, we'll see to that.'

Joe Steel held the glasses steady. At first he could only see the gun, poking at an angle down from the parapet of the roof seven storeys high. Then the men who manned it began

173

to pull the gun back out of sight, and for a second they were visible.

Everyone knew that was a police post on the roof. The police had been hanging about the Ministry entrance all morning, and those who came earliest to take places for the parade had seen the police take the gun in. About half an hour before the firing there had been movement on the roof, as Francis had noticed, obviously one police crew relieving another.

But the men in Joe Steel's lenses were not policemen at all. When he raised the glass again they and the gun had gone. But he was accustomed to be right on these matters. They had been civilians and they had been Arabs.

But he did not tell Richard. He simply agreed. 'Yes, we'll see to that.'

By this time they could hear firing in several parts of the city.

27

Richard Herbert and Guy Winter sat on either side of the Air Rajnaya Comet, willing it to take off.

The Arab van driver had been given fifty rupees on top of the enormous figure which he had named to get the Enterprise crew and equipment to the airport. The Inter Ocean Hotel had swarmed with journalists deciding whether to go or stay. Richard was clear that he had to go and Guy Winter, ranging the hotel lobby for someone who could find him a taxi, was of the same mind. His monogrammed soft leather cases had been jammed into the back of the van beside the two cameras and the reels of film. The driver had taken to the backstreets, on some of which R.L.F. flags were already fluttering.

Within an hour of the shot which killed Forster they were at the airport entrance. The airport police had parked a lorry across the road to form a barricade, and there was a good deal of shouting of instructions and haphazard rummaging among Richard's lotions and underwear. The grander cases belonging to Guy Winter were left untouched after the Lieutenant in charge had found his name on a list. But clearly this was just activity because on a day like this activity seemed to be required. There was no sign that the police had special orders or indeed any particular aim except to be mildly offensive in the service of the Republic. They took no interest in the precious reels of film. The van lurched into the parking quadrangle immediately in front of the departure building, and the driver, insisting on yet another payment because of the brush with the police, once again found that he was given more than he asked.

The incident gave Richard an idea, which he quickly negotiated with Guy Winter.

It was clear that no one in authority in Rajnaya on that difficult weekend had yet had time to punish Winter for his press conference by cancelling his V.I.P. status. It was equally clear that Guy Winter's next main concern was that nothing should prevent Enterprise from showing the extracts from his conference which Richard had filmed. Press coverage was important, but television would be the real clincher.

The Air Rajnaya staff were too preoccupied to object when the two men insisted that their personal luggage and the films should remain with them, so that only the cameras were checked in and carried off to the hold. All the kiosks and counters in the main lounge were shut. The clerks at the counter and then the stewardesses kept on saying that the flight would leave on time, but they did so with smiles which lacked conviction. They were constantly being called away to the telephone from which they returned muttering in Hindi. It was therefore a relief to be shepherded out on to the blazing tarmac not more than twenty minutes after the Comet had been due to leave.

The plane was elderly, with torn curtains and stained seat-covers. There were two pilots aboard, but as soon as the stewardesses had ushered aboard the English party and four or five Indians they clicked back to the airport building on their high heels, talking fast. Hope began to ebb. One of the pilots poked his face through the central curtains.

'Bad show, eh?' he said, grinning.

'Look, we're thirty-five minutes late already,' said Guy Winter in a first-class Southern Region commuter voice.

'Sorry, sir, can't leave till we get the orders.'

'But are there more passengers to come?'

'Maybe none, maybe plenty more.' The curtains closed on the grin.

His meaning became clear five minutes later. A Cadillac drove fast on to the tarmac and straight for the plane. A stout elderly Indian with snowy hair and glasses fussed his way on to the plane followed by his wife and a dozen cases carried by a bearer. Guy Winter got up at once.

'Why, Mr Singh.' It was the Director-General of the National Plan.

'I have been despatched on an urgent commercial mission

176

to London. At short notice, a matter of great delicacy and importance.'

Mr Singh began to recount his suitcases. These showed signs of hurried packing, squeezed fragments of clothing poked out of the sides of several of them.

'I'm afraid he's just the first,' said Richard.

'First of what?' asked Winter.

'First of a lot of distinguished Rajnayans with urgent business outside the country.'

But next to arrive were three police jeeps, weighed down by armed Indian constables. They ran towards the steps as if on an assault course.

Mr Singh and his wife began to bleat in alarm.

'At least it's not the R.L.F.,' said Winter.

'Not yet,' said Richard.

The constables under the command of a sergeant, took no notice of the Singhs. They went straight to the reels of film piled on the empty row of seats behind Richard.

'These are your films?'

'They are the property of Enterprise Television.'

'Here is my warrant to impound them.'

'But you can't do that, they're urgently needed in London.'

'I have my orders. They will be inspected and returned to you.' Richard shrugged his shoulders. Within three minutes the reels were loaded on to the jeep. As he drove off the sergeant gave a signal, and the plane's engines came to life. Five minutes later they were airborne.

The danger over, Mr Singh became smooth and talkative.

'Excuse me,' he said to Richard, 'but if I may say so you took that disturbing incident very calmly, very calmly indeed. That film must represent many days of devoted work.'

'The reels which they took away were all unused,' said Richard.

'But surely you have been filming . . .'

'Yes, indeed. The used film is safe in there. Luckily Mr Winter had left plenty of room for the shopping which in the end he had no time to do. Look.'

He unzipped one of Winter's big elegant cases, and they all laughed. Among the silk shirts and ties, more explosive than any bomb, lay the material for Wednesday night's 'Our Life'.

28

No one in the Rajnaya Broadcasting Corporation had known exactly why the fifth floor of the building had been cleared of its occupants, renamed the Special Projects Area and left empty throughout the last six months. They had only known that it had been done on Colonel Forster's orders; now they knew the rest. President Lall was installed in two of the rooms, and the rest were shared between the Army and the police. At the moment of crisis the broadcasting station was the right place for the seat of government.

'And so to you, citizens of Rajnaya, who love our country and wish it well, men and women of all races and creeds, who hate violence and long only for a life of peace under the law – to you all, my message as your President is this: stay at home, listen to this broadcasting station, keep your children off the streets, do not waste food or water, respond to every request made to you by the forces of order. This is a time of stern trial for us all; but with your help and stead-fastness we shall win through.'

The sound effects man put on the record of the national anthem for the fourth time that afternoon. Lall pushed the microphone away from him and lit a small cigar.

'How did that sound?'

But Kaul was looking through Forster's big Japanese field-glasses at the cluster of tall buildings in the commercial centre of the city. A smaller building near the Inter Ocean Hotel was burning, and bursts of small-arms fire could be heard at irregular intervals.

One advantage of the broadcasting station was that it lay a mile from the centre, standing ten storeys high and sepa-rated by a big asphalt car park from the network of narrow lanes and one-storey shops and houses which surrounded it. The car park provided an admirable glacis, and the fields of fire had been carefully worked out. Three army mortars were deployed around the statue of Truth at the entrance to the station, and the police had been pushing armed patrols into the lanes for the last two hours. The last patrol had run into some sniping, and the police helicopter operating from the forecourt had reported small groups of men entering the area. Kaul reckoned they would be under serious attack that night.

He lowered the glasses.

'It's happening just as Colonel Forster said.'

'I am interested now in what you say, Colonel Kaul, Forster served us well, and is dead.' To his own surprise Lall was enjoying himself. The timid little man juggling from his suburban villa with the details of political arithmetic seemed to have disappeared as effectively as Forster. 'What about the telephone exchange?'

They looked at the map of the city hanging on the wall. Operation Dragon provided that in the case of serious Arab insurrection the Government's forces should concentrate on holding five buildings, and they were circled on the map in blue chalk. Inside four of the circles was a blue tick: the broadcasting station, the airport, the Ministry of Foreign Affairs, the Bank of Rajnaya. But they had failed to secure the central telephone exchange.

'It's still out of order, of course. We don't know how the R.L.F. got in, or how many of them there are. And of course we're not counter-attacking yet.'

'Of course not.'

The strategy of Operation Dragon was that the Government, having secured the five vital centres of power, should remain passive for twenty-four hours. The calculation was that the R.L.F. and in particular Revani, would come out into the open in full strength to celebrate their easy capture of the greater part of the city. Once they were out of the shanty towns into the main streets, the Army and the police would move decisively against them from their positions on the fringes of the city. That phase could not start till Tuesday evening at the earliest, and it was still Monday afternoon.

An orderly came in with a scrap of paper for Lall. It led him to change the subject.

'How many of the schoolgirls died?'

'We cannot tell, sir, the Mountbatten hospital is not in our hands. Seven or eight, I should think.'

'The R.L.F. overpowered our detachment on the Ministry roof just fifteen minutes before the firing began.'

'You see what they are saying.' He handed Kaul the paper; it was a monitored report from Peking Radio's English language service.

'Ninety-two teenage schoolgirls were massacred in cold

blood by Rajnaya Government police as they took part in a peaceful demonstration. This act of deliberate provocation designed to cow the progressive elements in Rajnaya has badly misfired, and led to a popular uprising. Latest reports suggest that the reactionary government clique has fled from the city. In an act of popular justice the imperialist agent Forster, who commanded the government police, was shot dead by relatives of the murdered girls immediately following the massacre which he instigated.'

Lall lifted the grey telephone by his elbow. 'The R.B.C. internal exchange is still working? . . . get me the Director of News . . . I want you to interrupt your programme now and afterwards broadcast the following in every news bulletin for a full day . . . The Government has received incontrovertible evidence that the men who fired on the schoolgirls in the parade were members of Revani's illegal bodyguard acting under his personal orders . . . yes, incontrovertible – no, no further details. Thank you.'

Kaul looked at him. It wasn't true about the proof of course; they only suspected. But Forster would have done the same. He said nothing.

'Next thing,' said Lall, drawing a blank sheet of paper towards him. 'How do we get a message through to the British High Commission, now the telephones are out of order?'

'Helicopter,' said Kaul. 'The tennis court is big enough.' For a second Lall stared at his new Chief of Police. Kaul looked even younger than he remembered. There was much he would not learn until he had come out from under Forster's shadow. But Lall did not regret his choice.

'That's all for the moment, thank you,' he said. 'I'll need a secretary in five minutes to type this. Please check meanwhile that they managed to seize that British television film in time.'

Left alone, Lall wrote a letter out in longhand. He had rehearsed the text at the back of his mind for five years, hoping the day for it would never come.

Your Excellency,

I have the honour on behalf of the Government of the Republic of Rajnaya to inform you that a state of emergency exists in the Republic as a result of an insurrection inspired and assisted from beyond our shores. In these circumstances I have no alternative but to invoke with the utmost urgency, the assistance of Her Britannic Majesty's Government in accordance with the terms of Article 4(a) of the Treaty of Friendship between our two countries concluded in London on the 26th of June, 1969. I am ready at once to discuss with the competent British authorities practical steps for the immediate implementation of this Article.

I have the honour, etc.,

'May I ask a question?' Kaul was back in the room, and had read the letter. Lall noticed that he was already wearing the insignia of a colonel.

'Why is this necessary, sir?' Kaul spoke fiercely. 'We can deal with Revani ourselves.' He gestured at the map.

'We can check him,' said Lall. 'We can stop him getting what he wants at once. But then he will turn to his foreign friends, and say their investment in him is wasted unless they double it. Operation Dragon is admirably conceived for its own purpose – but not to deal with MiGs and parachutists.'

'They wouldn't dare.'

'How can I know that? I can only be sure of one thing. They wouldn't dare if the British are already here.'

'Will the British come?'

Lall shrugged his shoulders.

'It is impossible to say. For fifty years now they have been the least predictable people in the world.'

29

'Good morning. My name is Anne Charteris, and I'm the wife of your Conservative candidate.'

'Good morning.' A brisk small frizzy woman, drying her hands on her apron as she stood in the doorway. In the canvass return for last year's local election she was down as doubtful, her husband as Labour.

'I hope we can rely on your support on Thursday.'

'Well, I don't know really . . . I'll have to talk it over with my husband.'

No good wasting time. 'Well, you might find this interesting.' A copy of James's election address changed hands. Anne and her assistant walked down the crazy path to the gate.

'Labour for sure,' said Anne, looking at the hard-pruned roses. They used to say that you could tell a Conservative garden by its tidiness, but she had never found this reliable.

'How many more?'

'Only two in this street, then there are three council houses behind the post office which we're supposed to do before lunch.'

Anne was wearing sensible shoes, but already her feet hurt. She looked at her watch. Her call to Francis was due in an hour's time. She had booked it last night as soon as she heard of the fighting in Rajnaya on the television news. It was the earliest time they could give her. During election campaigns James Charteris slept more soundly and snored more loudly than at other times. Anne had not slept much, thinking of the danger.

'. . . hope we can rely on your support on Thursday.'

'Oh, yes, Mrs Charteris, my sister and I have always voted Conservative. My father, now, he was a bit of a Liberal, a picture of Lloyd George he had.'

The small council estate on the edge of this village was twenty years old. For ten years the local Conservatives had never canvassed it, believing that because the children were noisy and stole apples their parents were Socialist or worse. Now it was well established that the council tenants broke roughly fifty-fifty in a good year.

It would be evening now in Rajnaya. God knows what sort of a day they had had. Anne knew that the Residency lay just on the edge of the city. It might be a target for attack, she supposed, though she couldn't believe that Johnnie Revani would let Francis come to harm. But then she was thinking of Revani as he had been fifteen years ago.

'. . . support on Thursday.'

'Well, I suppose so . . . but I do think they ought to do something about our toilet. Rung up three times, I have, and no one's come.'

'I think that must be the responsibility of the council . . .'

'Flushes all on its own, it does, without so much as a touch . . . all through the night. I said to Bert at breakfast, not much good having these elections, I said, if they can't even make the toilets work properly. Stands to reason, really, I said . . .

The Resident Clerk at the Foreign Office had been less than helpful. Everyone was safe so far as they knew, he said. But what did they know, she asked. Not as much as we would like, Mrs Charteris, but as soon as we hear we will let you know. She had banged down the receiver.

'. . . on Thursday.'

'They're all the same, if you ask me . . . promise, promise, promise, there on the box night after night . . .'

A stout woman with a large blue rosette was panting up the road towards them from the café which served as headquarters for this operation. Every few yards she paused and shouted.

'Mrs Charteris!'

And then 'Telephone!'

The booked call to Rajnaya must have come through early. Anne pushed her fistful of election addresses at her companion, and sprinted down to the café

'It's a man,' said the teenage waitress who was treasuring the receiver. 'Long-distance, sounds ever so far away.'

'Francis,' said Anne. She was out of breath from her run, and there was nowhere to sit.

'Hallo, is that Anne Trennion?' It was not Francis, but it must be someone with news of him. Bad news almost certainly, if he had not been able to get to the phone himself The line crackled, but the voice was familiar.

'It's Richard, Richard Herbert here. I'm calling from Heathrow. Tried Ridingley first, and they gave me this number. I've just flown in from Rajnaya.'

'Richard.' She could not think what this meant.

'I thought I'd ring up to say that Francis was perfectly all right when we left yesterday. He was going straight back to the Residence after the parade broke up, and there was no sign of fighting in that bit of the town.'

Anne tried to compose herself, without success.

'Oh, Richard, I was so worried when I saw all that shooting on the news last night. I've been trying to ring him up.'

'That won't work. I've just heard they're not accepting any routine calls this morning. But I've got a priority listing as a journalist. As soon as I get into London I'll try to get through to someone and get the latest news.'

'That's terribly kind, Richard, it really is. We've only got two meetings tonight, we should be home by eleven. Could you ring around then?'

'Of course, sweetheart, of course.' He had always called her sweetheart in the old days. Anne felt better.

'How are *you* then?'

'I'm fine, Anne, we had a fascinating time. Listen, you must cancel all your meetings tomorrow night.'

'Don't be silly, it's the eve of poll.'

'Make old what's-his-name go alone. I mean it, Anne, I really do. You must watch my piece on "Our Life". It's all on Rajnaya and the best I've ever done.'

'What d'you think's going to happen there now?' She was still thinking of Francis.

'Three to one on Johnnie Revani being in power by Sunday. But he won't be too bad . . . Anne, I must get on into London. I've got to be there before they start editing my brainchild.'

'Goodbye, then, and thank you very much, Richard.'

'See you soon.'

As she munched her sandwiches and pretended to drink the washy coffee she realised that she had really been given no definite news at all. It was odd, then, that she should feel so relieved. Even her feet no longer hurt.

30

'We could bring up the twenty-five pounders,' said the detachment commander, but Kaul shook his head.

It was the remark he would have made himself a week ago, but that week already seemed many years. When they were first planning Operation Dragon six months ago, Lall had forbidden the use of artillery to clear barricades in the centre of the city; after an argument Forster had given way.

And anyway it shouldn't be necessary. Chowdhry was late. The first hour of the second stage of Dragon had gone well. The garrison of the broadcasting station had been reinforced during the night from the detachments at the airport. Just before first light Kaul had moved out quickly in his Land-Rovers, police and Army operating in separate units but both under his command. They had brushed aside some sleepy sniper fire and established themselves on schedule three hundred yards short of the Bank of Rajnaya.

The Bank had been built at the turn of the century as the chief Law Court of the colony. Its massive Roman columns and solid walls made it an ideal fortress, and the flag of the Republic still fluttered from the top of the pediment. The police inside were carefully picked, and had beaten off a substantial attack from Revani's men about midnight. Now Kaul had to raise the siege.

The shops and commercial banks all around carried the green and white flags of the R.L.F., and some had already been painted with the Party's slogans. Three main streets met at the Bank, and each of them had been blocked by the R.L.F. with elaborate barricades. Buses had been turned on their sides, wheels facing outwards, and linked with a wall of pavingstones. The strength of the R.L.F. lay in their rifles, and behind the barricades the marksmen were safe and formidable.

Forster had foreseen this. That was why the mortars had been bought in a hurry from France and men trained secretly behind the high walls in the main barracks outside the town. Chowdhry had had plenty of time during the afternoon and night to prepare his force and issue his instructions. The R.L.F. had not ventured near the barracks so far. Chowdhry claimed to be fully recovered from his mishap during the parade, and there was no reason for him to be late.

Smoke rose gently from a gutted department store to one side of the barricade which faced Kaul's men. He remembered going there four days earlier to order four silk shirts. Eight or nine bodies lay side by side on the pavement just outside the store. They must be the casualties of the R.L.F.'s abortive attack on the Bank during the night. Someone had lined up the corpses with mathematical neatness, stripping them of everything except underpants. A policeman shifted position on the roof of the Bank and drew a shot from a sniper concealed on the second floor of an adjoining office block.

Where the hell was Chowdhry? He had seemed enthusiastic enough first thing that morning, before they had agreed on radio silence. And yesterday, when Lall told him that Kaul was to be promoted over him to be Chief of Police, he had seemed far more relieved at being allowed to keep his job than hurt at not getting Forster's.

There was too much to do. Operation Dragon had cut it too fine. After raising the siege of the Bank, there was the Ministry of Foreign Affairs and the Inter Ocean Hotel to be secured and the whole docks area to be cleared. By nightfall the R.L.F. was supposed to be forced out of the whole centre of the city back to the shanty towns from which they drew their main strength. There would be a day's pause, and phase three would start on Thursday. The key fact in phase three was that there was no ban on the use of artillery in the shanty towns.

Kaul looked at his watch again. If Chowdhry didn't come by 8 a.m., he would himself attack the barricade in front of him, and gamble on reducing it before the R.L.F. reinforced it from the other two. At 7.55 precisely he heard what sounded like a burst of cheering. From the doorway of the bar which he had made his headquarters he could not see far enough down the third of the main streets which converged on the Bank. He stepped out into the street to take a better look, half expecting a bullet.

It looked as if the R.L.F. were dismantling the barricade in that street and there was some commotion just beyond which he could not account for. Could Lall have given in and reached a settlement? Then suddenly his glasses focused on a figure clambering over the barricade. No need to guess at the owner of that ungainly form even if the uniform had not been evidence enough. Kaul understood what had happened three seconds before the R.L.F. loudspeaker told him. It was Revani's voice.

'Members of the police force, you have been betrayed by corrupt politicians. You have been sent here to kill loyal and patriotic fellow citizens of the R.L.F., who have done you no harm and wish you nothing but well. Do not take my word. Here is your new commander Colonel Chowdhry to order you to lay down your arms and return in peace to your homes and families.'

Kaul jumped for his jeep. He thought he could rely on his own men. They had never liked Chowdhry. But they would need time to recover from this new blow.

He had left a strong enough force at the broadcasting station. There was only one way to win now, and for that it was vital to hold the airport.

'All five detachments are to disengage and move as fast as possible to the airport.'

'But, Colonel . . .'

'There is nothing more to do here. Now that Chowdhry's gone. We are outnumbered at least three to one. The British could be here tomorrow if we can keep the runways open.'

The journey to the airport took thirty minutes. Kaul spent five of them tearing up the closely typewritten sheets of Operation Dragon and throwing them out of the jeep.

31

That Tuesday morning, between nine and ten, the weather broke suddenly in England. On canvassers and pollsters, scurrying from doorway to doorway, umbrellas left at home after three weeks of sunshine. On James Charteris in the market place at Middle Trenbridge, more calves than voters gathered round his soapbox to hear about the merits of the agricultural levy system. On thousands of sodden posters, blue, red and yellow. On ten thousand tourists, peering at the traffic jams beyond the window wipers of their buses.

And on the Prime Minister, trapped in the New Circular Road on his way to the Enterprise studios. He reflected, as he often did, that London's hideous urban motorway had proved futile as well as expensive and destructive. Already it had generated enough extra traffic to make conditions worse than before. He jerked his thoughts back to the broadcast which he was about to record. The final party political of the series, and the most important. It was to go out the next night, the eve of poll.

Prime Minister, Prime Minister, Prime Minister – that was the card he must play again and again. Hint at knowledge which only a Prime Minister could have, at experience which only a Prime Minister could gain. He must seem to be above the fray, calmly working and planning, even during the election campaign, for the future of the nation.

Mistakes of course there had been, but they had learnt from them. That was the line. A bit of frankness at the start of the broadcast, a minute of quiet emotion at the end, a promise of calm times ahead – if only they stuck to the pilot who had weathered the storm.

Rajnaya, that was the difficulty. The Prime Minister never cursed his luck, for it had been more often good than bad. But it was hard that Rajnaya should boil up so fast and in such a crude and violent way. He had no idea how his colleagues would react at Cabinet tomorrow. An election campaign sharpened emotions, and sensible men began to talk nonsense when they were tired; he had seen that happen before. He was worried that one or two of them were already talking as if we were bound to send in troops at once.

Much would depend on Pastmaster, but he was swayed by his officials and they would make sure that he was sound. The Prime Minister did not need to make a single telephone call to know that as an institution the Foreign Office would be strongly against intervention. Even if other colleagues turned obstreperous he and Pastmaster between them could certainly get a decision postponed till after polling day. And if Lall foundered in the meantime – well, then, *cadit quaestio* and they could get back to more important matters.

In the studio he asked one of his standard questions: 'What's on before us tomorrow night?' Contrary to what most sophisticates believed, millions of people watched party political broadcasts at election times, and were influenced by what they heard. But exactly how many millions depended on what programme they had been viewing immediately beforehand. The Prime Minister's own breakthrough in politics had come in a current affairs programme immediately after the replay of a Cup Final. Thirteen million people lacked the energy to switch off, and a star was born.

'It's "Our Life" as usual,' said the producer.

'But rather a special number.'

'Election stuff, I suppose?'

'No, actually, it's Rajnaya from beginning to end, sixty bloody minutes of it. Can't see the logic myself, but they tell me it's an earthshaker.'

'You haven't seen it then?'

'No, nothing to do with me, they've given Richard Herbert a free run. He hasn't put it together yet. But he says there's never been a hatchet job like it in the history of television.'

'A hatchet job?'

The producer misinterpreted the sharpness in the Prime Minister's voice.

'Not against the Government here, it's aimed at that regime out in Rajnaya, race prejudice, genocide, suppression of basic human rights, the lot.'

'I see. Well, I suppose we'd better get on with our own effort.'

192

32

In the Inter Ocean Hotel the restaurant staff had left the day before, soon after the parade. The resident journalists lived mainly on cashew nuts and crisps from the bar. There was enough gin and Scotch for another four days. All communication with the outside world was cut. The lights in the main bar had always been dim, but now they went out completely for hours at a time. The air-conditioning had failed, and several of the more Anglo-Saxon correspondents lived without their shirts. Conversation tended to be repetitive.

'Let me prove it again. In front of the hotel there are converging streets and a total of nine visible corpses. Three per street.'

'Right.'

'There are five thousand four hundred streets in Rajnaya. It says so in the municipal guide.'

'Right. Mostly tiny alleys.'

'Never mind. Three times five thousand four hundred. That makes sixteen thousand five hundred corpses in Rajnaya.'

'Sixteen thousand two hundred.'

'Okay, okay, call it sixteen thousand. How's this, then? "The vultures wheeled overhead as for the second day running savage house to house fighting raged in race-torn Rajnaya. President Lall unleashed the full force of his British-trained police in a desperate bid to regain control of his capital city. Reports of fatal casualties vary widely but after careful checking I can assert that they have soared to at least the sixteen thousand mark" . . . There's lots more.'

'Good stuff. Pity you can't send it.'

'When the bloody hell are we going to get out of this hole?'

'What's Joe Steel up to?'

Joe Steel had been in this kind of situation before and he knew the rules. Get hold of plenty of money in different currencies. Pack your suitcase. Don't commit yourself to act with your colleagues. In a tight spot get your priorities right: journalists first, women and children later if there's room. Truth must at all times be served on the dot.

At the moment he was negotiating the rotating main door of the hotel suitcase in hand. The last man to attempt this had rotated back into the foyer with an R.L.F. bullet in his buttocks.

'What's the attraction, Joe? Taken out a new policy?' The attraction was a green and ancient taxi which had nosed its way into the square in front of the hotel. It stopped alongside the body of a young sniper, and a bareheaded Arab got out. By that time Joe Steel was there. For a clumsy gross man in bad training and carrying a suitcase he had moved fast.

'Whose side are you on?'

The Arab driver took the cigarette from his mouth.

'Revani, of course. Now he's won he wants the place cleaned up. Every taxi-driver's out collecting dead men at ten rupees each.'

He turned towards the corpse. The legs were twisted under the body, for the sniper had fallen from the top of the apartment block after the police bullet had hit him.

Joe Steel lifted the limp shoulders and between them they shoved the body into the boot of the taxi.

'Where are you taking them?'

'The slaughterhouse. We washed it down with a hose this morning. No cattle coming in from the villages today.'

194

'Take me to the airport and I'll give you three hundred rupees.' The wallet made yet one more bulge in Steel's ill-fitting brown suit.

The driver laughed. Steel saw now that he wore a red R.L.F. armband.

'Airport's the one place I can't go. That's where all the Indians have run to.'

'Is that where Lall is?' Different rumours on this point had filtered into the Inter Ocean Hotel at the rate of one an hour through the day.

'No, he's still at the radio station broadcasting lies.'

'I'll give you five hundred rupees to take me within half-a-mile of the airport.' He showed the money. Joe Steel found that his bribes usually worked better in soiled notes with random numbers.

The Arab smiled. 'You can't ride in front, we'll be stopped.'

There were four bodies stretched out tidily along the back seat of the taxi, three men and a girl. Joe Steel turned two of the men over so that they faced downwards on top of the others. They were no longer stiff. He took off his coat and spread it over their white shirts. One of them was crusted with blood between the shoulder-blades. Having placed his suitcase on the front seat, he climbed over the tangle of legs and stretched himself out on his back.

As the taxi drove off the journalists in the Inter Ocean could see Joe Steel's stomach heaving gently through the back window.

'Where's he off to, then?'

'Veteran journalist's dramatic death wish.'

'Wait till he files his story on the third day.'

*

195

It turned out to be a full mile of walking from the point where the taxi left him to the picket outside the airport, along an empty treeless road lined with bright billboards of every airline in the world. For the last hundred yards he was walking down the sights of a dozen police rifles. The suitcase was heavy.

They snatched at his American passport and took him straight to Kaul's office.

'He is a spy,' said Kaul. 'You should have shot him before he reached the picket.' He had not shaved and wore no tie. Already Forster's careful training and the Manual of Police Practice seemed years away. 'I am not a spy,' said Joe Steel, 'If I were a spy I would want to get back to Rajnaya. I don't. I simply want to get out.' A Lightning fighter was taxing along the tarmac beside the control tower. 'That plane will do.'

'That plane is taking me to Cyprus.'

'So you're getting out too. Room for a small one?'

Kaul had a hundred things on his mind, but suddenly he wanted to be as different as possible from this gross sweating man before him. He stood up behind his desk.

'I shall be flying back here tonight.'

'Flying back to this hole?' It was not often that Joe Steel let himself show surprise.

'I am going to liaise with the British Forces in Cyprus in advance of their intervention.' Kaul spoke formally.

Joe Steel thought hard. He did not believe the British would move. But here in front of him was a new man and a new story. Something over and above the story in his suitcase, of which he was somewhat ashamed because every fledgling drinking gin in the Inter Ocean had the same. He would have time in Cyprus to file the old story before any of the others got out of Rajnaya; then back to this crazy little airport if it lasted that long and this crazy young policeman masquerading as something out of the Indian Mutiny.

'You let me come, and I'll come back with you tonight. I'll help you.'

'You can fire straight?'

'Colonel Kaul, listen to me. You may need the British, but by Christ next to the British you need a Press Officer.'

33

Cold lamb, salad and lager – his favourite lunch, but otherwise Sir John Pastmaster's mood was bleak. To escape from the drone of his private secretary's voice he tried to see something of interest in Pembroke Square. The rain blurred the glass of the dining room window, but he noticed the puddles forming on the empty tennis courts, and his car drawn up opposite the house. Peaked cap, hunched shoulders and *Daily Mirror* visible in the driving seat; tweed coat, hunched shoulders and *Daily Express* in the other front seat, where the detective always sat. Rain equalled heavy traffic equalled at least two and a half hours to his Suffolk constituency. He finished the lager.

'Must get a move on,' he said.

'Just two more things, Secretary of State.' said Pringle. 'The P.M.'s on a whistlestop of South London this afternoon, but No. 10 said he might call you around two from Streatham.'

Another reason for getting a move on. Thank God they had taken the radio telephone out of his car in the last economy cuts. He raised a napkin to his grey moustache, and got up. The voice of his private secretary gathered speed.

'Then there are the papers for tomorrow's Cabinet. Rajnaya of course is the only subject on the agenda. All the papers are in the orange folder at the top of the box.'

'I'll read them in the car.'

'The Permanent Under-Secretary said he would be particularly grateful for an indication of the line you would be taking. He's very conscious that there hasn't been time for . . .'

'Can't tell till I've read the stuff.'

'If I could just summarise briefly, Secretary of State.' He had promised the P.U.S. to try and pin the man down. 'There's a joint submission from the official working party endorsed by the Chiefs of Staff recommending strongly against intervention. Obviously there are a lot of telegrams to be drafted for despatch immediately after the Cabinet decision. If in principle you could . . .'

'Is there a plan?' Sir John was on the move out of the room.

'A plan, sir?'

'A military plan for intervention.'

'Yes, indeed, there's an outline plan at Annex H of the paper. Someone from Rajnaya will be in Cyprus this afternoon for detailed contingency work on timings. But of course the unanimous official recommendation is quite in the other direction. They felt that the risks . . .'

'I'll read it all in the car,' said Sir John through the lavatory door. A small sane non-political room, with rude French sporting prints on the walls and a bad watercolour of his house in Suffolk.

Determined to avoid further discussion, he cantered out

of the lavatory, grabbed an umbrella from the stand in the hall, and so out into the square. The car drew away towards Suffolk, and within seconds the Foreign Secretary was fast asleep. Instant sleep was one political gift which he possessed in full measure. When they turned corners his shoulders sometimes brushed against the small pile of red boxes in the seat beside him.

34

That Tuesday night Rajnaya was a city of fortresses, strengthened against each other like the towers of an Italian hill-town. In between the fortresses the citizens of Rajnaya sat in their darkened homes obeying Revani's curfew, listening to Lall on the radio and wishing they were sure which of the two was going to win.

Francis had gathered almost all his staff into the compound of the High Commissioner's house. The billiard room had been turned into a dormitory – dark now, but alive with the rustle of excited children, each wrapped in a blanket on the floor.

The wives sat together in wicker chairs in the huge downstairs room which spread in three directions from the foot of the big staircase. Beside the front door was a pile of suitcases. Francis had made sure that drink would circulate freely. Indian servants passed from group to group with loaded trays. As the volume of chatter rose steadily, a glow of security spread through the room. Those who drank Coca Cola talked as loudly as those who drank whisky. Soon the Head of Chancery's wife would suggest that it was time for bed and they would all look at the roneoed sheet of room allocations. By using the adjoining Chancery offices as well as the High Commissioner's house a room had been found for each couple.

Some of the men were patrolling the fence which surrounded the garden. Inevitably there had been rumours running through the city that Revani meant to massacre all the British, but Francis was not afraid of this. A far more real risk was that the compound would be overrun by Rajnayan Indians seeking refuge. He had ordered that people with Rajnayan citizenship should be turned away at the gate unless they were close relatives of Rajnayans who worked and lived in the compound.

'Sir, my first cousin is at the gate.'

'He must go away, cousins cannot enter.'

'Sir, in the eyes of God he is not my cousin, he is my brother. We were brought up in one house, his thoughts are my thoughts, his friends my friends, sir, all his life he has spoken good things of the British, a picture of the Queen has hung in his shop, if you refuse him he will certainly be killed.'

'You have room for him in your quarters?'

'Of course, of course, even now we are only ten . . .'

'He may enter.' Francis scribbled on a card. 'Give this to the Administration Officer at the gate.'

'God's blessing be on Your Excellency.'

Francis walked off in the darkness towards the Chancery. The High Commission had its own generator, but the town below him was in almost total darkness and unnaturally quiet. The tropical grass squelched under his feet, and the cicadas competed fiercely.

The Cypher room was lit by three strong naked bulbs and smelt of human hard work. A fat orange folder of inward telegrams was waiting for Francis to read. Nothing from the Foreign and Commonwealth Office yet of course, he knew he would hear nothing till the next day at earliest. These were all telegrams from other posts repeated to him for information. Washington, Moscow, Bonn, Paris – they had all had the text of Lall's appeal for help by now, and were rushing in to comment before the Cabinet considered it.

'Anything to send out?'

'No, nothing just now.'

He knew they thought it odd that he had simply telegraphed Lall's letter without adding any recommendation of his own. A young man in a key position at a time like this was not usually so reticent.

Francis went out again into the garden. Beyond the fence he could just make out the wreckage of the helicopter which had brought Lall's letter. The R.L.F. had shot it down exactly one minute after it had left the tennis court on its return journey. The pilot and the messenger had almost certainly been killed at once. From inside the compound they had watched the R.L.F. drag the bodies out and drive them off in a truck.

Francis knew exactly what he wanted to say to London; but there was no hope of putting it into the style and vocabulary of Her Majesty's Diplomatic Service. Outside in the darkness, the smell of the smouldering helicopter in his nostrils, Francis hoped that in London in the intervals of weighing the pros and cons, of consulting and drafting and telephoning, they would find time to drum up a little courage.

35

'This is excellent, the best thing you've done yet.' Johnnie Revani smiled, and then turned the smile off. He handed the draft proclamation back to Katrakis. 'Now all we need is the broadcasting station to transmit it from.'

They were in the cellar to which Katrakis had brought Richard Herbert and the television crew the week before, but it had been transformed. The grubby tables and chairs had gone, and now the only furniture was Revani's modern desk and the chair behind it. Two young men in R.L.F. uniform stood by the door with rifles. There was nowhere for Katrakis to sit.

'You mean to storm the radio station tomorrow?'

'Of course.'

There was a pause, and Katrakis wondered if he should go. Here he was, Revani's adviser on public relations, virtually his only civilised supporter; but somehow the old easy relationship had become obscure.

'Do you think anyone believes what Lall says in his broadcasts?' asked Revani. He too was in uniform. He had hardly slept for two nights, and the lines on his face were hard.

'No one believes him when he says the Government still controls Rajnaya. But when he says the British will come . . .'

Johnnie laughed.

'Perhaps even you believe that?'

'No, no . . .'

'You've been a lackey of the British all your life, you've only seen them from below. No, they won't do anything. I know them, they'll postpone a decision until they can tell themselves that it's too late to do anything. No, it's not the British who will be coming tomorrow.'

'What do you mean, Johnnie?'

'No, no, you leak like a sieve, it's better you don't know – Tell me, who is this man Kaul?'

Katrakis relaxed. 'He was Forster's adjutant – young, ambitious, said to be brave, not clever.'

'He has made a good job of protecting the airport. They tell me he flew to Cyprus this afternoon.'

'He won't come back, then.'

'That's not what they tell me.' A pause. 'I want you to buy him. He is in my way.'

'It would be easier to do the other thing.'

'No, I want him alive and willing. Like Chowdhry, but better.'

Katrakis hesitated. This was not the kind of argument he deserved; it was uncomfortable, difficult and trivial. Chowdhry was fat and by nature venal, quite a different proposition.

'I'll do my best,' he said.

'Of course you will.' Revani got up. 'I want you here at seven o'clock tomorrow morning. It will be a busy day.'

As Revani went through the door the two sentries came to attention and saluted. That was something which, so far as Katrakis knew, had never happened in the R.L.F. before.

'Here is a special communiqué issued by the Government of the Republic of Rajnaya. Our forces continued to make headway against the terrorists. Loyal police and troops continued to defend the airport and the broadcasting station, inflicting heavy casualties, and recapturing a number of important positions. The Government has announced that a reward of 30,000 rupees will be paid for information leading to the arrest of the outlaw Revani.'

Lall switched it off. He had just recorded a personal message for broadcasting later in the evening, and the Director of Broadcasting was with him, a stout silvery Indian with a British Council background, an English wife and an air of gathering fear.

'What is your estimate of reception?' asked Lall. He sat behind the microphone, head in pudgy hands. Now that it was dark the studio which he used as an office looked particularly bleak.

'Oh, they listen all right . . .' the Director waved his hands.

'But they don't believe?'

'The only thing that would help would be if you said the British were coming.'

'No, I cannot say that today.' Lall knew that if he let out anything in advance about his request for help his chance of the right answer from London was nil.

The Director overflowed. He was not a traitor, nor in small things a coward. But the store of fears which had piled up in that silver head over the last forty-eight hours now swept aside his self-respect. The engineers were leaving, the food was running out, there was no one to maintain the generator, the police were damaging his wife's furniture, it was said that Revani himself would lead an all-out attack on the station at dawn.

Having gone so far, the Director drew a deep breath. 'So I must respectfully, Mr President, ask you to go. In the remaining helicopter, during the hours of darkness, to the airport. There you will be safe, Prime Minister, till the British come or people return to their senses.' He had rehearsed these phrases with his wife, and they came out rather fast.

'And you will stay and broadcast for Revani?'

The Director spread his hands.

'Mr President, I have a wife, I have children . . .'

It was like a bad film, thought Lall. He never went to the cinema, but had sometimes watched old films on television. He had noticed before that Indians under stress talked like a British parody of themselves; he sometimes did it himself.

'I will go at once,' he said.

36

'Gentlemen, the Queen.'

Kaul thought that he had never been so happy in his life. It was not the food, for the R.A.F. Mess at Akrotiri made no special claims in that respect. It was not the service, for the waiters with red, scrubbed hands who banged down the plates in front of him were no match for those smooth Indians who waited in the big barracks on the outskirts of Rajnaya.

It had something to do with the wine, for Kaul was used only to weak and occasional whisky. It had something to do with the combination of candlelight and ceremonial silver. The R.A.F. shared the mess with the one surviving squadron of a famous cavalry regiment. It had something to do with the music pumped out by a small military orchestra concealed behind a long green curtain. Not tunes of glory exactly, but tunes from twenty-year-old American musicals which had been appropriated by the armed forces of every English-speaking nation.

The C.-in-C. was on his feet again.

'Gentlemen, I give you – the President of the Republic of Rajnaya.' First the scrape of chairs, then the approving echo, and the gulp of port.

There had been a small scurry about this, for the gazetteer in the Political Adviser's office was eight years old and listed Rajnaya as a monarchy. So they had guessed. Looking at Kaul's face, the Political Adviser saw that they had guessed right.

He was not so sure they had guessed right about Joe Steel, sitting on his right. No one had expected him, but Kaul had introduced him as his information officer. They had asked him to dinner, told the Political Adviser to look after him, and placed them both towards the bottom of the table out of earshot of the C.-in-C., who had Kaul on his right. Out of normal earshot, that is; but Steel had pushed away the Chablis, the claret and now the port. He had insisted on neat whisky throughout. He did not rise to drink President Lall's health, and felt the need to explain this at the top of his voice.

'No point in drinking the little doctor's health. Poor little bugger, he won't last the week.'

He pushed his chair back and tried without success to put his feet on the table. He had filed his story as soon as he arrived. He had left out anything about the appeal to the British because he didn't want to ruin Kaul's chances. The scoop of a lifetime, and he had thrown it away for reasons which he found increasingly unreal.

The Political Adviser could not decide whether Steel's hair was dirtier than his fingernails; both were certainly too long. He hoped that neither the C.-in-C. nor Kaul had heard the last remark.

He need not have worried. Kaul let the waiter refill his glass, and for the first time in his life took a cigar. He had no idea how to work the cutter. A golden haze was clouding his mind, but he did not care. For six hours that day he had worked with British Staff officers twice his age on the details of Operation Andromeda. He knew now exactly how the British would help him to save Rajnaya. If he closed his eyes he could see splendid events unrolling as on a newsreel. The parachutists rescuing Lall from the broadcasting station: the four VC 10s of Support Command landing on the single runway at the airport, one every fifteen minutes; the Marines and the infantry moving quietly and quickly out on to the tarmac and into formation for the advance into the city: the rocket attack by Lightnings on the main buildings held by the R.L.F., and the final knock-out blows synchronised for just after dawn, with his own loyal police taking the lead.

At the back of his mind he knew that this was still only a chance. He knew that what he and these friendly polished men had been doing all afternoon was called contingency planning: that in London, far away from this cheerful island, another group of men, equally polished but not so friendly, would be meeting in a few hours to decide if it was all to be real. In the same way, at the back of his mind, he knew that the silver and the drink and the music were not organised to do honour to Kaul, Colonel of Police. It was a guest night which had been skilfully expanded at the last minute to include Joe Steel and himself. But it did not spoil his happiness: reality was at arm's length.

He caught the sound of Steel's thick voice and looked down the table to where the American sat, scowling and drunk. It was a mistake to have brought him. He could not be trusted. Kaul turned away to talk to the C.-in-C.

'You have been very kind.' It was all he could think of to say.

The Air Marshal was embarrassed. He had made his name in the corridors of Whitehall, he knew the form. He thought he knew exactly how a Government fighting for its life in an election would react to Lall's request. It would postpone a decision and eventually say no. He, the Air Marshal, had done nothing amiss, he had simply used the authority given to him as C.-in-C. to work out a detailed plan of action with Lall's emissary. It was not his fault that Kaul was so enthusiastic and trusting. But he felt embarrassed. He tapped the table with the cigar box in front of him and stood up.

'None of us here are politicians,' he began, loud enough to silence the chatter of such as had not noticed he was on his feet. 'Except of course the Political Adviser, and I'm never quite sure how good he is at it.' Small titter. 'I'm not going to say anything political tonight. I haven't the slightest idea how our masters back at home will react to the nasty situation which has blown up in Rajnaya. I'd just like to say one thing, though. We all of us here in this room wish Colonel Kaul well, and hope that he and his country can find the right answer to their problems. And we look forward to welcoming him again here in happier circumstances.' He turned to Kaul, drank to him, and sat down feeling better. Kaul did exactly the right thing: he got up, smiled at the murmurs of approval, raised his glass, said nothing, sat down.

In Rajnaya the R.L.F. militia had just shot dead the Director of the Broadcasting Corporation in front of his wife and his family. He had surrendered the station, but Lall had got away, and they were angry. Because Revani was strict in these matters they did not rape the daughter; but they took her clothes off, tied her to the chair which Lall had been using, and walked round her most of the night. Because she was Anglo-Indian her skin was fair and interesting to touch.

In Cyprus, Joe Steel pulled himself together and spoke in a quiet and friendly manner to the Political Adviser.

'I had no idea you British were such bastards,' he said.

'What d'you mean?'

'When we Americans are going to let a man down, we kick the chair away quick, and that's that. You do it the slow way.'

'There are worse anaesthetics than port,' said the Political Adviser. He too thought he knew what would happen. Not far away, on the vast airfield beyond the scattered huts and oleanders, they had finished refuelling Kaul's Lightning for the flight back to Rajnaya.

37

That evening at Lo Scandalo in Berkeley Square they were drinking brandy. It was a new and horrible restaurant owned by the principal shareholder in Enterprise Television who took a close personal interest in its clientele. The senior staff of ET ate there to the extent that their ambition was stronger than their good taste.

'All we need now is luck,' said Barney Tyrrell. He spoke as if he had spent the whole day like Richard and the 'Our Life' team, agonising over several hundred feet of film, cutting, discarding, running and re-running in different sequences, sweating and swearing, bringing to birth tomorrow's programme. Tyrrell had arrived at six, inspected the result, cut out a couple of Richard's comments as too provocative, and pronounced the whole thing the best 'Our Life' had produced since his own film on Vietnam two years before. Then he had asked Richard out to dinner.

'What sort of luck?' said Richard, who felt drunk with his own talent. Luck seemed superfluous.

Tyrrell had the affectation of smoking cheap cigars in expensive places. He lit something Swiss and nasty.

'I've been trying to find out all day what's actually happening in Rajnaya.'

'That's easy. The place is falling to bits.'

'Of course. But none of our viewers cares a damn for that so long as we're not involved. The only question is – has Lall asked for British help? If he has, and this gets out tomorrow, then our programme won't be just good, it'll be history.'

'There was nothing in the evening papers.'

'The lobby boys know nothing, the Foreign Office News Department say they know nothing. Pastmaster's gone off to his constituency, the P.M.'s making a speech tonight in Croydon about value added tax. No smoke signals from any of the usual wigwams.'

'But here's your favourite squaw.'

Across the room in full sail came Betty Bradshaw, Labour's No. 2 spokesman on foreign affairs. Four years ago she had become Tyrrell's mistress, a handsome smiling woman of thirty-five with a mane of black hair and a brilliant political future. Things had not worked out, and she had lost her seat on the National Executive Committee. As Tyrrell rose to become Enterprise's Director of Current Affairs he began to mix on easy terms with politicians of all parties, and Betty, having done her bit to launch him, became a liability. But she still nosed out little secrets which she would come and lay at his feet.

Tonight Richard could just about see her tail wagging. The hair was still tremendous.

'Hallo, Barney, didn't know you'd be here.' Except that she had rung up five restaurants to find out where he'd booked a table. 'What d'you think? I'd been set to do a debate with Pastmaster on the radio tomorrow morning, but he's just cried off. Special Cabinet meeting been called. Must be Rajnaya.'

'Must be Rajnaya,' Barney repeated her words as if she had not spoken them.

'They wouldn't call a Cabinet on the eve of poll unless Lall had invoked the Treaty,' said Richard, with a question in his voice.

'No, they wouldn't, my boy.' Barney got up, his eyes glistening. Up went the big brandy glass. 'Here's to our luck and happy ratings,' he shouted across the room.

Mind if I join you?' said Betty Bradshaw.

Half an hour later Barney and Betty had gone off together to her flat behind Westminster Cathedral. He preferred to pay his debts quickly.

Richard walked alone down the dip of Piccadilly towards Hyde Park Corner. He should have felt on top of the world, but the sight of the two of them lurching into a taxi together had spoiled it. He liked his moments of happiness to be complete, and there was a hole in this one.

Anne – she would still be out and about in Central Downshire, politicking with that ass of a husband. No use even to ring up.

Roberta – large, unhappy and cantankerous in Barnes. He could not face the thought.

Nancy, the girl who made the coffee in the office. She had helped him out once before. She helped other Enterprise executives in the same way, and her flat was full of pop-up toasters, electric blankets and other tributes. Warwick Road, wasn't it? Richard began to look for a taxi. He would ring up from the kiosk on the corner.

38

The Prime Minister had called the Cabinet for twelve noon, an hour later than usual. The excuse was that most Ministers had to travel that morning from electioneering in their constituencies. The reason was that he needed the clock on his side. Clocks rather, for there were two loudly ticking against each other in the Cabinet room, and a third chiming from the Horse Guards beyond the garden. By one o'clock, or one fifteen at the latest, his colleagues would feel it was high time to take a decision.

The Prime Minister sat in the only chair which had arms, under the portrait of Sir Robert Walpole. It had ceased to worry him that the table was coffin-shaped. There was only one paper in his folder, but it was bulky.

'I'm sorry to have to call you back so hastily from your duties in the country. Please don't minute this, but our efforts seem to be having some effect at last.' The National Opinion Poll published in the *Daily Mail* that morning put the Conservatives three per cent ahead. And of course as the incumbents the final TV broadcast that night was in their hands. They were in quite good spirits, and the Secretary of State for Education wore a rose in his buttonhole.

'We have a tricky little decision to take on Rajnaya,' the Prime Minister continued. He had wondered if he could get away with 'little', but it was important to set the right tone from the start. 'As you know, there's been no time for the External Affairs Committee to take this at Ministerial level before it came to Cabinet. But at official level all the departments concerned have been busy, and we are in their debt for a most comprehensive and workmanlike document.' He paused, and there was a mutter of approval. That was a good sign. 'Would you like to lead off, Foreign Secretary?'

This was a calculated risk. The P.M. knew that Pastmaster had gone to Suffolk the afternoon before without telling his officials what he thought. He knew that Pastmaster had deliberately evaded his own efforts to talk on the secure telephone. But neither of these things was unusual. It was rare for Pastmaster to take a definite personal line in Cabinet, and unknown for him to quarrel with a clear recommendation of his officials.

'I have looked at this paper and all the telegrams very carefully,' said Sir John, 'and I have come to a clear conclusion.' He wore a thick tweed suit with a waistcoat; the rest of them were in dark blues and greys. He spoke slowly. The Prime Minister realised a few seconds before the others that his Foreign Secretary had taken one brandy, perhaps two, just enough for a little extra courage and a slight slur of the voice.

'As I see it, the guts of the matter is our Treaty obligation. We can't play about with these things. If we have an obligation, then we ought to meet it.'

'Of course, of course, I don't think any of us would disagree with that.' The Prime Minister saw that a smokescreen was

213

needed. 'But the legal part of the official paper, section four, shows that in these particular circumstances, the nature of the obligation is far from clear. Trennion has perhaps rather overstated the case in some of his telegrams.'

'There's a lot of clever argument, that's true, but it misses the point.' Sir John's voice rose a fraction. Subconsciously he had waited for this moment for a long time. Too often he had been persuaded that things were complicated when in fact they were simple.

'The Treaty says that if Rajnaya is threatened from the outside and if they ask for help, then we must give it. There's no doubt at all that this fellow Revani has been financed and armed from outside Rajnaya. Trennion's telegrams and the intelligence reports make that very clear. Now that Lall has put in a definite request we are bound to meet it. Annex H, at the back of this paper, shows how it could be done. Lall sent his police commander to Cyprus yesterday, and he dotted the i's and crossed the t's with the C.-in-C. I'm told it's all feasible and could start at once.'

Then, with varying degrees of conviction, the colleagues fell on him. The Chancellor of the Exchequer was worried about the cost, and the danger of a run on sterling. The Lord Chancellor was far from clear about the justification for intervention in terms of Article 51 of the U.N. Charter. The Secretary of State for Defence drew attention to the possible need to send reinforcements to Northern Ireland. And, since every man is his own Foreign Secretary, they all prognosticated about the effect in Washington, Moscow, Paris and Bonn.

At five past one the Prime Minister summed up. Several senior ministers had not spoken, but he thought he could take the chance. He had to stop the talk while the balance of

214

argument lay against Pastmaster. The brandy courage would have worn off by now.

The summing up was one of his best. They had had a most useful discussion. Several new and useful points had been brought up. They agreed that the official paper was a useful basis for their decisions. On the main question of armed intervention, the general feeling had been that the risks outweighed the advantages, and that the obligation was not entirely clear. Some of them felt that possibly President Lall had been a little unwise to press quite so specific a request so urgently at this particular juncture of affairs in Britain. On the other hand they all felt deep sympathy for his predicament. Whatever the shortcomings of his domestic policy he had a claim on their help. For this reason he, the Prime Minister, strongly favoured the suggestion set out in Section V of the official paper for an immediate British initiative in the Security Council designed to bring to an end any foreign help which Revani might be getting. The necessary telegrams were, he understood, already drafted and could go off at once. The Security Council could meet within forty-eight hours, perhaps less. He himself would send personal messages to the heads of the governments represented on the Council stressing the importance and urgency of the matter. Etc., etc., etc. The Prime Minister, speaking with much force, dealt further with the details of this proposal until the Horse Guards clock struck quarter past one. Several of the colleagues including Pastmaster had already looked at their watches. When the Prime Minister had stopped, he began to collect nods round the table.

'Yes, I think that's probably best.'

'A very good summing-up, Prime Minister.'

'I suppose that's all we can do at this stage.'

215

'Could I just make two points?' Pastmaster cleared his throat and spoke rather more loudly than was necessary. 'The first is that Lall could not have acted in any other way or at any other time. His country is being destroyed, and won't last another day. That's the fact of the matter. The Security Council can say a prayer over the grave, but that's all. We're the only people who can act in time. And the second point is this.' Pastmaster tugged for a moment at his moustache. 'Unless we decide to go in at once, I shall have to resign. This afternoon.'

They sat appalled, lunch forgotten. The possibility of such a wild act had never entered their minds. Except the Prime Minister's: he always made it a point to consider in advance of any great matter the most disagreeable contingency of all. He had decided over breakfast that this was the one outcome which would be worse politically than a decision to intervene. The trump had always been in Pastmaster's hand; the surprise was that he had recognised it.

'Well, that of course creates a completely new situation,' he said briskly. 'I don't think we can carry our discussion any further now. But I will be in touch with each of you during the afternoon. Foreign Secretary, perhaps you and I could have a word.'

The two men settled it together in five minutes. The troops would go in to Rajnaya that night, with modified instructions to stay on the defensive round the airport. No announcement would be made till 6 a.m. next morning. This timing meant that the national dailies on polling day would be full of speculation, but nothing hard. The morning's radio bulletins and the evening's would be a different matter. But, lunching off an omelette and a peach, the P.M. thought he could just get away with it.

39

The furry taste in Joe Steel's mouth was familiar, but the bed was not. Indeed it was not a bed at all, just a couple of blankets on an office floor. On the door Steel could read back to front the red letters 'Meteorological Officer'.

Would the meteorological officer at Rajnaya airport have vodka and tomato juice secreted somewhere in his office? The answer was no. Grimly Joe Steel began to make sense of the world without his usual early morning aid. He recalled the dinner at Akrotiri, his row with the British, stumbling to the plane in the grip of a military policeman, Kaul's furious silence on the flight back to Rajnaya. They had circled the airport three times before the control tower finally convinced the fighter pilot that it had not been captured by the R.L.F. in their absence.

Now what? The sun was already high in the sky. Steel lifted the internal telephone, jigged the rest up and down, and as soon as there was a reply, said, 'I want two eggs sunny side up, an electric razor and a clean shirt size seventeen. I've slept in this one three nights running . . . I'm the Chief Information Officer of the Republic of Rajnaya, on the personal staff of the Chief of Police.'

Joe Steel put on his old shirt and found a basin down the corridor in which to wash the Cyprus dust off his neck and two-day beard. Then he looked out of the window to see how the cause of the Republic was faring.

The meteorological officer's window did not give on to the runways. It faced outwards from above the main entrance to the airport, looking up an avenue of palm trees which quickly degenerated into the avenue of billboards for airlines and soft drinks. Two hundred yards up the avenue the police had built a substantial road block out of two tanker lorries turned on their sides and jammed together. Trenches had been dug on either side of the road, and Steel could see the sun glint on steel helmets and rifles. It looked to him exactly like a sequence from a World War II movie and he strained his eyes to see Kirk Douglas advancing alone and indomitable out of the desert.

But it wasn't Kirk Douglas at all. A familiar figure, yes, clad in cream suit with brown and white shoes and carrying a smart fawn-coloured despatch case. Whoever it was, he clearly did not enjoy walking down the avenue from the roadblock with a policeman poking a sub-machine gun in his back. Jack Lemon, perhaps. It was a comedy, anyway.

In the doorway Steel collided with an Indian police sergeant carrying a tray with a plate of eggs, a razor also on a plate, a clean white shirt and an abundance of napkins.

'Colonel Kaul's compliments, sir, and when you have finished your breakfast he hopes you will see Mr Katrakis on his behalf. That's the gentleman out there, sir, the one with the gun in his back.' The sergeant grinned.

Of course, Katrakis, the smoothie who had compered Winter's press conference. But Joe Steel's immediate business was with the eggs.

'Where the hell did these come from?'

'Colonel Kaul said you were to have everything you required, sir. The cook in the airport kitchen is not bad for an Arab.'

'O.K. then, bring Katrakis in. I'll see him while I eat.'

'If I might suggest it, sir, it might be better to keep him waiting. Until his heels are cool. That is our way in the police.'

Joe Steel laughed. 'What's your name?'

'Ralli, sir.'

'Tell me one good reason, Sergeant Ralli, why you're still a sergeant. By the way, where is President Lall?'

The sergeant looked serious.

'He is here, sir, in the commandant's flat down the corridor in this flat. But he is sick this morning. The doctor is there now.'

'What sort of sick?'

'I do not know. He came from the broadcasting building last night before you and Colonel Kaul came back from Cyprus. The terrorists fired on the helicopter. The pilot was hit and they made a bumpy landing. Maybe the President too was hit, or maybe he was just bumped. Anyway this morning he is sick.'

By the time Katrakis was shown in Joe Steel had shaved, put on a clean collar and tie and established himself sternly behind the meteorological officer's desk.

'It's a pleasure to see you again, Mr Katrakis.' Joe Steel put on the clipped accent of a British official, though it fitted oddly with his shaggy hair and bloodshot eyes.

'I asked to see Captain Kaul.' Katrakis was already disconcerted.

'There is no Captain Kaul here. Colonel Kaul, the Chief of Police, is busy with urgent matters. He has asked me to see you in my capacity as Chief Information Officer.' Vintage Alec Guinness.

'But I know you, you're Joe Steel of the *Messenger*. There's no point in talking to you.'

'And I know you, you're Katrakis who runs the seedy P.R. business down by the Customs House. And you won't get to talk to anyone else.'

Katrakis thought for a second; but he had no choice.

'Johnnie Revani wants to save a lot of people getting killed. He wants Kaul to give himself up. Ten thousand rupees and Kaul to keep his present job.' Katrakis had invented these terms; they seemed to him the minimum required.

'And for me?'

'The first exclusive interview with the new President. Revani is formally taking over today.'

'Tell him to hurry up then.' Steel leant over his desk and lowered his voice to a confidential whisper. 'The British are coming tonight. Kaul and I were in Cyprus last night. We fixed it all up. I'll say this for the British, when they move, they move quick.'

Katrakis did not believe it. But if it was untrue, why had Kaul and this impossible American come back from Cyprus at all? And then the whole look and feel of the airport puzzled him. He had expected a shambles of worried Asiatics huddled together, whom a few clever words could finally defeat. But here were checkpoints and guns pointing outwards and discipline and people sitting behind desks. Almost as if Colonel Forster were still alive.

Swiftly Katrakis changed tack. He sat on the desk and leaned forward. The smell of his sweat was just stronger than his perfume. It had been a hot walk.

'Look, Joe, you and I are nothing in this, nothing at all. Why should we get mixed up in a lot more trouble? You've got a marvellous story, you need to file it before all those guys in the hotel get loose.'

'I filed it in Cyprus yesterday. And don't call me Joe.'

'Yes, but a heap of things have happened since then. I

could tell you a lot you don't even guess at. And I've got money, not much, but quite a lot for a man like me.' He pointed to his despatch case. 'I need to get it away, get myself away. Whoever wins there won't be much in Rajnaya for Katrakis any more. Now, you've been here a day now, you know the planes down there, you know the pilots. There must be one of them who'd take me out and save himself at the same time. Johnnie will attack before the day's out, that's for sure.'

Joe Steel laughed. It was the first funny thing which had happened for several days.

'Sergeant Ralli,' he shouted, and as he expected the door opened at once.

'Take Mr Katrakis back to the checkpoint please, point him in the direction of Rajnaya, and give him three hard shoves with the butt of a rifle to start him off. He's got a long hike ahead of him.'

It was just four minutes later that bullets began to enter the room through the roof and the window. Steel was aware of the bullets before he heard the roar overhead. Through the shattered window he could see three unmarked planes disappearing towards the city, flying low and in close formation.

Physical courage had never been his strong point, and he waited under the desk for the next attack. It never came. After three minutes he got up and looked again out of the window.

Below in the car park they were loading on to a stretcher what remained of Albert Katrakis, public relations consultant.

40

Evening Star, June 17, 19—

CABINET IN EVE-OF-POLL CRISIS MEETING

MYSTERY DEEPENS IN TROPIC ISLE

by our Political Editor

Cabinet Ministers hurried away tight-lipped from a short-notice meeting at 10 Downing Street this morning. The meeting was called to discuss one item only – the rapidly deteriorating situation in the Indian Ocean Republic of Rajnaya. There was no confirmation of reports that Rajnayan President Lall, former Guy's Hospital medical student, had backed up his desperate fight for political existence with an appeal for British armed intervention under the Anglo-Rajnayan Treaty. Whitehall sources said after the Cabinet meeting that no decisions had been taken and that Ministers would be remaining in close touch.

Meanwhile the news blackout from Rajnaya deepened. There was no word of the safety of dozens of newsmen from the world's press trapped in Rajnaya by a total breakdown of communications. Latest news published in a national daily this morning by American journalist Joe Steel who escaped to Cyprus yesterday, reported renewed fighting and many casualties in Rajnaya itself, with rebel forces led by handsome Cambridge-educated Johnnie Revani in firm control of the city centre. Evidence of a further deterioration in the position of President Lall's loyalist forces came later in the morning when the Rajnaya broadcasting station monitored in Beirut began to broadcast revolutionary slogans and bulletins after four hours off the air. This suggested the fall of another key government strongpoint.

Meanwhile at home the leader of the Labour Party, Mr Jack Wellcome, issued an appeal to the Government to take the whole question at once to the U.N. Security Council. In a statement from Transport House, Mr Wellcome warned sternly against any direct British intervention in Rajnaya which would he said 'smack of old-fashioned imperialism and send a shockwave of revulsion round the civilised world'. Mr Wellcome later left for an eve-of-poll rally in his Cardiff constituency.

Another comment on the rapidly developing situation came from Lord Smiley, President of the Newspaper Proprietor's Association, who praised the British newsmen in Rajnaya for their selfless courage and integrity in reporting the truth. Interviewed at his Belgravia home Lord Smiley said 'Once again, without thought of personal risk and without favour to any man, the representatives of the press have been true to the highest standards of British journalism.'

41

It was at 4 p.m. that afternoon that the three-day Siege of the Inter Ocean Hotel was lifted. Afterwards the thirty-four journalists inside the hotel wrote many thousands of words about the Siege. The nature of their ordeal was not entirely clear in all these accounts. It consisted of one large militia sergeant with a sub-machine gun stationed outside the revolving doors of the main entrance, and a slightly smaller corporal outside the exit to the underground garage. Both had orders to prevent anyone leaving, which they made clear with silent motions of their guns whenever the question was raised.

It had been clear that morning that the situation was changing. First, there was the shift of allegiance by the radio station. Then, some of the staff trickled back into the hotel. A boy in a white coat staggered across the square under the weight of a big wooden tray loaded with loaves and bottles of Coca Cola. When the sergeant had let the boy in, he dumped his tray on the table in the Air Rajnaya kiosk by the entrance. Then he began to empty the brimming ashtrays in the main lounge and sweep up the bottles and empty tins of soup and fruit which lay scattered around. A little later three elderly maids appeared and began to make beds.

They were sure by now that the R.L.F. had won. Indeed dozens of articles were being pounded out on portable type-writers explaining why this had been inevitable and foreseen from the start by everyone except the British Government. Seasoned observers of the Rajnayan scene had long been convinced, they noted, that President Lall with his unpopular and reactionary policies was sitting on a powder keg or barrel. Now that he had gone the way of Nuri Said, King Idris of Libya and the Sultan of Muscat and Oman the question was – would the British never learn?

A tiny minority of two, one British, one Italian, disagreed. The two men had gone up together on to the roof with their cameras. They saw from four miles off the fighter attack on the airport and the Italian thought the unmarked planes were MiGs. But the interest downstairs in their story was quickly overtaken by the news that the telephone system was working again. There was no overseas operator, and so no chance of phoning stories out. But it gave them a chance to harry the British High Commission. What steps had been taken to secure their release from the hotel? Had the Acting High Commissioner been to see Revani on the subject? Had he arranged for an R.A.F. plane to come in and fly them out? Could they use the diplomatic wireless system to send their messages? Eventually they got on to Francis, who took down the thirty-four names and promised to telegraph that they were alive and well. Then they asked him questions about Lall and Revani and Kaul and the British Government. Some of these he could not answer, others he would not; so they concluded that the High Commission was falling down on the job.

Some of them then rang Katrakis, but there was no reply from his office.

At three thirty the radio announced that General Revani had been proclaimed President of the Revolutionary Republic of Rajnaya.

At 4 p.m. he was there in the hotel in a tight-fitting light grey uniform buttoned up to the neck, no insignia, no epaulettes, bareheaded and very cheerful. To all of them he was a figure of legend. He was also the winner and they gave him a scattered clap. He marched straight into the ping-pong room adjoining the lounge, four militiamen at his heels.

'Gentlemen, I have come to introduce myself and to answer your questions. But first of all, let me make it clear that you are the guests of the Revolutionary Republic, which will take care of your bills until the airport is in our hands. After that you will leave at once.

'Secondly, an announcement. The whole of the Republic of Rajnaya is now in the hands of the Revolutionary Government with the exception of the airport. I sent my

Minister of Information, Mr Katrakis, to the airport this morning to offer the remnants of the former regime fair terms of surrender. I regret to have to tell you that he was murdered in cold blood. Events must therefore take their course.

'Now, Gentlemen, I will gladly answer your questions.' And so he did, for fifteen minutes exactly, as if he had been holding press conferences all his life.

The air attack at midday? That had been mounted by a flight of the Revolutionary Air Force and had inflicted severe damage on the reactionary forces. No, he could not at present, for reasons of security, say exactly where these planes were based.

The British? They had of course, no grounds for intervention, even under their neo-colonialist Treaty, and he understood that anyway they would have other things on their minds in the next day or two. Titter. Elections? Yes, they would be held at once on the basis of lists submitted by the revolutionary parties.

Ex-President Lall? He was free to go or to stay. If he stayed he would of course face charges of maladministration and corruption.

Diplomatic relations? The Revolutionary Republic was prepared to let bygones be bygones and enter into relations with every peace-loving state.

External help for the R.L.F.? Surely no one of intelligence could believe that sort of nonsense. Was that all? Then he would just like to add that they were from now on entirely free to send reports back to their papers. The necessary technical facilities had been arranged, and all reports should be submitted to the new Office of Press Guidance round the corner in MacDonald Street, which would ensure onward transmission with the least possible delay.

They were also free to circulate in the city outside certain security zones, and the necessary protective escorts had been detailed. They would of course respect the hours of curfew.

There was nothing else? Then as he had a lot to do, perhaps they would excuse him.

And so the siege was lifted. Later that afternoon they heard a good deal of firing in the centre of the city, and the melodramatic Italian thought it was execution squads. There was no evidence for this. When the bus came in the early evening to take them on a tour of the city they saw only open shops, portraits of Revani, and smiling crowds. The Italian said he did not see many Indians, but by then they suspected that the Italian might have Fascist sympathies.

42

The snatch from the Knightsbridge March died away, the bass voice intoned 'Introducing OUR LIFE to those that live it' and the 193rd edition of the programme was on the air.

The politicians were not watching. They were speaking on the platforms of Corn Exchanges, or driving breakneck through the rain down twisting country lanes to the fourth meeting of the evening, or walking with collars up down drab streets where the canvass returns showed the most doubtful voters.

Anne Charteris was watching, at home in front of blazing logs. She had pleaded a savage headache, and James had gone off to his meeting, grumbling mildly.

Barney Tyrrell was watching on the closed circuit in the Chairman's room at Enterprise.

Most of the political correspondents of the daily papers were watching, because Tyrrell had rung them up earlier in the evening. Some of them had been bold enough to ask their editors to keep space on the front page for a completely new story.

It was for some reason cold in the studio, but Richard Herbert wore no coat over his bright blue shirt with the pointed button-down collar and jade cuff-links. He thought he was young and graceful like this, and anyway it looked more suitable for Rajnaya.

One minute of film first, the start of the independence day procession in Rajnaya, flags fluttering from the saluting position, Lall smiling and talking, a shot of the tankers in the harbour, back to the diplomatic corps in tail coats and pretty dresses, a zoom on to Francis Trennion looking British, the police band marching past, the first few seconds of the school children.

'A friendly simple scene – a new country celebrating its birthday in the sunshine – on the surface that was Rajnaya only three short days ago.' Richard's voice was smooth and civilised. Rough Midland accents were several years out of date. 'But what lay underneath this happy surface? A story of bitter tensions and racial strife, a story in which Britain was and is intimately involved. For whether we like it or not we in Britain are linked by Treaty with Rajnaya, a Treaty of Alliance and perpetual friendship. Now what exactly does this Treaty mean for you and me? I put that question to Donald Wiskerton, Professor of International Relations at the University of Cambridge.'

Wiskerton was young and had a ginger beard which looked particularly splendid in colour. But it was wrong to suppose that the beard was the reason for his success on the box. This was mainly due to his courage in leading a small group of students which a few months before, in the interests of free speech, had broken up a meeting being addressed on ancient sculpture by a Greek archaeologist. For a week or two after this his professorship had been in doubt, but his fame on television was assured.

Professor Wiskerton spoke at length about the old Sultan and how he had been deposed, then about the revised Treaty. With a sneer visible beneath the beard he read out the clause containing the British commitment. Richard cut in.

'And this surely is the crunch of the matter, Professor. That clause is nearly twenty years old now. With your experience of international law, do you believe that in this day and age Britain should really send forces to Rajnaya on the strength of that clause?'

The Professor bared his teeth. 'Well, it is a complicated business, involving the U.N. Charter as well as this particular Treaty. I for one would be very doubtful if that clause could now be legitimately invoked.'

'Thank you very much, Professor. Obviously, as you say, it's a complicated business. But there's one man who doesn't find it complicated at all – and that's the man who has the closest responsibility for it – the Foreign and Commonwealth Secretary, Sir John Pastmaster. You remember the surprise just over a year ago when Sir John was promoted to this office without any previous knowledge of foreign affairs. Indeed the unkind crack then was that the only foreigners Sir John knew were the waiters in the Carlton Club. Ten days ago I went with Sir John to a Conservative fête in Downshire.'

A minute of Ridingley – Sir John in shirtsleeves missing a

coconut – guessing the weight of a cake offered by two ladies in flowered hats – saying, 'Lovely day, isn't it?' to the world in general – cut to the pensive face of a bullock in the park back to Sir John speaking to 2,000 people without words, mouth flapping open and shut.

'After completing his duties at the fête, Sir John was persuaded to answer my questions about Rajnaya.'

A snippet from the interview in James Charteris's study, antlers on the wall, Sir John loud and emphatic '. . . of course we shall stand by our friends.'

'Well, that was clear enough.' Richard put the edge into his voice and leant towards the camera. 'What wasn't so clear was whether Sir John and his advisers really understood what was going on in Rajnaya. Enterprise Television asked me to fly out to make a special up-to-date investigation on the spot.'

Shot of Richard striding purposefully behind the slim calves of a Heathrow stewardess, briefcase in hand.

'What sort of country is this Rajnaya, with which we in Britain are involved? Well, first of all it's a poor country. Not of course, poor for all.'

Shot of Lall's suburban bungalow, taken almost from ground level so that the roses in the garden looked six feet high and the house a viceroy's palace. 'This is the private house of President Lall. No one knows how much it cost. Like almost everyone at the top in Rajnaya, Lall is an Indian. But, as Professor Wiskerton has just told us, Rajnaya was originally an Arab island. And life for the Arab inhabitants has more thorns than roses.'

Richard picking his way down an alley in the shanty town on his way to Revani's headquarters. There are potholes, and outside one doorway stands a donkey so thin that its ribs are showing. Close up of ribs, then switch to a naked Arab child relieving itself in the gutter.

'But though the Arabs are poor, they have not lost their pride or their political determination. One of my first experiences in Rajnaya was to listen to their leader Johnnie Revani.'

Scene in the R.L.F. underground café, Johnnie's fierce Arabic oratory, the camera slowly swinging round the tables, catching intent faces, a sweating forehead, a young hand tightening on a coffee cup, the naked electric bulbs gently swinging, an old man's lips moving. Then Johnnie's climax, a second's silence, and the camera swinging back across the same tables, but this time quickly to catch faces come alive again and the thunder of applause.

'But we were not the only people interested in Johnnie Revani's meeting that night. For political meetings in Rajnaya do not enjoy the same kind of comfortable security as Sir John Pastmaster's Conservative fête. In fact, though we did not know it, a warrant had gone out for Revani's arrest that very day.'

The police bursting into the café, the batons swinging, Revani's escape, Kaul's discomfiture. Shot of an old man crouching in a corner. Blood from a broken tooth trickling down his chin on to the white shirt.

'Next day, in very different circumstances, we spoke to President Lall.'

Now the camera is inside Lall's bungalow, and for a moment it lingers over the comfortable bric-à-brac, the pipestand, the plate of sweet cakes, the tank of gorgeous fish. Then on to Lall, a small man occupying a large chair. He shifts from time to time in search of an impressive position. He has never before in his life given a major television interview.

Richard begins by thanking him gravely for the President's courtesy in receiving him. Lall speaks too quickly in reply, and through the strong accent his politeness becomes a gabble. Richard by contrast is even and suave.

'Now on 24th November last, speaking to the Anglo-Rajnayan Chamber of Commerce, you spoke about the way in which Rajnaya had followed British traditions in setting up her institutions.'

'Yes, I remember, I spoke on those lines.'

'Would you say that free speech was one of the British traditions which you had applied in Rajnaya?'

Lall remembers just in time what Colonel Forster told him about the Enterprise team's expedition to Revani's meeting the night before.

'Yes, indeed, there is free speech guaranteed for those who are prepared to pursue constitutional objectives by legitimate means.'

'Those are rather long words, Mr President, and perhaps their meaning isn't always clear to simple people. For example last night we went to a meeting addressed by your principal opponent, Mr Revani.'

Lall cuts in. It is very hot now in the sitting room and his forehead glistens with sweat. 'Revani is a revolutionary dedicated to violence. There is a warrant issued in proper form for his arrest.'

'So we gathered last night, Mr President. Of course he says that he is simply fighting for basic human rights denied to all Arabs.'

Lall launches into a powerful defence of his policies. He reminds Richard that the Indians are now a majority in Rajnaya and that they created almost all its wealth. He speaks of his plans for getting the Arabs to play a bigger part in political life. He quotes the key clause in the Bill extending universal suffrage to the Arab villages. He gives precise and detailed examples of the new opportunities open to Arabs in clerical and managerial jobs. He gives figures showing that the standard of living of the Arabs in Rajnaya is quickly catching up the standard of living of the Indians. He ends with an eloquent summing up:

'Already Arab and Indian are equal before the law. They are not equal in terms of prosperity because the Indians have taken opportunities which Arabs have never been offered. That too we can put right in the next few years. Already we begin to think not as Indians or Arabs but as Rajnayans.'

Lall had rarely spoken so well, and it was an impressive statement. Not an inch of it was used.

Much later Joe Steel, who heard about it from Lall, asked Tyrrell why this part of the interview was cut. Tyrrell agreed that it had been impressive, indeed moving, 'Well Joe, you know how it is, it just didn't fit the theme of the programme as it ended up.' And that indeed was true.

The editing is skilful, and there is no apparent break as Richard sweeps on to his final questions.

'Mr President, you are holding an independence parade in a few days' time. Is it true that the British Government and indeed your own British advisers have all urged you to cancel it?'

'That is a decision for me to take, not for anyone else.'

'But you wouldn't deny that there is a serious risk of violence, and indeed of people being killed, if the parade goes on?'

Lall begins to show honest anger and Richard, seeing the danger of this, puts another question before the first one is answered.

'If that upsets you, Mr President, let me put the point in a slightly different way. If there is a major outbreak of violence after the parade on Monday, would you appeal to the British for help under the Treaty?'

Lall had been told that this was to be a relaxed conversation about life in modern Rajnaya. Enterprise Television entirely understood, they said, that it would not be possible for him as Head of State to deal with controversial problems. But just at the moment when for his own good, like Sir John Pastmaster, he should have lost his temper he recaptured it with an effort.

'The British have always been our good friends.' Dissolve. 'So the Indian President Lall of Rajnaya relies on the British as his good friends.' Over to the little gilt chairs in Guy Winter's suite in the Inter Ocean Hotel. 'Here is one young British businessman who came out to Rajnaya without any preconceived ideas. He had firm plans to be this country's good friend. A few days later I asked him what his impressions were.'

Shots of Winter's press conference, but not much. Tyrrell said it was good stuff but even Enterprise viewers would spot that Winter was an ass if he went over two minutes. Winter himself, watching in the Savoy on black and white as well as colour, was so disappointed that he rang up his solicitor. A final shift of scene, and Richard's voice-over becomes quicker and more urgent.

'At the start of this programme you saw the opening moments of the Rajnaya Independence Day parade. Flags, sunshine, laughter – all just as President Lall planned it.

'Now let us see how it ends . . .'

They had moved fast that morning, the cameramen, and the result was tremendous television. Chowdhry sitting, stupid and immobilised in his Land-Rover, the stir in the saluting base, Forster elbowing forward, Forster dead on the ground. They even brought the group of machine-gunners on the Ministry roof into rough focus a few seconds after they opened fire. But by then it was mainly the schoolgirls, first a tidy and self-confident column, within a minute transformed into a scatter of frightened hens. One seventeen year old stumbled towards the cameramen screaming and clutching her side. As she came nearer the lens zoomed to meet her, and as she fell the final shot of the blood flowing from her mouth was particularly powerful.

Then Richard to sum up, straight to camera and judicial: 'Civil war is now raging in Rajnaya. President Lall has been thrown out of the house which you saw and has taken refuge at the airport. Though the position is still confused, most experts seem agreed that Lall's only chance of surviving is to call in British troops. Has he yet done so, and if he has, how will our government respond on the very eve of a general election? Will it send in British troops to fight Revani and his determined revolutionaries? Or will it take the line that this is essentially a quarrel between Rajnayans of one race and Rajnayans of another, with which Britain has no real concern? The Cabinet met today and Rajnaya was on the agenda, but no statement was issued afterwards. All I can say for certain tonight is that the parade which I saw in Rajnaya marks the end of an era. Whichever way the decision goes, Rajnaya will never be the same again.'

It is the end of the edited film. But a telephone rings at the studio desk and twelve million people see Richard answer it, with just the right air of grave urgency. As he listens he jots with a pen on the pad before him. Then his voice is measured and sombre.

'We have just received a report from Cyprus that British forces in the Sovereign Base Area have begun to embark tonight in transport planes of R.A.F. Support Command for an operation in Rajnaya. This report is reliable but not yet confirmed.'

Then the final throwaway line which made television history:

'Let's hope they know what they are doing.'

43

The British were supposed to come at 8 p.m. This was the plan which Kaul had agreed with the Staff Captain in Cyprus. But that seemed a long time ago. They had no link with the outside world now. The MiG raid had destroyed even the short range radio in the control tower.

Kaul sat looking at two eggs brought by his batman. His mind was a blank, but it did not matter now, for the whole thing was out of his hands. He had beaten off the R.L.F. attack at midnight. They had come down the road after a few bursts of fire shouting slogans in the darkness, expecting to find a handful of demoralised men waiting for a chance to surrender. After they had learnt their mistake they tried again, three small groups of men with wire-cutters edging through the desert by the side of the road. But Kaul's searchlights, borrowed from the main runway, caught each group as it reached the perimeter. There was no escape, and they screamed as the bullets pelted them. Kaul was not cruel, but the sound of the screams comforted him. Those men on the wire were politically trained revolutionaries, Revani's shock troops. But they made mistakes and died in fear, just as his own men had done.

So he had held on until the appointed time. Forster could not have done more. If the British came, then the Republic of Rajnaya would be saved.

If the British did not come by nightfall, then he would surrender, getting what terms he could. They were running out of water at the airport and before long food too would be short. After that it would be Revani's Republic, and a new kind of police.

On the floor below, in the airport commandant's flat, President Lall dozed uneasily. There were no nurses, and no one had thought to pull down the blind to shelter his bed from the morning sun. His temperature had been very high ever since he arrived from the radio station, but the airport doctor could not find any specific illness. 'Rest,' he said, and indeed Lall had no wish to do anything else. Kaul had come and stood by the bed and talked about the British, and through waves of weakness Lall understood that there was still a hope. Kaul had done well, he thought, but it was not only Kaul. He himself had done his bit. He remembered the television interview with Richard Herbert, how it had begun badly, and how he had been provoked into strong defence of what he and his government were doing. They would have shown that interview in England by now, he thought; it would have done a lot of good. One day, when all this was over, he would do another. Meanwhile he must force himself to sleep.

Lall poured a sedative powder into the glass by his bedside, and turned away from the glare of the window. He pulled the sheet up over his ears, and so was slow to catch the sound of approaching aircraft engines.

Joe Steel heard the engines while he was being driven back to the airport from the roadblock which had beaten back the R.L.F. a few hours before. He was determined to get out of this situation, however it ended, with a whole skin and as many first hand stories as he could contrive. The men in the roadblock talked well and vividly, as men do after they have won.

'Take cover,' shouted Joe Steel, grasping at the steering wheel.

'What is the matter, sir?' The Indian driver found himself heading for the ditch.

'Those bloody MiGs again.'

The ditch was full of thistles and because of the trees along the road did not command a good view of aircraft overhead. The planes, it sounded like four at least, flew close overhead without firing. That meant they would come again, and Joe Steel stayed in the ditch.

He was the only person in the airport, he thought, to know about England. Not the make-believe England of High Commissioners, treaties and service messes, but the comfortable lazy intelligent England in which he had lived for five years, the decayed little England of Richard Herbert and Barney Tyrrell. The England he knew would not help Rajnaya because it was long past helping itself. And anyway today was polling day; the whole thing was too bloody absurd. It was no use talking to Kaul about all this. Lall might understand, but Lall was too ill to care; and anyway what was the use? Things, thought Joe Steel, as he emerged from the thistles, are what they are and will be what they will be. But if people want to deceive themselves they're welcome.

He had broken cover too soon. But this time there was

something different in the sound of the aircraft engines. Hardly believing, Joe Steel scrambled into his Land-Rover as fast as his bulk would allow. He reached the tarmac just as the first of the four Lightnings touched down. The VC 10s of Support Command arrived fifteen minutes later.

44

Anne could see from a long way off the little cluster of ladies gathered at the gate of one of the cottages in the village street. Her sixth Conservative committee room that morning, and nine more to visit before the polls closed at ten. The only way she and James could get round every village on polling day was to split the constituency and each take half. This time Anne had the western half, which she preferred because it included the villages which she knew best round Ridingley itself.

Last time she had enjoyed it enormously – the posters on the farm gates, excited faces in tiny cottage parlours, endless cups of tea and once in a while a glass of sherry or a nip of sloe gin, the scurryings of canvassers with huge blue rosettes, the happy little rumours, the total enthusiasm for a cause from whose success very few of them had anything direct to gain.

It was just the same this time, with a touch of anxiety to spice the excitement. It looked as if the nationwide result might be close, though for Central Downshire there could still be little doubt. But Anne's heart was not in it. As she drove through the deep and narrow lanes, accelerating or slowing down to match the itinerary lying face up on the seat beside her, Anne could not keep her mind off last night's broadcast.

This was because of Francis of course. Though Whitehall had still made no announcement, it was pretty clear that Richard's dramatic final words had been right. She kept the car radio on and fragmented reports from the area all suggested that the British were moving into Rajnaya in strength. The South Yemen radio reported bitter fighting, mass bombing of civilians and ten thousand casualties. Moscow had issued a solemn warning, the State Department had expressed surprise, but had no report yet from their man on the spot. Whatever was happening must mean that Francis was in danger. It was natural enough that she should be worried.

But it wasn't really that. A university education made a woman think clearly about her own emotions, and Anne sometimes wondered if this was a mistake. Sitting there last night, alone in front of the big hearth at Ridingley, she had been maddened by the sight and sound of Richard Herbert. So sure of himself, so professional, riding the world like a god, sitting in judgement on nations. In that very room he had come back and offered himself again on the day of the fête. She had turned him away with hardly a thought because he seemed run to seed, degenerating in a crude and ridiculous profession. Now . . . now it was polling day, and the ladies had begun to wave.

'Going very well, I think, Mrs Charteris, of course only a light poll this early.'

'Do hope your headache is better. Such a shame your missing the eve of poll meeting like that.'

'The Major made a beautiful speech.' James was still the Major in the smaller villages.

'Have another cup of tea, do.'

'Of course the Labour people mostly vote about tea time.'

'Mrs Snowitt was taken poorly in the night, but we've sent the car to see if she's fit to come down.'

'Funny business this in Rajnaya, isn't it, Mrs Charteris? I wonder what the Major makes of it. Didn't he serve in those parts?'

'Do try these scones, they're fresh from the oven.'

Anne looked at her watch – just twelve o'clock. 'I'm sorry to be a nuisance, but could we possibly turn on the news? You see my brother's out in Rajnaya . . .'

'Of course, Mrs Charteris, now let me see . . .'

The dark brown knobs of the ancient radio on top of the bookcase were hastily twiddled.

'The following announcement was made from No. 10 Downing Street fifteen minutes ago: Her Majesty's Government have acceded to a request received from the Government of the Republic of Rajnaya for assistance in accordance with Britain's Treaty of Friendship with that country. British forces landed at the airport of Rajnaya last night without encountering resistance and are co-operating with Government forces. A communiqué about the further course of operations will be issued from the Ministry of Defence this evening. That is the end of the official announcement. Reports from Middle Eastern sources of heavy bombing and street fighting in the city of Rajnaya are discounted in Whitehall. But at the U.N. after a twenty-minute meeting the Afro-Asian group issued a . . .'

Anne switched off the radio and put her smile back in place. There was a pleased chatter around her.

'Nice to see the country acting with a bit of spirit.'

'There was some Rajnayan President or other on the

241

television last night. He seemed to be a shifty sort of person, and he was sweating fit to melt.'

'I suppose I must be getting along now.' Anne looked at the typewritten sheet. 'All Pennings 12.45, and that's a good fifteen minutes from here. Well, my husband asked me to thank you very much for all you're doing here today. I'm meeting him for lunch, and I'll tell him how hard you've been working. I expect we'll be seeing some of you at the Corn Exchange tonight.'

She was shown to her car down the path lined with roses and lavender by the son of the lady who kept the post office. He worked at a bank in the nearby town and was the only Young Conservative in the village.

'D'you really think it'll be all right about Rajnaya, Mrs Charteris?'

'I expect so, John. More noise than fighting, I imagine.'

'They were saying in the pub last night any fool could see we ought to keep our noses out of a place like that. And this morning Mrs Staggs up at Glebe Cottage said with her rheumatism she wasn't going to go and vote for a Government which went in for that sort of foolishness. She's voted Tory for fifty years.'

'You can explain it to them better than I can, John. You put them right about the Treaty and all that.'

'I'll do my best, Mrs Charteris.'

As she drove away past the polling station with its policeman outside, Anne thought that she should have listened more carefully to what the Prime Minister was trying to tell her that evening at Ridingley just over a week ago.

45

Francis sat at the High Commissioner's big rosewood desk under the portrait of King George V in full robes, trying to think of something to do. For the whole of the staff this was the real problem, and the key to their morale. At the eye of the storm, boredom led to discontent. Here they were, just under a hundred Britons, living in cramped but adequate conditions with plenty of food and drink on top of a hill overlooking a city with which they had lost all contact. The telephone stayed cut, and the R.L.F. were now patrolling the perimeter of the garden so intensively that there was no chance of anyone slipping in or out.

The last British subject to arrive the night before, bribing his way through the gate, had been old Paton and his Indian mistress. He had reported, what was indeed obvious, that the town was almost quiet. In the small hours Francis had heard firing from the direction of the airport, and the Air Attaché swore that noises he heard at breakfast time meant flight movements in or out. In or out, it made a certain amount of difference, either H.M. Forces in or Lall, Kaul and Co., out. Unluckily, neither flight path brought aircraft near the High Commission, so they could not be sure.

The women had set up a school for the children in a corner of the ballroom which had been cleared of mattresses. The ratio of pupils to teachers was about one to one. The men were set to patrol the garden and observe the city through binoculars from the roof of the main house. The swimming pool was a great boon, and the Head of Chancery had spent an hour drawing up revised instructions to show which categories of staff could use it at which times. The

Naval Attaché's staff had taken over the duty of keeping it swept of leaves.

Not only cut off from the city, but from the world. Of course Francis listened to the radio, indeed he had a small team monitoring the main stations. But the jabber of their rumours that morning just about cancelled each other out. His only connection with reality was the diplomatic wireless and the flow of telegrams which it transmitted from the Foreign Office. But even these inhabited a realm of higher fantasy.

Flash No. 874 arrived just after breakfast.

You should at once inform President Lall that H.M.G. have decided to accede to his request for assistance. You should add that this will take broadly the form worked out with his representative in Cyprus. The timing and content of any announcement of this decision in Rajnaya are important. You should impress on the President that . . .

An hour later another Flash.

President Lall will be aware of the importance of convincing world opinion that his request for British assistance is fully defensible in terms of Article 51 of the Charter of the U.N. My immediately following telegram contains supporting material prepared by the Legal Adviser. You should inform the President that I see great advantage in an early meeting of the Security Council to be summoned at the initiative of the Rajnayan, repeat Rajnayan delegation.

Where was Lall? No one knew, except that he was no longer broadcasting. This might mean he was a prisoner, or escaped to the airport, or dead. In none of these situations could Francis arrange an interview.

The situation was absurd.

The Head of Chancery entered.

'We still have six or seven men with nothing particular to do. They've even offered to start weeding files, but they're not security vetted far enough for that.'

'What do you suggest?'

'I thought of organising a table-tennis competition.'

46

Richard Herbert had not lived in vain. Indeed up till that morning he felt that he had not lived at all. The telephone at his secretary's desk in Enterprise House never stopped pealing with congratulation. Tyrrell had come in first thing to say no commitment mind, but he was thinking of suggesting Richard might be the star of Ad Hoc, the forthcoming weekly programme of uninhibited chat and comment. He also offered to put him up for the Garrick Club.

The next caller was Roberta to say a good many bills had arrived, and should she send them to Enterprise House? This might have been her way of edging towards a reconciliation, but Richard could not be bothered to find out. Wives and bills could come later, if at all. It was not every morning that a star was born.

'Is that you, Richard? This is Henry Hampton here.' Richard had met Labour's Shadow Foreign Secretary twice at dinners, but there had been no question of Christian names. 'That was a splendid broadcast last night, an excellent piece of work, and I congratulate you.'

'Thank you very much. I . . .'

'Well, to come to the point, we're determined to take over where you left off. There's a great deal of excitement, particularly in London. I'm setting up a rally in Trafalgar Square 4 p.m., march on Downing Street 5 p.m., in time for the first TV news bulletins. I want you to speak second. Not political stuff, of course, just your eyewitness account, very personal. Seven minutes will do.'

'I've never really made a speech to a meeting before. I'm not sure . . .'

'That's why we want you. That can be your opening line. There's no problem. We'll sketch something out here in Transport House. You can come round at three to rehearse it.'

Richard tried to be sensible. He tried to remember the terms of his contract and what Enterprise's Code of Conduct said about political appearances. But Hampton had been at the game long enough to read other men's hesitations over a telephone.

'Don't worry, we're going to sweep the country on this issue today. Thanks to your programme, of course. The signs from all over say we'll win in a canter. You've helped to bring this about, and now you can do a bit more. We won't forget, and you've burnt your boats with the Tories already.'

So Richard agreed. Outside in Park Lane the cars of the rich were carrying them to hotels, clubs and boardrooms for lunch. Before lunch one thing was needed to fill his cup. But the housekeeper at Ridingley Hall reported that both Mr and Mrs Charteris were out. They'd be back for a bite of cold supper before driving over to the Corn Exchange for the count.

He'd forgotten that a candidate's wife would be out and about all polling day. As if it mattered. All those simple people at that silly fête had been wasting their time. How on earth could he have let himself be impressed by such an ordinary event? He left a message at Ridingley to say that he'd called.

'Oh, Mr Herbert, yes, of course, the television gentleman. I'll tell Mrs Charteris the minute she gets in.'

The television gentleman ordered a taxi to take him to the White Tower restaurant. He had received three invitations to lunch in the course of the morning, and had chosen one from a well-known female literary agent. The next upward step, as she had wisely pointed out, should be a book. The prospects for serial rights were excellent.

47

Johnnie Revani shook hands with the fat man with the bald white head. Revani had decided to operate that afternoon from the Inter Ocean Hotel, and had commandeered the suite which Guy Winter had occupied ten days earlier. He changed his headquarters every day, which was good for security but bad for efficiency.

The bald man thought he had seen several men like Revani in his life and read of many more in the textbooks of his trade. Thin, good-looking, restless men who made their revolutions but went on afterwards as if they had to make them all over again. But perhaps this one would learn the trade of a ruler. If he lasted long enough – and that was the point. The bald man repeated what he had said two minutes earlier.

'As much money as you want within reason, but no more direct operations from South Yemen.'

'But this is just when I need the MiGs. Without them the Lightnings can terrorise this town.'

'You should attack the airport at once before the British consolidate.' Revani had not told the bald man about the attack which had gone wrong in the night. But the bald man knew of it, and of the desertions which had followed.

'I must formally ask you to report that direct operations by the MiGs are essential if we are to consolidate our success.'

'I will report what you say.'

'And when can I expect a reply?'

'Three days, perhaps four.' By then he would have won or lost on his own.

The two men looked at each other across the gilt furniture. Revani understood his friends. He was a small piece on their board, and in their game small pieces were never worth big risks.

48

'Won't be long now,' said a blue rosette encouragingly. 'No, I suppose not,' said Anne.

Together they looked at the growing piles of ballot papers on the table in front of the returning officer. The Labour votes on the left half of the table seemed stacked rather higher than the Conservatives on the right. But in Central Downshire this was normal, because the three main towns with their rings of council estates delivered their ballot boxes to the Corn Exchange before the outlying villages. Central Downshire had gone Liberal once in the twenties, but since then had been steadily Conservative; never by a big majority, but whatever the national swing against the Party they had managed to hang on.

An exhausting day driving, talking and smiling had given Anne a bad headache, a real one this time. Their timetable had slipped badly, and she and James gobbled a cold supper in five minutes. The housekeeper told her of Richard's call. James said she need not come to the count, but she insisted. So he gave her two stiff whiskies and from then on she felt unreal.

No one was allowed into the Corn Exchange except the returning officer's staff and accredited representatives of the two parties. No one was allowed out at all once the count had begun. Everyone in the big hall, familiar to them all from lesser occasions, felt the rising tension of a closed community.

Anne went into a little side room where a carroty and freckled Young Conservative had been allowed to install a portable television. He was taking down the early results from other constituencies as they came in. He made a face when he saw Anne, and handed her the sheet.

On the screen a hatchet-faced don was speaking fast to get his long mid-Atlantic sentences launched before he was interrupted by further results.

'The swing to Labour on the results so far declared is little short of sensational, going far beyond the calculations of any of the opinion polls. I have no doubt in my mind that the news of British intervention in Rajnaya, so dramatically highlighted on the "Our Life" programme on this channel last evening, has had a determining effect. The fact that the Foreign Secretary, Sir John Pastmaster, lost his seat in S.W. Suffolk on an above-average swing of 11.7 per cent adds powerful support to this thesis Although it is still too early to make any definite . . .'

'What has actually happened in Rajnaya?' asked Anne.

'Oh, nothing much, our forces successfully consolidating round the airport, that sort of thing. Bit of an anti-climax really so far.'

'Anything about British subjects living there?'

The friendly young man remembered what he had heard about Mrs Charteris's brother.

'Nothing in particular. I'm sure that means they're all right.' More results began to chatter across the screen, superimposed on the voluble don.

Anne went back to the main hall. James was already on the platform with the Returning Officer and the Labour candidate. He smiled at her across the room, and she remembered how four years ago she had gone up there and chatted charmingly to the Labour candidate for twenty stilted minutes. This time she could not manage it. Richard, Francis, James – they had all got mixed up in this impossible situation now near its climax. And of the three the most remote seemed the one who was in the room with her. She turned away to avoid catching James' eye.

This would never do. There were tears behind her eyes. It must be the whisky acting on the headache the wrong way. She bent over the trestle table nearest her and watched the teller emptying out the last ballot box allocated to him. Only a handful of papers came out; it must be one of the smallest villages tucked away in the downs. First of all the teller had to count the ballot papers to make sure that the total tallied with the number of votes recorded as having been cast. In real life he was a bank clerk at the National Westminster, and Anne had often smiled at him through a grille. Tonight, in the tense hall, where the shuffling of papers was louder than the occasional mutter of talk, he was the arbiter of her future.

At last he had begun to sort out the votes according to the crosses marked against the names of the candidates.

Two for James, one for Labour, three for James, two for Labour, one James, three Labour. The young man shared an Anglepoise desk lamp with his neighbour because the ornate Victorian chandeliers in the roof were too dim for concentrated work. Two Labour, one James – then someone had written 'Tory warmongers out!' below his X. The teller put this paper aside. Technically it was spoiled, but if the result was close the Returning Officer would certainly allow it to Labour.

The hall was getting very hot, and the bank clerk paused to take off his coat, and wipe the sweat off his spectacles. Anne tried to think of the next few hours. If they won, she knew exactly what would happen. A good deal of cheering and a little booing in the Market Place, and then they would walk two hundred yards along the High Street to the Conservative headquarters. The agent would throw open the door of his refrigerator, and the champagne which it held would keep everyone happy for at least an hour. Then she would look at her watch and say 'Well, I really think . . .' and they would say 'You must both be absolutely fagged out' and James would say 'I'll stay a bit longer. You take the Mini home if you like darling. After all we won't get champagne like this again for another five years', and everyone would laugh, and she would stay and eventually, eventually they would get to bed.

If they lost – well, there was no precedent for that, so she would make her own. She crumpled a piece of paper in the pocket of her coat.

At last up on the platform they were moving. The Returning Officer had turned towards the door which led out on to the balcony, and he motioned James and Martin, the Labour candidate, to follow. He must have shown the result to both of them while Anne was not looking, but neither James nor Martin had any expression on their face. Then Anne saw Mrs Martin, who was also up on the platform. She wore a rather vertical black hat, which bobbed up and down like a brig in a storm as Mrs Martin nodded and smiled to her friends below her in the hall.

So Anne knew that they had lost. She saw James look around for her, then file out on to the balcony. He was a thoroughly nice man, and it was a pity he was so far away. She heard the Returning Officer begin to boom his announcement into the Market Square. 'I, Reginald Arthur Biggs, Returning Officer, do hereby by virtue of the authority entrusted to me . . .' The microphone crackled and blared, and she heard no more.

Labour had won Central Downshire that day by 900 votes. On the balcony there were formal little speeches of thanks, and outwardly everyone was very calm. Even the crowd seemed more surprised than enthusiastic. The Conservative agent wondered how he would deal with the unused champagne.

'Well,' said James. 'I think our best plan is to go straight home and sleep it off. Has anyone seen my wife lately? She didn't come out on the balcony.'

There was a scurry and a bit of a search, which James soon cut short:

'We brought both cars, I imagine she's slipped off home to make me a nightcap.'

And so he got away, too tired to think or feel. They all said you couldn't help feeling sorry for the Major, he'd taken it very well, but then you'd expect that from a man of his type. Funny his wife disappearing at the last minute like that.

As the crowd dispersed, Anne was still in the telephone booth in the dark corner of the Market Place, the crumpled paper with the telephone number spread in front of her, waiting for the Enterprise switchboard to find Richard Herbert and bring him to the phone.

49

The Enterprise election night party, given by Lord Outward himself in his personal suite at the top of Enterprise House, was a famous event. Everyone of note in the interlocking worlds of politics and communications was asked, though understandably the winners turned up in larger numbers than the losers. By half past midnight the air-conditioned rooms, brilliantly lit with curtainless windows opening on Hyde Park, contained four or five likely members of the Labour Cabinet which the coming day would bring to birth. Each was the centre of a cluster of journalists and minor politicians who drew out of them happy explanations of the past and even happier prophecies for the future. Lord Outward, standing plumb in the centre of the largest of his three drawing rooms, had a similar audience for his familiar impersonation of a plain blunt man denouncing all politicians.

The only other person in the room with the same magnetic effect on fellow guests was Richard Herbert. He stood in a corner, wearing a white dinner jacket and a dark red carnation. His fair hair was just slightly awry, and no one could guess that his tan came from no farther east than a sunlamp in Jermyn Street.

'What did it feel like on Trafalgar Square this afternoon, with all the thousands of people waiting to hear you speak?'

'Oh, well, just like an enormous studio,' Richard laughed modestly. 'You can't imagine how alarming it was to have to say something myself after five years of asking other people questions.'

'The Labour Party owe you a peerage.'

'Or at least a safe seat.'

Richard prepared to reissue the modest laugh, but a waiter intervened.

'The Honourable Mrs Charteris to speak to you on the telephone, Mr Herbert.'

He spoke loud enough for the little circle to catch the name.

'Oh, isn't that her husband who's just lost in Central Downshire?'

'He looks a bore, but I'm told she's pretty.'

So James Charteris was out, and Ridingley had had its day. As he followed the waiter to a little alcove by the lift Richard was glad.

Three minutes later he was back in the drawing room, a fresh glass of champagne in his hand, and a look on his face so triumphant that Tyrrell marked it at twenty paces. Not only had Ridingley Hall fallen, but its mistress was running from the ruins. She had given no explanation, he had asked for none. It was enough that Anne needed comfort and that she would be in Carlyle Square by 2 a.m.

It was at this point that Tyrrell moved in. Few people recognised him at a party like this, and of these only the cleverest actually sought him out. Liking power, he despised those who preferred glory, and looking at Richard he knew that he was right.

'Could I have a quiet word with you? . . . Sorry to interrupt your little seance with the press . . . How's the house?'

The house in Carlyle Square belonged to Tyrrell. He had let Richard use it until the rift with Roberta had been resolved one way or the other.

'It's fine. Look, there's no reason for you to move out. There's plenty . . .'

'Of course, but I like a change, every now and then. Now, down to business. The M.O.D. have agreed you should fly direct to Rajnaya in a service plane. It'll be a press party of only about six, but I managed to get you in. I'm afraid it's short notice but the plane leaves Northolt at ten, and one of our cars will pick you up in Carlyle Square at 8.34 – that's just eight hours' time.'

'What the hell's this all about?' Then Richard saw that Tyrrell must be joking. 'For God's sake, Barney, you nearly took me in.'

'I've never been more serious in my life. Sit down a minute.' They found two fragile chairs. 'Look, the Rajnaya story isn't over, it's just warming up. These boys,' he waved at the nearest Labour politicians, 'will pull out the troops, I've checked that tonight, but that'll make an even greater mess than before. We must cover it and after last night you're the only man to do it.'

Richard was surprised. Tyrrell, usually so quick, did not seem to realise that their relationship had changed since last night. Richard Herbert was no longer a minion to be sent hither and thither without a word of consultation. He must make this clear at once.

'A good deal has been happening today,' he said, 'and I don't think I could possibly go to Rajnaya again – certainly not as soon as tomorrow. There are several other projects that have come up; and I think I'm right in saying my contract allows me . . .'

'I read your contract again as I fixed my bow tie this evening,' said Tyrrell. 'Particularly the clause about consulting the Board before accepting commitments with a political party. That's a standard clause which Lord Outward is distinctly keen on. I felt I had to tell him about this afternoon's matinée in Trafalgar Square.'

'That's nonsense, it was an all-party protest.' But Richard saw how he was hooked.

'Yes, of course, all the parties that sing the Red Flag as a finale and march down Whitehall shouting "Tories out, Tories out." Look here, Richard,' Tyrrell softened his voice. He did not want Richard as a successful rival, but he did not want him as an enemy either. 'It's fairly simple really. You've had a break, part luck, part your own skill. Now everyone's painting little pictures of your brilliant future and dangling them before you. In our job these choices come quickly and go quickly. You can grab whatever offer looks brightest tonight and wish Enterprise goodbye. Outward won't sue you for breach of contract, it's not worth his while, there are plenty of thirty-year-olds ravenous for your job. But if you stick with me, Richard, you must be on that plane in eight hours' time. You know very well we can't run this bloody profession any other way.'

Richard looked round the room and thought. There, anchored alongside the buffet was the Labour millionaire who had half-promised to set him up in his own P.R. business if he helped make the Party's political broadcasts on the side. There, sprawled in front of the television, was Hampton, who would be Foreign Secretary by dinner time, and had talked about a safe seat in Lancashire.

The champagne inside him pushed him towards the break. But the real Richard Herbert was cautious and did not drink champagne. Until he knew who was paying for it.

'I'll be there,' he said. 'I'd better go and pack.'

50

It was past two by the time Anne drove into London off the Hammersmith Flyover. She had kept herself awake by listening to the election results on the radio, but their story of Labour wins had become monotonous. After that she fought sleep simply by driving too fast. In her exhaustion she had deliberately stopped thinking about her future. 36 Carlyle Square, 36 Carlyle Square, 36 Carlyle Square, and the morrow must take care of itself.

Richard opened the door and kissed her. She noticed two big suitcases, where the entrance widened into a little hall. She herself had no case.

'Haven't had time to unpack yet,' he said. He took her up one floor to the big drawing room, ornate with Tyrrell's collection of French furniture. There was a little Corot above the mantelpiece and a hunting tapestry on the wall behind the sofa. Richard pointed to the drinks.

'I'm sorry,' she said. 'I just don't want to talk.'

Upstairs again the bed was single, for Tyrrell's affairs were conducted elsewhere. Anne undressed herself quickly.

Richard, as she remembered from the past, hung up his suit carefully, making sure that the trouser creases were in the right place on the hanger. They were both naked, as had been their custom.

For Anne indeed it was all part of the past, and this pleased her, for she was running hard from the present. She remembered how the flesh of his back folded in her grip, the roughness of his hands on her breasts, the quick movements which then had to be checked until she was ready. She had been afraid that she might not manage, but all was well.

'Comfort, comfort,' she whispered as they moved together at the end. The words too were traditional. They had sounded odd years ago, but now they were right, as if all that had been a rehearsal for this.

Physically it was not brilliant, indeed it was more like James than the excitement she remembered from before. But the comfort was there and afterwards, pressed closely against him in the narrow bed, she regretted nothing.

She woke an hour later and saw that he was watching her face.

'Can I stay?' she asked, still in the dream of comfort.

'Let's talk in the morning.'

'But can I stay with you?'

'Of course, sweetheart, it's just that I have to fly off somewhere pretty soon.'

She was wide awake now, remembering the suitcases by the umbrella stand.

'Back to Rajnaya?'

'Yes, just for a few days. After that we can sort things out. You can make my breakfast, and we'll discuss it then.' Anne sat up in bed.

'Take me with you. You asked me to go last time. You must take me with you.'

It was almost a shout, and Richard thought hard. It was a Service plane, he certainly could not get her on to it, and the other end there would be complications, troubles, danger.

'I can't, sweetheart, it's just not on. This time is different.'

'Why?'

'Well, for one thing, I'm going on a Service plane . . .'

Anne let the explanations flow over her. She was not a girl, and after a moment of shock the dream was over and she knew herself again. She was the wife of James Charteris, loving and beloved mother of his sons, mistress of his house.

In a few hours she would drink some coffee, climb into her Mini and be back in Ridingley in time for a cold lunch. James would ask no questions, and be just that more considerate than usual for a few days. This sort of thing happened to his friends and now it had happened to him. After his defeat there would be much to do and much to decide. Life would go on being pleasant, interesting and worthwhile. Like Joe Steel in the ditch, she saw that things were what they were, and would be what they would be. She did not really want to be deceived.

When Richard moved towards her she held him off with a kiss. He was the first to get up, and as he dressed she noticed how his waistline was thickening. There was coffee, then vague words and goodbye kisses. When the Enterprise car drove him off into the Kings Road there were few doubts in his mind, for he was not stupid in these matters, and none at all in hers.

51

'So there it is,' concluded Air Vice-Marshal. 'You see that my orders are very precise, they don't give me any leeway, beyond the twenty-four hours.' His manner grew even stiffer. It was hard work apologising to a man one hardly knew, but in this case he felt it had to be done. 'I need hardly say that this is not what any of us in Andromeda Force would have wished. Most of us would have wanted to go through with it.'

The Brigadier sitting beside him grunted agreement. 'But you will understand, Colonel Kaul, that orders are orders.'

'Of course,' Kaul was numb. It was exactly what Joe Steel had predicted. 'Your orders are clear.'

Joe Steel had been trying to keep control of his temper. Kaul had brought him along yesterday to the first of these joint meetings, presenting him as the Rajnayan Government's Chief Information Officer. Now he flared up.

'Why don't you shake him by the hand, and say you'll never forget the service he's done you?' he asked Kaul. 'We could get that slob of an R.A.F. photographer in, it would make a fine recruiting poster. Nothing like a first-class act of treachery for boosting service morale.'

The Brigadier had disliked the look of Joe Steel from the start – too fat, too clever, too American.

'Surely we can keep this discussion on a practical . . .'

'Surely you can at least pretend to be a soldier instead of a goddam filing clerk.' Steel was in orbit now, brushing aside Kaul's nervous gesture. 'Look, you don't like me, I don't like you, no need to pretend this is a love feast. But you know without my telling that you've got here a proper man called

Kaul who can do this godforsaken island a lot of good, and stay your friend while he's doing it, and that's a rare combination, God knows. Lall's too sick, but this guy will take over and do the new job a lot better. You've given him what he needed most, and that was two days. You've manned the defence of this airport without any loss, not so much as a sergeant's nose bleed. That's given him time to rest his men, talk to them, pull them together, make a plan to use them. Another couple of days, and they'll be ready to move against Revani. After that it's up to them, and you lot can skip off and collect your medals from Buckingham Palace.'

The Air Vice-Marshal stood up, but Steel took no notice. 'Just one more thing. You've seen the reports from the city that I've been putting together. We've had more intelligence out of that stinkhole in the last twenty-four hours than in all the rest of the time we've been here, and that means something in itself. No one's seen those MiGs since you arrived, and Revani told his men they'd be blasting us to pieces day and night. The R.L.F. is coming apart at the seams, ten deserters shot in Constitution Square yesterday, a whole company drifted off back to the villages yesterday. When their C. O. came to inspect them, they weren't there any more. The Indians are beginning to keep shops open during the curfew, steal guns from billeted soldiers, that sort of thing. A couple of days at this rate, and the Revani set up will be rotten. But there has to be someone still around to shake the tree.'

The Air Vice-Marshal had decided on the soft answer, but he gave it to Kaul.

'Let's be quite clear about this. I sympathise with most of what Mr Steel has just said. You've done a marvellous recovery job since we got here, and on the other side of the hill

261

they seem to be running out of steam fast. But I'm a serviceman, not a politician. I can't query the policy behind these instructions. It's not made in my Ministry, it comes across from the Foreign Office, way beyond my reach. All I can promise is whatever help I can reasonably give before our evacuation is complete in twenty-four hours.'

'Will Revani know of your instructions?' asked Kaul.

'No, they say specifically that no announcement will be made until all our forces are out. The official line will simply be that the new Government is reviewing the situation.'

Kaul still looked unsure, and the Air Vice-Marshal guessed why.

'We of course, shall have no contact of any kind with Revani,' he added.

'Then I shall attack him tomorrow,' said Kaul simply, as to himself.

'There's another piece of news,' said the Brigadier, keen to change the subject. 'Half a dozen journalists are flying out from London, should be here any minute. Blasted nuisance of course, but we'll try to stop them getting in your hair.'

But Joe Steel had been following another train of thought.

'If the policy is made in the Foreign Office, then their man here could query it and ask that it be changed.'

'Yes, in theory, but of course . . .'

Steel felt much better for having had an idea. 'You said yesterday you've got authority to send a patrol to the High Commission.'

'Yes, it's the only exception to the general instruction about avoiding offensive action. But we can only act if lives in the High Commission are known to be in danger.'

'Hold it a second.' Joe Steel found on Kaul's table a sheet of notepaper with 'Republic of Rajnaya' on the top, and scribbled six lines. 'That's for your files.'

The Air Vice-Marshal read it aloud.

'08.00 Saturday June 20 R.L.F. intensified containment British High Commission area. Secret reports from inter-rogation deserters indicate possibility of attack under cover darkness this evening.

Signed

J. Steel, Head of Intelligence
Republic of Rajnaya.'

'Will that do?'

The Brigadier stared and puffed. The Air Vice-Marshal stared too, then laughed.

'I take it you wish to accompany the patrol?' he said to Steel. 'It will leave at 11.00 hours.'

52

'The Chief of Government has been given your name. He still says no interview. You understand, he has other more important things to do.'

The young Arab in R.L.F. uniform smiled. He was still in the stage where it pleased him to be rude to an Englishman. But Richard had not come so far to be turned away at the last obstacle. He unzipped his briefcase and took out a small scribbling pad.

Dear Johnnie,

You are very busy, but you ought to give me ten minutes. I had to leave my camera team at the airport, so it would be for sound only. I'm sure this is a crucial moment in which you ought to put yourself across to the British public. Opinion has been moving your way fast, but they know too little about you. You've got a lot to gain, and from me nothing to lose.

Yours, Richard.

He thought for a moment, sitting on one of an army of long shiny black seats in the main lounge of the Inter Ocean Hotel. At some moment since he was last there each seat had been methodically ripped open with a bayonet. He unslung the tape recorder from round his neck. He felt separated by thousands of miles, or perhaps by many years, from the constraints which might have held him back. There were risks, but they were acceptable, and any other considerations were kept well at the back of his mind. So he added the postscript.

P.S. I have of course just come from the airport where I spent two interesting hours, looking around. You may have some questions of your own to put to me about this.

While he waited for a reply, Richard absorbed the changes which had transformed the Inter Ocean Hotel into the seat of revolutionary government. Gone were the turbaned Sikhs at the entrance, gone too the magnificent girls in saris who had staffed the dozen kiosks in the lounge, colourful little fortresses from which they had dispensed newspapers, airline tickets and the nasty quartz jewellery with which Rajnaya sought to attract the expensive tourist.

Gone were the journalists, packed off by Revani the night before in an Italian liner, which had surprised everyone by making its usual call in Rajnaya. Now that things were turning sour, they were better out of the way.

The kiosks in the lounge were now in the possession of uniformed Arab girls fiercely attacking ancient typewriters, apparently determined to destroy them for good as relics of a colonial past. There was a constant ebb and flow across the lobby of Arabs in Western suits or in the rough bulky uniform of the R.L.F. Richard knew no Arabic, but thought he detected an uneasy atmosphere – people walking a little too fast, thinking too hard, flaring up in angry talk over what seemed to be trifles. Three of the four lifts in the main bank were out of order, and when the captain reappeared he motioned Richard towards the service stairs. It was a long twisting walk up, and by the sixth floor Richard was out of breath.

'Why not the lift?'

'The lift is for soldiers and officials only.'

On the eleventh floor Johnnie Revani still occupied the suite where Guy Winter had given his press conference. Everyone else had been cleared from the floor, and the space in front of the lift was occupied by a guard of seven men. There were more soldiers fingering sub-machine guns in the ante-room where the bar had been. Revani was alone in the main room, desk in one corner, bed in the other – Richard noticed that he had removed the standard hotel bed with padded headrest and gilt trimmings in favour of a simple truckle bed and rough grey blankets.

Richard had last seen Johnnie Revani in the underground café, and watching him had found it easy to trace a line back to the tense undergraduate whom he remembered. Somewhere

265

in the last few days that line had snapped. It was a different man whom he now saw – thin, weary, grim, already isolated by power from ordinary contact with ordinary men, and from his own past.

'No calls,' he said to the captain, and motioned him to withdraw. Then he turned on Richard almost savagely.

'Well, what is happening at the airport?'

Richard was taken aback. He had not realised his bait was so important. But he did not lose all sense of the bargain which he believed he had made.

'You'll give me an on the record interview?'

'Of course. But the airport?'

'I flew in with my colleagues three hours ago. The Service commanders would tell us nothing about their orders. But it was clear to me that they were on their way out. '

'How was that clear?'

'If they'd still been acting on the old orders, they'd have been willing to talk about them, explain how successful they'd been in improving the defences, that sort of thing. The services are very talkative these days when they're pleased with themselves. That's point one. Point two is that the VC 10s were being moved out of their hangars, into the loading bays. Point three, a British platoon was marching away from the advance post on the road. They'd been relieved by Kaul's men.'

'None of that's conclusive.'

But Revani was listening intently. 'The thing that clinched it in my mind was that they let me come here to you.'

'How was that?'

'I said I was determined to see you and asked for an Army tank to take me in. They argued they could not guarantee my safety outside the airport perimeter. I had to agree to leave the camera team behind, and finally they whistled up an old taxi with a driver who'd been hanging around the airport since the fighting started. It was touch and go, but they'd never have let me come if they still thought of you as an enemy.'

Revani paced the room. He picked two or three grapes from a bowl of fruit done up in yellow cellophane paper which stood on the table and swallowed them without tasting. Suddenly he opened the door and shouted into the corridor in Arabic. The captain returned, followed by a group of other officers.

'You'll have to leave,' Revani said to Richard. In his self-absorption he had been talking to Richard without expression as to an unwelcome stranger.

'But the interview?'

'You must wait.' A thought struck him. 'You have the questions you want to ask?'

Richard pulled a sheet out of his inside pocket. He had jotted down a dozen questions in the plane, making sure the other journalists could not read over his shoulder.

'I'm not sure if you can read these. And in any case I'd rather . . .'

'That's all right. Now, would you please wait outside?' And so Richard found himself sitting with the soldiers in the space outside the lift. He could not speak to them nor they to him. People hurried in and out of the lift, up and down the stairs, more officers, a girl secretary, an orderly with cups of black coffee. There were no windows, and he had nothing to read. Moreover the plane flight from Heathrow had been bumpy. Almost an hour passed.

He was woken up by the odious captain, who thrust a small box into his hand.

'Here is your interview. Now you are to go.'

'But I must see Revani again. He promised . . .'

'The Acting President has dictated the replies to your questions. Here they are on a tape of ours. Now he is busy.'

Richard would have lost his temper, but there were ten guns within ten yards of him.

'For how long will he be busy?'

'He stays busy. The stairs are there.'

The same group of officers came out of Revani's room. They looked different now, they were relaxed and laughing. One of them shouted something at Richard as he pressed the lift button. The captain interpreted as he edged Richard to the top of the twisting service stairs.

'The Colonel says you'd better hurry away if you want to catch those VC 10s back to London.'

53

It was to be a long day. The first telegram reached the High Commission just after 9 a.m.

FLASH

Confidential

Foreign and Commonwealth Office telegram No. 1068 of 20th June to Rajnaya r.f. Washington, Cairo, Aden, New Delhi, G.H.Q. Cyprus.

My telegram No. 1065: Andromeda Force.

H.M.G. have decided to terminate this operation as soon as feasible. The officer commanding has been instructed to complete withdrawal of all forces from the airport area by midnight to-morrow 21st June. He is authorised to offer

President Lall and senior members of his entourage passage to Cyprus and eventually to the U.K.

2. For security reasons no announcement will be made until withdrawal is complete. The British journalists now in the airport area under MOD auspices will be offered no transmission facilities until they return to Cyprus.

3. You should abstain from all contact either with loyalist forces or the revolutionary regime. For your own information my colleagues and I are urgently considering the contents and timing of an approach to Revani to establish conditions for British recognition of his regime. Further instructions will follow as soon as possible.

4. We have all admired the calm way in which you and your staff have conducted themselves during this protracted period of danger. Well done.

The first visitor reached the High Commission almost exactly at eleven. It was the ragged old Arab, who for more years than anyone could remember had brought baskets of fresh red lichees to the kitchen door every morning when they were in season. He had not come for six days. This morning he walked slowly up the centre of the asphalt drive, shoulders bowed under the wooden yoke from either end of which the wicker baskets of fruit were suspended. No one stopped him, for the R.L.F. picket had melted away. The old man told the Arab houseboy who told the Goanese cook who told the Punjabi butler who told Francis that they had slit the throats of their two officers, buried them in a thicket by the side of the road and disappeared to their villages. Francis did not believe this; but it was true that the men had gone and the siege was raised.

He sat at his desk, above which the big white fan slowly revolved. He was in shirtsleeves, and though it was still early the sweat ran down the inside of his forearm on to the blue telegram forms in front of him. Several crumpled balls of discarded paper had already been pushed to one side. Then he abandoned the idea of a telegram, and took out of the top drawer a stiff sheet of crested white paper.

Sir,

I have the honour to submit the resignation of my Commission as a member of Her Majesty's Diplomatic Service. Pending the acceptance of this resignation I shall of course continue at my post and carry out to the best of my ability whatever instructions I receive.

I should welcome an opportunity to explain to you in person the reasons which have led me to this decision.

Francis did not sign or date the letter. He put it in an open envelope and slipped it back into the drawer. It was time for his morning inspection of the compound. The Head of Chancery appeared punctually in the doorway to accompany him. The Head of Chancery was wearing a jacket and tie. Reluctantly Francis put on his.

The second visitor was Joe Steel, in a Ferret scout car, accompanied by a Land-Rover and six loyalist policemen with sub-machine guns. On the journey from the airport they had fired only once, at a youth in an R.L.F. uniform who had scuttled away from them up a back alley. In the recesses of his soul Joe Steel was sorry that he had not had to battle his way through against hopeless odds. But as he strode up the drive he felt as if he had shed ten years and twenty pounds of flesh since he became a man of action.

'Take me to your leader,' he said to the Chancery guard who stopped him at the entrance to the High Commission building.

Francis too was a surprise, the kind of Englishman Joe Steel had read about but never met. Tired, pale under the sweat, lines of kindliness and worry mixed up on his face, a good mind underpowered with will, a man who listened and groped.

In normal times the two men would have found no meeting place. As it was they came quickly to the point and agreed on what Francis should do.

'. . . For all these reasons therefore I recommend most strongly that the withdrawal of H.M. Forces should be postponed for forty-eight hours, during which time they should continue to play a purely defensive role in the vicinity of the airport. I believe that this delay, while involving virtually no extra risk, will give the loyalist forces under Colonel Kaul a chance which they deserve to reassert themselves in a situation which thanks to our intervention is now rapidly changing in their favour.

'They are our friends, and whatever their imperfections they offer the best chance of a decent and reasonably progressive government for this country.'

'It won't work, I know it won't work,' said Francis.

'Anyway it'll do for the Oxford Book of English Prose,' said Joe Steel. For a few minutes they both felt better.

Joe Steel decided to wait in the compound until a reply came to the telegram, and Francis invited him to lunch with the senior members of the staff in the big dining room. They sat

271

on high cane chairs, backs to the cream walls and dark shoulder-level panelling. They ate corned beef and tinned potatoes off the High Commissioner's silver plate. The butler had also produced a decanter of port. Thus it was, he thought, that the Sahibs had eaten and drunk in the days of the Mutiny at Lucknow, Cawnpore, and Delhi.

The dining room windows opened on to the lawn on the opposite side from the drive, so they did not see Richard's ancient taxi grind up to the house.

'Good afternoon, Francis. May I join you?' It was a stagey entrance, quickly spoilt because he was as surprised to see Joe Steel as Francis and Joe were to see him. Explanations followed quickly, Richard had washed his face, brushed his suit and run a comb through his hair in the downstairs cloakroom. Francis, mousey and worried, felt resentful at the old spell of those assured good looks. Joe recognised the bounce of the journalist with a scoop. Richard had the tape-recorder still slung over his arm.

And sure enough, after a few mouthfuls of corned beef: 'Do you mind if I play something on this? I haven't heard it myself yet.'

At that moment the firing started in the city. The noise came up the little hill, across the lawn and into the room loudly enough to halt conversation.

They went out on to the lawn, Francis taking his binoculars. A warehouse was burning on the edge of the city just off the airport road, and as they watched, another crackle of irregular fire reached them from the same direction. They could distinguish between the crack of rifles and the rattle of old-fashioned machine guns. Through the glasses Francis could see R.L.F. trucks speeding towards the trouble along the raised road from the centre of the city.

'What the bloody hell's he up to?' Joe was visibly shaken.

'What do you mean?' asked Francis.

Joe Steel was silent for a moment. It was completely quiet in the compound. The children were asleep on their mattresses in the ballroom, and instructions had been given that they were not to be disturbed.

'Kaul must have thought I was a joke,' said Joe. 'He never took seriously the idea of getting an extra two days out of you British by coming here and sending goddam telegrams. So he's attacked out of the airport before he is ready. He's run on his own bloody sword.'

'What chance has he?' asked Francis.

'One in ten, I guess, provided of course Revani hasn't heard that his gallant British allies are pulling out for good tonight. Kaul is badly outnumbered, and his men are still tired, but they're a good bunch.'

The heavy clouds which had hung over the city all day, trapped between mountain and ocean, began to close in. Faraway sheets of rain fell over the harbour, blotting out their sight of the tankers and the big jetty. The firing below them died down, flared up, stopped.

'Better go in,' said Francis. He looked at his watch. 'When it rains it always starts at three o'clock.'

It was a remark he had made a dozen times standing on the same lawn at the same hour. Indeed it was the damnable normality of the whole scene which upset Joe. Clerks and typists were making their way along the asphalt drive down to the Chancery building, as they always did at five to three. The only difference was that they kept voices low so as not to wake the children.

'When the devil will you get an answer to the telegram?' asked Joe.

There was an isolated burst of firing out in the city, some-where beyond the advancing curtain of rain, but perhaps closer than before.

'It'll be some time yet,' said Francis. 'They're only just getting to the office in London. Bound to need a lot of talk-ing and telephoning.'

'I'm going inside to listen to my tape,' said Richard. 'Can you telegraph it for me to London through the diplomatic wireless?'

'I don't think the rules . . .'

At that moment the rain arrived, and with it the fourth visitor of the day. Colonel Kaul was soaked, his whole body with water, his left thigh with blood. As soon as his motor-cycle stopped he toppled sideways on to the asphalt. Richard and Francis carried him half-conscious into the house.

'Excellency, there's an R.L.F. sergeant at the gate, with five men in a jeep. They say Fascist terrorists have come this way. They want to search the compound.'

'Tell them that they cannot do so. Tell them this is the house and garden of the British Queen. Tell them they will be in trouble if they try to force entry.'

'Yes, sir. I will tell them.'

'. . . we pushed very quickly right ahead towards Central Square, no fighting, not even snipers.' Kaul's whisky tumbler was almost empty. He looked flushed and frail in Francis's dressing-gown, open to show his tightly bandaged leg. 'There was a barricade in front of us round the corner by the Ministry of Foreign Trade. I sent twelve men into the side streets on the left to turn it, but they got pinned down by a gun on the roof of the Ministry. There was no way round on the right. So it meant a frontal assault. It was not strong, we could have carried it. But then the loudspeaker started . . .'

Outside the rain was slackening. Francis had set his staff patrolling again, and from the drawing room they could see mackintoshed figures cross and recross the lawn. Soon it would be dark.

'. . . it was Revani. He told my men the British were going at once. He said the VC 10s were loading up. He said he knew for sure because a British friend had come from London to tell him so that morning. He laughed a good deal. He told them to throw away their guns and go home. I shouted that it was all lies, but they would not obey the order to assault.' He raised his voice a fraction. 'They would not obey my order. I was going to shoot the man nearest me, but a sergeant jerked my arm. Then I tried to regroup some way back, but by then there were less than fifty of them, and Revani had a post behind us on the airport road.'

Kaul talked fast, without emotion, as if to an empty room.

Richard rejoined them after an absence of five minutes. He looked cross.

'Was it worth it?' asked Joe Steel. He was sprawled in a basket chair, stomach straining through a missing button, whisky bottle on the floor beside him. He was finding the courage to go back with Kaul to the airport when Kaul felt strong enough.

'What do you mean, worth it?'

'You've been out there playing the Revani interview on your machine.'

'Yes.' Richard's answer was abrupt. To his dismay the interview on his machine was unbelievably trite. Revani had doled out a dollop of platitude in answer to each of his written questions.

Joe laughed. 'You mean to say you paid all that and it's no bloody good?'

Richard did not understand. 'I paid nothing.'

'He says different,' Joe pointed to Kaul. 'He says Revani was told the British were pulling out tonight. Told by someone who knew. It knocked the last bit of stuffing out of his attack.'

Richard turned away to the window. 'He had no chance anyway.'

There was no answer. The rain was beginning to slacken, it no longer beat against the windows.

The telephone rang. Through the open doors they watched Francis, at his desk in the study, pick up the receiver. The conversation was one-sided and Francis scribbled on a pad. Then he came in to them and went over to Kaul, glancing at the notes he had made.

'That was Chowdhry, Commander-in-Chief he calls himself now. First call I've had in a week. They know you're here, and Revani wants to talk to you. He wants you to go at once to the Inter Ocean Hotel, under his personal guarantee of safety. Otherwise he says your men whom he has taken will be shot as traitors.'

Kaul tried to haul himself to his feet.

'Thank you for the whisky,' he said.

'You can't go, you're not fit,' said Francis. 'Stay the night, and decide in the morning. They won't come for you here.'

Kaul for the first time in his life lost his temper with an Englishman.

'I will go at once. My clothes are upstairs,' he shouted. 'Why should I fear Revani? I will go if I have to drag myself all the way.'

'Your bike's a write-off,' said Joe, to his own surprise. 'We'll take the Ferret car I came in this morning.'

'I will go alone.'

'You can't even walk without help. I'm going to find the driver.

Richard and Francis went down to the compound gate to see them off.

As he walked down the drive Francis counted twenty fires in the city. Two or three had been normal for some nights now. The Indian store-keepers were unlucky that the rain had stopped at dusk, particularly the ones who had opened during the curfew or been rude to looting soldiers. In the future even Indians would be needed, with their money, in the new Rajnaya. But that night the R.L.F. decided that they needed a lesson. There were of course no journalists in the city to count the bodies in the morning.

'Did Chowdhry say anything else?' asked Richard.

'Yes.' Francis paused, but it seemed useless to hold back. 'He said Revani had much to discuss with me, and would come for a glass of whisky before dinner.'

Neither Kaul nor Joe came to say goodbye. They clambered into the car, Kaul lifting in his damaged leg with his hands, and a minute later it had passed the white stone gate with the royal arms on the arch.

The road to the city dipped sharply a hundred yards from the gate, where the bamboo thickets closed in to within five yards of the verge.

Just as the scout car was about to pass from their sight, down the slope, it disappeared in yellow flame. The noise of the explosion reached their ears an instant later. Francis ran across the drive to the staff car park, found a Vauxhall with the keys in and drove out of the gate into the darkness towards the burning wreckage. Five minutes later he was back, alone. For a few minutes he said nothing and looked at no one.

It was a most regrettable mistake. Chowdhry said so on the telephone. The R.L.F. had mined the road when they withdrew their detachment from the High Commission that morning. They had forgotten about these mines when suggesting that Kaul should use the road. Revani had given orders that those responsible should be severely punished. He would be coming to the High Commission as planned, and would present his apologies in person.

Richard sat in the window seat of the drawing room, feeling sorry for himself. He should never have come back to Rajnaya. All right, his life was trivial, self-important, even silly. But almost everyone he knew lived like that, playing the same game by the same rules. By those rules he'd made good, scored a brilliant success. Everyone had said so.

Then he'd come back to this bloody country, where people shouted and did mad things like driving out of a safe High Commission into a murderous jungle. Even a debauched cynic like Joe Steel. Nothing at all to do with Richard Herbert, he was just there to report the truth as he saw it, and that was what he'd done.

Richard used his tiredness to stop thinking. The only important thing was to get a plane out of Rajnaya as soon as he could, and not come back. No one in London would know exactly what had happened. He could carry on where he'd left off. Francis would tell no tales. There'd be no nasty taste in his mouth. That seat in Lancashire. Or Tyrrell's job in a month or two. And plenty more money. A current affairs programme of his own. No one he knew would care a damn about Rajnaya in a month's time. Except Anne. And even she had not seen the scout car in its halo of yellow flame.

Francis had sat at the other window seat for almost half an hour. It was dark now. He had wanted to work out what to say to Revani but the thoughts did not come. Then he went to the desk, took out his letter of resignation from the top drawer, dated and signed it. He had been a member of his Service for eighteen years. The ink was still wet when they brought him a short telegram from London.

> I have carefully considered your recommendation of a delay in evacuating Andromeda Force. I am grateful for these views but for reasons of general policy the operational instructions already issued must stand.
> 2. The Officer Commanding has been instructed to offer Colonel Kaul as well as President Lall safe passage to Cyprus. I hope that this meets at least part of your concern.

Francis put the letter of resignation in an envelope and sealed it. The door into the ballroom was ajar. He could see the corner of a cot, and hear the rustle of young children settling to sleep. They had been remarkably quiet all day. If they remembered the day at all it would be as a vague excitement, and sleeping all together in a vast splendid room.

The cicadas were loud through the garden among the dripping trees and bushes.

Down in the city the night's work reached its climax. Even those who were neither killing nor being killed found it hard to sleep.

At the airport the preparations for evacuation progressed smoothly and quietly. The soldiers and airmen swore more often than usual as they stowed away their gear in the VC 10s. They carried Lall gently on his stretcher up the steps into the leading plane.

In the High Commission the silver plate had been set out again for dinner and the candles were lit. The portraits of Kings, Viceroys, Admirals and Governors loomed from the dark panelling, each meticulously labelled and framed in gold. The two brass cannon on the lawn in front of the portico still pointed outwards as they had for a hundred and fifty years, one over the harbour, the other to the mountains. Because the sun had set the flagstaff was empty.

In the huge white drawing room, sitting separately and in silence, Richard and Francis heard through the darkness the sirens of the approaching dictator.